IAN JEFFRIES
IS NOT
FOR SALE

BOB McCABE

Ian Jeffries is Not for Sale

First Edition Published 2019

ISBN: 978 1 78645 369 3

Copyediting, typesetting and formatting:
Beaten Track Publishing
www.beatentrackpublishing.com

IAN JEFFRIES
IS NOT
FOR SALE

Prologue

Laura Anne was only joking. Well, that's what Addie thought. It was the 21ˢᵗ October 1960: lunch at the Shelbourne Hotel. The two friends were on their second bottle of Chablis when Laura Anne offered £10,000 to buy Addie's son, Ian.

***

Addie Jeffries and Laura Anne Robinson met for the first time on the school sports day. Addie's son, Ian, was struggling through the three-legged race attached to a small, pale-faced boy. Ian, several inches taller than his partner, practically carried the smaller boy across the line to a stumbling finish.

"Who matched those two up? That little fella is hopeless!" Addie protested, turning to the stylish-looking woman beside her, receiving a polite smile in reply.

Laura Anne Robinson was becoming more accustomed to the outgoing informality of the Irish, and this woman, with dramatic flashing eyes and spectacular mop of auburn hair who was so incensed over a three-legged race, was of interest to her. Laura Anne had intentionally positioned herself beside the unsuspecting Adelaide Jeffries.

"Absolutely," she said with a laugh, "but they're good friends. I'm the little fellow's mother."

Addie's attempt to apologise was brushed aside by the wave of a well-manicured hand and a generous smile.

"My Christopher is no athlete, I'm afraid." The smile stayed in place as she held out her hand. "I'm Laura Anne Robinson, and I'm so pleased to meet Ian's mother."

Ian had never mentioned a friend called Christopher Robinson, and Addie was curious. She took the proffered hand, receiving a vigorous handshake. Before she could frame a question, the Audrey Hepburn look-alike began to hastily unbutton her jacket.

"It's the mothers' egg-and-spoon race next, and I promised Christopher I'd take part. Are you going in it?"

"No, I've got to help with the teas." Addie hesitated, gesturing towards the tea tent.

"Would you mind holding these for me? I'll only be a minute. I'm always the first to drop the egg, there's a darling."

Addie took the beautiful jacket and shoes.

"Oh! And this!" Laura Anne removed her scarf and placed it on top of the precious items in Addie's arms.

Addie held the exquisite headscarf and designer jacket close to her face as she watched the slim-figured Laura Anne, in stockinged feet, tiptoe across the grass to join the start of the race.

The pure silk was light and soft against her cheek, the scent of expensive perfume invading her senses. She closed her eyes and was transported, imagining herself owning such things, shopping at the stores in Grafton Street, stepping from her sports car to the gate of Ivy Lodge—*"Addie Jeffries, pleased to meet you. Would you please park my car? Keep the change—it's only ten shillings."*—the builders arriving to fix the roof, the outstanding grocery bill paid at the corner shop, school fees taken care of—*"I'll write a cheque."*—Roy taking her and the kids for a drive in a beautiful car...

She smiled in her reverie, burying her face deeper into the world of Laura Anne's possessions.

"I came fourth." Laura Anne, breathless and smiling from her efforts in the egg-and-spoon race, had returned.

Addie, unaware, didn't feel the touch on her arm.

"My things?" Laura Anne looked enquiringly. "Adelaide?"

"Oh! Sorry!" Addie raised her head as Laura Anne gently removed the silk scarf from her tight grasp.

"Oh dear!" Bright red smears of Woolworth's cheap lipstick merged with the en vogue Dior design. "No matter. I have another one just like it." Laura Anne released the scarf and reached for her jacket and shoes. "You keep it. It's a present," she said generously, with a smile.

But to Addie, the smile and the generous gesture only added to her feeling of mortification.

"I'm so sorry, I'll have it cleaned and return it to you." She appealed to the top of a perfectly coiffured head as Laura Anne bent to slip on her shoes.

"Please don't worry. I have lots of them." Laura Anne stood upright as Addie held out the jacket. There was a very slight lipstick smudge on the suede collar, but neither woman commented.

Nor were they aware that this encounter signalled the beginning of events that would influence both their lives for many years to come.

Chapter 1

New Year's Eve 1955

*I*HOPE SHE DOESN'T KISS ME *on the face when she's leaving,* was the thought paramount in Ian Jeffries' mind, his eyes transfixed by his mother's smiling lips, bright red with newly applied lipstick.

Hands on hips, Adelaide twirled and posed, her eyes shining, *Greta Garbo, Bette Davis* style. Ian's dad, tall and dapper in his rented tuxedo suit and with a large box of Tara Chocolates gripped in a strong, tanned hand, beamed his approval.

Ian's older sister Debbie and brother James watched their ma and da make the final preparations for the New Year's Eve Company Dinner Dance.

"You look like a movie star, Ma." James, the eldest, held up the corsage, his eyes level with his mother's.

Roy Jeffries put down the box of chocolates and carefully took the flower from his son's hand.

"A beautiful flower for a beautiful lady."

Addie twirled and looked up into Roy's handsome face. He leaned down, doing his best to attach the tricky pin arrangement to the low-cut bodice. The grand gesture, though well intended, was doomed to failure. Fingers strong and weathered from gripping the handlebars of the bike and hauling the heavy gas company collector's money bag from house to house were not suited to the delicate task.

"It's OK." She smiled. "Here, I'll do it."

Taking the fragile arrangement from his hand, she smoothed it between her fingers and expertly pinned it in place. "Now the coat."

Across the back of a dining room chair, it lay like a beautiful, sleeping, furry Persian cat. The coat itself was much like it had always been: cream with a cinched-in waist. It was, however, the huge fur collar newly attached by Mrs. O'Neill, a talented neighbour, that made the difference. Addie admiringly held it at arm's length and then, with a twirl and the willing attention of Roy, the beautiful coat was around her shoulders. Running her hands up under the heavy collar, she lifted it on both sides to frame her face.

Debbie clapped and started to dance and sing, "She wore red feathers and a hula-hula skirt," skipping and cavorting around the room while Ian held on to her hem and tried his best to knock his big sister off her feet. Addie hitched up her evening dress and danced with them while Roy rescued the box of chocolates from the table.

"She lived on just coconuts and fish from the sea." James, at fourteen, older and wiser, held back until, unable to resist, he grabbed his mother around the waist to attempt a *slow, slow, quick, quick, slow* quickstep.

"With a rose in her hair and a gleam in her eye and love in her heart for me..." they sang. The doorbell rang, but nobody heard it.

***

Standing on the doorstep, Owen Ferris, the taxi man, rang the bell again. *It's going to be a long night.* With a resigned sigh, he plunged his hands into his pockets and did a soft-shoe shuffle against the cold.

This small village on the coast south of Dublin City was a lively place, especially on New Year's Eve; its inhabitants and those from the surrounding countryside would need ferrying on this celebration night.

Owen bent his large frame and peered through the letterbox, feeling the warm breath of the house on his cold face. At first, all he could see was the ornate tiled floor of the porch. Stooping lower and adjusting his position, he was greeted with the view of a long hallway, the floor covered in linoleum with a fairly threadbare carpet running along its centre. Down the hallway, a light came from a doorway, and he heard voices, mainly children, making a hell of a noise.

Returning to his warm-up dance, Owen looked back along the gravel path to the love of his life. Beyond the high laurel hedge, the car, sleek and stylish—a Wolseley Ten—was parked on the road, engine running and the lights on.

"Why were they not waiting, looking out the window, ready to open the door, watching out for me?" It was a cold December evening, and the Wolseley was not a great car for the cold weather. If he turned off the ignition, it might be difficult to restart. He blew on his hands and shuffled from foot to foot, some people have no consideration.

Ringing the doorbell again, he kept it pressed down this time with a large, nicotine-stained finger. Eyes raised to heaven, bending double, he pushed the brass flap of the fancy letterbox. The racket from inside could still be heard. "TAXI!" he roared. "It's fuckin' freezin' out here!"

The door suddenly opened, and the portly Owen was presented with a close-up of a set of pearly shirt buttons.

"Sorry, we didn't hear the bell. Come in."

"Yer chariot awaits." With a sweep of the arm—and still bent double—Owen stepped back and indicated the Wolseley that could just be seen through the small gate in the gap in the hedge that ran the width of the large garden.

Three kids appeared behind the tall, handsome, smiling man standing in the doorway.

"Ma's not ready," said the smallest one with a grin, looking at the other two. "She had to go to the lav."

"Now then," the dad admonished with a raised finger. "Don't be rude." He turned to Owen. "Would you care for a drink?" he asked with a slight nod of his head and an inviting smile. "It's New Year's Eve."

"No, no, you're grand," Owen replied unconvincingly as, with a grimace, he straightened up, holding the small of his back.

"Are you sure? It's a cold night." Roy repeated the invitation.

Owen paused. "Well, maybe a quick one. I'll just turn off the engine."

Stepping back, the man introduced himself, "Roy Jeffries." He stuck out a hand. "This is James, Debbie, and the little fella is Ian."

With exaggerated gravity, Owen introduced himself. "The Lone Ranger," said he, shaking each of the children's hands in turn and then to Roy, "Owen Ferris is the name. A whiskey would be nice. It's a cold night, much appreciated." He rubbed his hands together and stepped into the warm porch.

Addie appeared down the hall and overheard the last part of the conversation. "Come in, come in!" she invited with a smile.

"This is Owen Ferris," said Roy. "Go on, go on. I'll turn off the engine of your car for you."

"Your husband is a nice man, Mrs. Jeffries," said the cold taxi man as he followed her down the hall to where a Jameson waited.

***

Roy opened the door of the large, sleek, black car. *What a beauty!* He ran his hand over the heavy, shiny leather upholstery, his eye taking in the beautiful rosewood dashboard. Slipping in behind the steering wheel, he listened to the purr of the engine. On his salary, owning such a car wasn't even a remote possibility. The interior was warm, luxurious and comfortable. Roy sat back with a sigh and ran his rough palms over the smooth, polished steering wheel.

If he got the inspector's job, the Company would give him a van to drive. That would do him. Some of the inspectors took their vans home for weekends, depending on the proximity of the area they had to cover on the following Monday morning.

Collecting from house to house, especially in the winter months, was not a job for the physically weak or fainthearted, the big leather money bag getting heavier as the working day wore on, facing down angry dogs and coping with hard-pressed individuals short of cash. A part of Roy resented the toughness of the work; that was what had driven him towards applying for the inspector's job.

"Nobody deserves it more than you." Addie's words echoed in his ears. But Roy, not by nature one of the world's most ambitious individuals, had his reservations. With the inspector's job would come a lot more office work—reports to write and meetings to attend, responsibilities—and there would be a trial period. What if he wasn't up to the job?

He sighed again. *Well, never mind. Count your blessings; money isn't everything.* Turning off the ignition and removing the key from the dash, he stepped into the cold night air.

"Good night, Roy, it's a cold one. Happy New Year!" two neighbours greeted as they passed on the country road heading in the darkness towards the lights at the crossroad and the local pub. They eyed the car but didn't comment, and Roy didn't enlighten them. He smiled. *That'll be a bit of gossip for them.*

He went through the doorway in the high wall. *Ivy Lodge*: the brass plate with its engraved letters stood out against the green paintwork. He headed on under the arched laurel hedge to the gravel path bisecting the lawn leading straight to the lighted porch.

***

"A very nice house, Mrs. Jeffries." Owen Ferris took in the big marble fireplace and the crackling fire in the hearth. "Yeah, and a very nice man, your husband." He cradled the large whiskey in a practised hand and held it up to the light, admiring the amber liquid, smacking his lips. "Mmm, they broke the mould, Mrs. Jeffries." He downed the whiskey in one. "Yes, they broke the mould when they made that husband of yours."

"Yes, they did," replied Addie with a smile at the obvious attempt at flattery. "You know, I don't believe I have ever heard anyone say a bad word about him. Would you like another, Mr. Ferris?"

The taxi man nodded, his big shiny cheeks glowing red from the effects of the whiskey and the fire. "Owen, Owen," he corrected her lightly. "Don't mind if I do, thanks. A little bit of what you like does you no harm, am I right? Well, speak of the devil."

He raised his glass as Roy joined them and handed over the car keys.

"Better make tracks." The comfortable taxi man reluctantly clambered to his feet. "Duty calls. Do you mind if I use your toilet before we go? Or do you mind if I go before we go, if you get my meaning." He gave a little chuckle at his own humour, finishing off the second neat whiskey in one glorious gulp.

**

Roy was waiting in the hall when Owen, having completed his ablutions, joined him.

"A fine size wooden toilet seat you have there." He chuckled. "If I had the time, I might have lingered awhile. Very comfortable." They headed to the front of the house.

Grandad Hugh, Addie's father and a man not given to frivolity at the best of times, stood in the porch flanked by his daughter and grandchildren.

"And who is this?" He eyed the tipsy taxi man approaching him.

Owen, taking in the severe face, the waxed moustache and stiff upright tweed-suited stance, did not miss the note of disapproval.

"Evening, sir. I'm here to whisk your daughter away to the ball in my golden chariot."

"A taxi, no less," Grandad Hugh muttered disapprovingly. He transferred the severe look to Addie. "How can you fritter good money on a taxi. What's wrong with the bus?" He rocked on his heels, hands clasped behind his back in his best Duke of Edinburgh imitation.

Ignoring him, Addie was saying her goodbyes to the kids. "Be good for your grandad, no fighting." She managed to grab a dodging Ian. "And you do as your brother tells you. He's in charge."

"But Ma!" he began to protest. "Don't kiss me!" he pleaded, too late; the bright red lipstick had done its work.

"Now, be good." She hugged the squirming Ian before turning to the two older ones, who dutifully received their lipstick kisses. With a last parting glance of warning and another "be good!" she quickly followed the two men out the front door.

***

"Good boy." Grandad Hugh, showing his softer side, ruffled Ian's dark curls with a gentle, blue-veined hand. "Here." He bent down, producing a well-laundered white handkerchief from his top pocket. Spitting on it, he rubbed at the lipstick mark. The action only resulted in making things worse as the boy's upturned face took on a pinkish hue.

Ian obediently looked up at his grandad. He always hated it when grown-ups spat on handkerchiefs and cleaned him.

"Can I borrow your sharp scissors? We've got a shoe box, and James is going to help me make a house."

The three children waited expectantly. A request for Grandad's coveted sharp scissors was often refused, but it seemed Ian had judged the mood of the moment to perfection.

"Please?" he said, his voice soft, head to one side, looking into the old grey eyes.

The boy has his father's looks and charm, but his mother's eyes, the old man thought as, handkerchief poised, he peered down into the upturned face.

"All right, but be careful, and James is in charge. Just wait till I lock the front door." Folding the lipstick-stained handkerchief to return it to his top pocket, he thought better of it and stepped into the porch, just in time to give a cursory wave to the figures departing down the path.

"A taxi, and them without two brass farthings to rub together," he muttered to himself. "Whatever next? Well, that's it," he mused as he turned the key in the lock. "New Year's Eve. Another year gone—another year without Betty."

Two years previously, Addie's mother Elizabeth had passed away. Hugh Arthur, not a man given to much emotion, stood for a moment in the porch reflecting on how she had been on that spring day: a minute figure lying in the bed, bedecked with pink and white apple blossom from the garden, the neighbours all coming in to say goodbye. She had informed them all that morning in her beautiful lilting voice, "I want to say goodbye and I want the bed to be covered in apple blossom."

That afternoon at around five o'clock, she had passed away, the cancer in her system having the final say.

With a sigh, Hugh straightened his back and stood ramrod straight, hands clasped behind him, always the composed gent, and eyed his three grandchildren waiting in the hall.

"Come with me, you little scallywags, and I'll get the blessed scissors for you."

Chapter 2

Outside the Centre City Hotel, one of Dublin's finest, the taxis came and went, depositing the would-be Errol Flynns and Van Heflins along with the Deborah Kerrs and Lauren Bacalls. If the truth be told, there was a pretty liberal smattering of Mickey Rooneys and Sophie Tuckers, all dressed in their best, no expense spared, the one night in the year when Dublin splashed out: New Year's Eve.

In the large reception area, Roy stood by while Addie mingled, eyes flashing. She was in her element, moving from group to group.

"Wow, you look great!"

"Haven't seen you since last year! How are the kids?"

"Try these—they're called Craven A. What a name for a cigarette!"

The drinks were flowing, glasses of gin and tonic, and vodka and orange, pints of Guinness and Carlsberg Special passing from hand to hand. Waiters buzzed at high speed, swerving skilfully, trays aloft in the smoke-filled air. Roy watched with amusement as his popular and attractive wife moved ever closer to her goal, smiling to himself as Addie eventually manoeuvred to a position back to back with the chairman of the board.

Mr. Roger Blackwell was regaling some of his cronies with an anecdote or two when he thought he had jostled a person behind him. Turning to apologise, glass in hand, his face transformed to a welcoming smile.

"Why, hello." He knew she was the wife of one of his collectors, but her name momentarily evaded him.

"Hello, Adelaide." One of his cohorts came to the rescue. "How is Roy? Don't tell me you're here without him?"

Recognising one of the company's managing accountants, Jim Bradley, Addie assumed an exaggerated impersonation of a Hollywood femme fatale and struck a pose.

"Not tonight, Boogie Boy. He's over there and you're out of luck." The couple of whiskeys in the house earlier and a swiftly downed gin and tonic when she arrived were taking an effect.

"That's put you in your place, *Boogie Boy*," laughed Roger Blackwell.

Ultra-conservative Jim Bradley was on the verge of a testy retort but thought better of it. He took himself and his position in the firm very seriously, especially in the company of the chairman, and was offended at the familiarity shown by Addie, whom he considered to be merely the wife of an underling. In an effort to regain some ground, he placed a patronising hand on her elbow and tried to deflect her from the management group and the presence of Mr. Blackwell.

"Now then, Adelaide, why don't you join the girls? Joan is over there—she's been looking forward to some girlie talk." His grip tightened as he redirected her towards his wife: a shrewish-looking woman standing alone.

"Au contraire, Au contraire," the chairman interjected. "Adelaide...Addie, it's a night for celebration. Join us, join us. I see your glass is empty, what are you having?"

"A gin and tonic, please." She smiled as she felt Boogie Boy's grip loosen.

"Where is your husband, did you say? And what's he having?"

Addie pointed across the room. "The best-looking man at the ball," she proclaimed and then, with a laugh, "Present company excluded, of course. He likes a Jameson."

Roger Blackwell accepted the light-hearted banter in the fun and spirit it was offered. He had an aversion to these evenings of toadying up and fawning, and enjoyed the light relief this refreshing, pretty woman offered. He looked across the room at Roy Jeffries, taking in the aspect of the man. On impulse, he turned to Jim Bradley.

"I'll have a brandy, and fetch a gin and tonic for the lady. I'm sure you know Jeffries over there. Ask him to join us. I believe he likes a Jameson."

"Of course, Chairman." Immediately releasing Addie, he hesitated, flustered at the reversal of roles.

"Go on, go on, Jim, there's a good chap," the chairman urged.

Roy, who was unaware of the scrutiny from across the room, felt a touch on his arm and turned around.

"Hey! What's the jazz?" Mick Moroney, fellow collector and a decent bloke, beamed and rubbed his hands together, full of the New Year spirit. "Come and join the gang," he invited. Mick's wife Gladys, a big, blowsy, peroxide blonde, smiled by his side.

"Of course, yes. Hello, Gladys." Roy returned the smile.

"Where's Addie?" Mick looked around and spotted her across the room. "Ah! There she is, hobnobbing with the boss, I see. God! Look who's heading this way—that Creeping Jesus Bradley. What does he want? We're not in working hours. He'd best behave himself or I'll flatten that big beaky nose for him."

Head erect and with a slightly sickly smile, Jim Bradley made his way through the throng. For some reason, he always felt ill at ease in Roy Jeffries' company. There was a quiet confidence about the man along with his obvious physical stature and apparently imperturbable calmness that Jim found disquieting, even though, as his immediate boss, Jim had a lot of power over him. The last thing he needed was the chairman taking an interest in Roy Jeffries. He adjusted his bow tie and pulled down on the sides of his perfectly tailored dress-suit jacket as he approached the two collectors, the last few yards taken in a purposeful stride.

"Hello, Jeffries, Moroney…mm…Happy New Year."

"Mr. Bradley," the two collectors nodded in unison. Mick's reference to Jim's beaky nose lingered in the air and the men found it hard to contain their amusement at the pompous figure before them. Jim Bradley misjudged the expressions.

"Jeffries, Royston...Roy." He beamed as he put out a friendly hand to grasp the taller man's arm in an over-the-top attempt at sociability. "Your chairman would like you to join him in a celebratory drink."

Taken aback at the invitation, Roy glanced at Mick and Gladys then back again, his natural sense of loyalty coming to the fore. "I was just going to join the lads."

"Of course, no problem." A much-relieved Bradley looked into the open, friendly face, anticipating and savouring the prospect of telling the chairman that one of his collectors preferred not to drink with him. A little smile tweaked at the corner of his mouth as he took a step backwards, turning on his heel, and spotted Addie across the room, glaring angrily at her husband. She made a minute but violent beckoning motion with her right hand from waist height and out of sight of all except Roy and the observant Jim Bradley. *There's one to watch out for...* He made a mental note.

"Go on, ya big eejit," Mick encouraged Roy. "Put in a good word for me. Tell him I want the inspector's job."

"Are you sure?" Roy hesitated. Addie was still looking fierce.

"Go on, see you a bit later."

It took two strides for Roy to overhaul the retreating figure. "I'll have a Jameson please, Mr. Bradley," he said.

Mick Moroney, an ambitious grafter in the process of trying to better himself but lacking in much of the basic equipment for success, looked after the retreating figure of his colleague.

"That fella hasn't got a clue," he said, turning to his wife. "If I had half of what he's got, I'd own the bleedin' place. Look at him—'The chairman would like you to join him in a celebratory drink,'" he mimicked. "My arse—that Bradley fella hardly gave me a rec, and he didn't even say hello to you!"

Gladys Moroney looked at her downcast husband. "Never mind, you'll get your chance." A good four inches taller than Mick, she hung a fairly hefty arm around his neck, pulling him to her and giving him a big lipstick kiss. "Cheer up, lover, it's New Year's Eve." Holding hands, the two of them headed towards the group of co-workers.

"Hiya, Mick. Put that woman down and have a pint."

"Are you going to give us a song later?"

"Who are you sittin' with for the dinner?"

"Where's Roy disappeared to? I saw you talkin' to him a minute ago."

The party was really getting going as Mick and Gladys joined the group. Mick held up two hands in front of him, palms out.

"Wait till you hear this. You'll never believe it. We were invited by the chairman to join him for a drink. It's no lie, am I right, Gladys?" Mick regaled them. "Up came auld Bradley, the Creepin' Jesus, and invited us for a celebratory drink." He did a pretty good impersonation of the unpopular accountant's voice and manner, much to the amusement of all.

"And Roy went and you didn't?" a voice came from the amused group. "Good on ya, Mick."

There were a good few nods and sounds of approval.

Mick hesitated a moment but then honesty won the day. "Well, not exactly, ye see. Like, Bradley put the emphasis on Roy, like, he was lookin' at Roy when he said it."

"Ya weren't asked, were ya?" came a voice from the crowd. "Get out o' that—he wasn't asked, sure he wasn't, Gladys." The general good-humoured banter continued.

But Roy went. The possibility of gaining the inspector's job lurked in most of their minds and Mick was a decent bloke; he couldn't betray his friend.

"No, I have to say, in fairness, Roy turned him down—said he was goin' to have a drink with the lads. Am I right, Gladys? I think it was his missus, the beautiful Adelaide. She gave him one of those looks." Mick made a mad face. Tipping his head back, he downed the remains of his pint, then smacked his lips as he examined the empty glass with a minute scrutiny. "Get's another one of these," he said, to no one in particular.

***

Roy was unaware of the effect he was having on the assembled company as he joined the chairman and management group. Many curried favour and toadied up, but very few were invited.

"Jeffries, Roy." Roger Blackwell extended his hand, "Happy New Year. Your wife has been regaling us with your great virtues. You know all here." With a sweep of his hand, he indicated various members of his management team and their wives.

The tall, quiet-mannered Roy, appearing totally nonplussed by the occasion, smiled his big smile and greeted the company with a slight bow.

"Thanks, Mr. Blackwell, and a Happy New Year to all." He turned as he was handed a whiskey by a far from happy yet smiling Jim Bradley. Addie positively glowed with pleasure at her husband's calm finesse.

"A word." The chairman took Roy to one side, his expression grave and concerned as he excused himself from those in the immediate vicinity with a cursory wave of the hand.

"Your wife here was telling me that you are acquainted with the Murdochs?" He looked enquiringly at the younger man and received an affirmative nod. "How are they? I haven't seen them for a while—lost touch, you know. You see," he went on earnestly, "I can remember Geoff Murdoch mentioning a good friend of his called Roy Jeffries. He was full of admiration for this man, often talked about him. Am I in the presence of the same Roy Jeffries?"

"Well, yes. I would consider Geoff Murdoch and Barbara friends of ours. We're on the parish committee together."

"Well I never!" Roger Blackwell looked at the younger man. "Small world! You're a bit of a dark horse, aren't you?" He hesitated as if considering whether to continue the conversation, then abruptly made up his mind. Leaning closer, he confided,

"You're probably aware that Barbra Murdoch is my sister?" Not waiting for a response, the obviously tipsy chairman of the board proceeded to unload some family details that normally would not have been divulged. He explained in detail how there had been a falling-out and he and his sister had drifted apart.

Nearby, Addie was engaged in conversation with a couple and gave the appearance of being totally unaware of the exchange, but she heard every word.

"Perhaps you might mention that you were talking to me the next time you meet the Murdochs?" the chairman continued. "You know, remind them of my existence so to speak. You know what I mean, you're an honest broker. It seems that they have great respect for you."

"Of course, I understand. You'd like me to break the ice," Roy replied, quite astonished at the revelations and equally surprised at the fact that the chairman of the board, was confiding in such a personal manner. He felt sorry for the man, who was so obviously sad about the rift in his family.

"Yes, that's right. You know what I mean. You're a good man." Roger Blackwell patted Roy on the shoulder and raised his half-empty brandy glass to his lips, making another visit to the golden liquid.

"Yes, Roy, old chap, it's a sad world, and things aren't always as they appear to be." With a sigh and a shake of the head, he looked at the floor, brandy glass poised.

Roy could detected moistness in those eyes that had, in their time, stared down many a challenge across the boardroom table.

"I hope you don't think I have been too indiscreet." The chairman offered Roy a slightly apologetic smile.

"Not at all." Roy often found people confided in him. He had never tried to analyse why. It wasn't in his nature; nor was it in his nature to criticise or judge.

"Well, well, I think dinner is about to be announced." Roger Blackwell was back to his normal self. The exchange had only taken a few minutes. "Perhaps you'd join us at our table."

He turned to the astonished Jim Bradley, "Bradley there's room for two more, surely?"

Those in the immediate vicinity pricked up their ears, including Addie.

"Why, yes, of course. We'd love—" She didn't finish the sentence.

"Thanks." Roy smiled openly. "But I arranged to sit with Mick Moroney and his wife and a few of the others. I hope you don't mind? Nice talking to you, I'll remember what you said about the Murdochs." With a nod and a smile, Roy said, "C'mon Addie," and took her hand, leading her across the floor towards a group making their way to the dining room.

Roger Blackwell watched them. "Well, now, there goes a unique man," he said to nobody in particular.

"Bad manners, if you ask me." Jim Bradley couldn't resist the comment.

"No, Bradley, to the contrary. Loyalty and a bit of style." The words hung in the air as the chairman looked after the two figures.

"Are you right, dear?" Doris Blackwell, who had been circulating, joined her husband, and the two headed for the dining room, Jim Bradley and his wife dutifully tagging along. "Bradley, that Jeffries chap is one of our collectors, isn't he? Has he applied for the inspector's job?" the chairman enquired.

***

"It would have been nice to sit at the chairman's table," a slightly miffed Addie commented as they moved away. "Can you imagine the comments?"

"But we'll have more fun with the others." Roy laughed. "It wouldn't be very nice after arranging to sit with them. They're a great bunch. There's Alex Matthews and his wife, and Mick Moroney is a gas man." Roy had no regrets whatsoever.

"Did you mention anything to Blackwell about the inspector's job?" Addie persisted with a raised eyebrow and a sideways glance.

"There they are." Roy pointed with his glass, ignoring the enquiry, as they were greeted by the sight of round, white-cloth-covered tables flanked by gold-backed, red-velvet-cushioned chairs, floral decorations, balloons and the excited sounds of five hundred people searching for their places beneath glittering chandeliers stretching the length and breadth of the vast ballroom. Dress-suited men guided their charges to their seats with a feeling of spontaneous and unaccustomed grandeur.

"Over here! We saw the two of you hobnobbin' with Blackwell and his cronies!" Mick Moroney shouted from amongst a group gathered round a table near the centre of the room. "There are place names—you're here."

The good-natured banter continued as Roy and Addie took their seats. Word had spread quickly through the room.

"Invited to the Chairman's table, no less."

"More fun here." Addie laughed, grabbing Des Lennon by the ears and giving him a big lipstick kiss on the top of his bald head.

As the ultimate celebration, the Annual Company New Year's Eve Dance never failed. World War Two, an event of the recent past, with the misery that goes with such a conflict—ration books and meagre living—was still fresh in the minds of all. Ireland was just beginning to recover, and the people felt they owed themselves a party. Women were coming more to the fore, playing a more dominant role in every aspect of Irish life—the cinema had a great influence. Smoking cigarettes was an art—how to hold a cigarette, silver cigarette cases, cigarette holders and Zippo lighters—head back, blow smoke rings in the air...now that was something to aspire to.

The menu boasted five courses, an impressive feast to those who rarely, if ever, dined in a restaurant other than the Company canteen. Waiters deposited bottles of red and white wine amongst the forest of drinks on the already laden tables. The Jeffries sat with their friends and exclaimed at the choice of delicacies.

"Prawn cocktail, vegetable soup, grapefruit in a glass with a cherry in the middle..." They scrutinised the menu.

"A prawn cocktail to start? No, thanks!"

"What is it? God, no thanks! Grapefruit, please."

Most went for the vegetable soup. The waiter patiently stood, pen poised taking the orders.

"Prawn cocktail, please." Addie couldn't resist. "I'll have the prawn cocktail, whatever that is." With a giggle, she nudged Roy as heads turned.

"Addie, you're never!" Gladys exclaimed. "There's vegetable soup and grapefruit with a cherry! I'm having the grapefruit with a cherry. I had the soup last year. Mick, Addie is having the prawn cocktail. It's a drink, you know," she said knowledgably, nodding her head to add gravity to the statement, displaying her fount of knowledge.

"Now there you're wrong," Alex Matthews, well known for his great wisdom, interjected. "I'm sorry to say you're wrong there." Pausing for effect, he removed his cherry-wood pipe from his mouth and tapped down the tobacco with his thumb as everyone waited. "It's fish, in a sauce—a crustacean presented in a wine glass." Well, nobody was going to argue with that.

"Are you still having it, Addie, after what Alex just said?" enquired Gladys. "I wouldn't."

Thinking of how nice a bowl of vegetable soup would be, but seeing that the waiter had moved on, Addie nodded positively. "Of course I'm having it. It's probably like sardines in tomato sauce."

The good-humoured conversation swung back and forth. Cigarettes were exchanged: Gold Flake, Players Please and Sweet Afton.

"There's a poem on the back of the pack. 'Flow gently Sweet Afton among thy green braes,'" Des Lennon read aloud, "by Robbie Burns."

"What's a brae?"

"It's what a donkey does."

"No, it's a little town about ten miles from Dublin on the coast."

Amidst the laughter, all-knowing Alex could not be heard as he attempted to give the correct definition.

Then the starters arrived. Cigarettes were extinguished into overloaded ashtrays as the soup and grapefruit were placed in front of the anticipating diners. Heads bent, spoons moved rapidly, buttered bread rolls in some cases were dunked, cherries were immediately plucked from the centres of grapefruits.

"Nice soup, pass the butter."

But all eyes followed the waiter's hand as he placed the prawn cocktail in front of the not-so-sure Addie, who managed a confident smile.

It stood in solitary magnificence: a shallow champagne glass on a dish with a small, delicate spoon and fork. Transfixed, they watched, soup spoons poised, grapefruit without cherries on top forgotten momentarily.

Addie looked around the table as she lifted the miniature fork. She then gave the prawn cocktail her complete attention. It seemed innocent enough. There was a creamy, light-brown sauce and some lettuce. She glanced again at the spectators; not a word. They waited. She plunged the little fork into the middle of the concoction and rapidly withdrew it.

"It's a caterpillar!" Mick Moroney cried out, breaking the silence. "It's a caterpillar! Don't eat it!"

"There's a caterpillar in your prawn cocktail."

"That's a prawn," the all-knowing Alex Matthews interjected. "Perfectly edible, and though I have never had one myself, I believe very good for you."

"Nothing will convince me that *that thing* is not a caterpillar," Mick persisted. "Addie, call the waiter and complain."

A passing waiter overhearing the comment stopped. "Is everything all right, sir?"

"Well," said Mick, not used to being put on the spot. "My soup's grand an' all that, but there's a caterpillar in this lady's prawn cocktail." He pointed at the fork still held in front of Addie.

"It's all right." Alex rescued the situation. "May I?" He reached across the table and, politely taking the fork from Addie's hand, popped the prawn into his mouth.

The waiter hurried on about his business finding it difficult to keep a straight face but making a mental note to regale the kitchen staff later.

Adelaide looking around at the other tables spotted a few prawn cocktails being consumed enthusiastically, especially by some at the management tables. She took the spoon and helped herself to a prawn, reaching for the wine glass at the same time, just in case. The taste of the sauce was nice but the caterpillar description persisted. Quickly, she downed half the glass of wine.

"Mm," she said, "very nice."

"The French eat frogs," someone said. "And snails."

"Ah, stop, you're putting me off me soup."

"Here, did you hear the one about the fella in the French restaurant? 'Have you got frogs legs,' he said to the waiter. 'Wee, wee,' said the waiter. 'Well, would you ever hop over to the counter and get me a cheese sandwich?' said the fellah. Ha! Ha! Do yah get it?"

The joke provoked such laughter several heads turned to see what was going on.

"I see our collectors are having a good time," Jim Bradley commented to one of the inspectors sitting beside him. The inspector turned to look, slightly enviously, at the happy group. He turned back to his soup without commenting. Bradley tucked into his prawn cocktail.

Back at the Jeffries' table the main course of beef or salmon was going down a treat.

"Did you ever see so many knives and forks?"

"You start from the outside and work inwards—the one that looks like a putty knife is for the fish."

There was a whip-round and more drinks were ordered. The waiters were working overtime keeping up. The coffee, after the sherry trifle, didn't get much of a look-in.

Speeches followed. The head of the social committee had his moment of glory...well, too many moments. A bit on the longwinded side, he was eventually heckled into silence.

As near as possible to a respectful silence, in spite of the amount of alcohol consumed, prevailed during the chairman's speech. Roger Blackwell, a man of much experience, knew how to work this particular audience with a nice balance of complimentary comments and some humour.

Then Bradley was introduced to give a few words on the financial situation. He didn't stand a chance.

"Give us a song, Beaky!"

"Why don't you stand up? Oh! you are standing up."

"Len's us a fiver, Beaky!

Voices coming from every corner of the room provoked laughter, drowning out the unfortunate man's attempts to speak.

The chairman of the social committee came to the rescue.

"Now then, now then, a bit of hush, please, please, a bit of respect." The laughter and heckling gradually subsided. "Thank you, thank you very much." The head of the social committee was a popular man. As the hubbub quietened, he turned to the accountant. "The floor is yours, Mr. Beak— Mr. Bradley." He corrected himself but not quick enough. Pandemonium broke out as the entire company collapsed into uncontrolled laughter.

Roy felt a bit sorry for the man, but really, he couldn't stop laughing. People said afterwards they thought Mick Moroney was going to have a heart attack. Roger Blackwell, the chairman, did his best but had to hide his face in a big white handkerchief and turn away, his shoulders shaking uncontrollably and tears streaming down his face. One of the great moments in The Company's Social Club history.

The floor was cleared and the dancing began.

"Ladies and gentlemen, tonight you are dancing to the fabulous Rhythm Kings!" The strains of Victor Sylvester's 'You're Dancing on my Heart' filled the room.

"Happy New Year, everybody, it's a quickstep."

The spotlights bouncing off the MC's suit, dazzling and sparkling, were only outshone by the largest crystal ball in Ireland revolving slowly high up in the ceiling. Millions of coloured light-dots played over and around the dancers as they took to the floor.

The printed programme for the dancing promised quicksteps, slow waltzes, the foxtrot, a Paul Jones, tango and, of course, the much-anticipated spot prizes.

"I love to tango." Addie read the card carefully. "There's a Hokey Cokey, even a military two-step."

Everyone took part. Long dresses whirled as the women strutted their stuff, and the men felt grand in their tuxedos and dickey bows. The Rhythm Kings played their hearts out.

The spotlight jerked and swivelled around and around, and side to side, adding to the excitement. When the music stopped, whichever couple were captured in the spotlight would win a spot prize.

The prizes were displayed at the front of the stage, and if you were a lucky winner, you could take your pick. Every couple made a point of dancing near to the stage to see what was on offer.

"Wow! A radio, there's a radio this year and a record player and cash tokens for Cleary's!"

The spotlight swung, and the excitement grew. Suddenly the music stopped. The spotlight swung and bounced around the excited, expectant upturned faces.

"And the winners of our first spot prize of the night are..." The MC built the tension. The room went dark, highlighting a young couple, who became frozen in disbelief with a mixture of excitement and embarrassment at being picked out. The spotlight followed them as they made their way to claim their prize.

The dancers applauded the young couple as they stepped onto the stage.

"Jim and Laura Jackson!" the MC declared. "Jim works in the stores." He bent his head close to the girl, who spoke in his ear. "And they got married last month! Give them a great round of applause!"

Some enterprising member of the orchestra played a few notes of the Bridal March as young Jim punched the air and claimed the beautiful new Bush four-valve, with special feature tuning eye, radio set.

"Lucky blighters, there goes the bleedin' radio...ah look, they're only just married, I'm glad for them."

"Now, ladies and gentlemen, take the floor for a lady's excuse-me. Don't be shy, here's your chance." The dancing continued as midnight approached.

There were novelty spot prizes, a great new idea. The lights went up and everyone crowded around the stage.

"For our first novelty spot prize..." The MC paused, and the dancers shuffled forward.

"...the first person up to me..." He hesitated. The dancers waited in anticipation.

"...with a pair of nylon stockings over his arm!"

"Quick! Get your stockings off!"

Some had their suspenders half undone when the prize was suddenly awarded.

"Ah, Jaysus!" one or two exclaimed, in the process of trying to coax a wife or girlfriend to hand over their stockings. Standing on the stage was one of the young lads from the accounts department, his girlfriend held high, knees bent, her stocking-clad legs dangling over his arm.

A good few heads turned as Addie tried to readjust her suspenders. Many similar spot prizes followed.

"The first person up to me with a complete set of black teeth!" The compere laughed as he delivered the challenge.

Nobody could produce a complete set of black teeth, though a good few were close. With a flourish, some bright spark produced a black comb and another prize was claimed.

"First man with a couple of redheads!"

"It's a matchstick," the all-knowing Alex exclaimed. "A friendly match with a sulphur head, quick!"

There was a mad rush for the stage, people holding matchboxes aloft.

"I'll never get the hang of this," said a disappointed Mick Moroney. "Last year I won two prizes with the spotlight."

"That's progress for you, Mick," came the reply.

"Maybe you'll win the raffle."

"I wanted the radio."

The Rhythm Kings took a break and an interval prevailed. Various performers were summoned to the stage. This was a highlight moment.

The compere had been furnished with a list of names. "Would Mick Moroney take to the stage, please." He looked around expectantly. "We all agree he's a great singer." Mick strutted up amidst howls of approval and whistles.

"Give us Danny Boy, Mick."

Mick stood on stage, the showman, milking it for all it was worth, savouring every delicious moment. Drawing himself up to his best height, a portly five feet five inches, with his left hand he loosened his dickey bow, letting it hang, Johnnie Ray style. Two buttons popped on the rented frilly shirt revealing a bunch of reddish-brown hair. The crowd howled and whistled and called, "Go for it, Mick!"

With a chubby hand, he readjusted the mic to a lower level. The crowd quietened to a respectful silence.

Now, Mick didn't know much about prawns and he didn't look much like Johnnie Ray, but he certainly could sing. His voice had a beautiful tenor quality that belied his rotund and diminutive physique.

The well-known classic air of Danny Boy soared and filled the room. One by one, the crowd quietly joined in until the whole room was singing, Mick's beautiful voice rising above them all.

Gladys dabbed an eye with her handkerchief. "He's got a beautiful voice, hasn't he?"

Addie put a friendly arm around Mick's wife's shoulders. "He sure has, Gladys," she said.

He finished to thunderous applause and calls of, "More! More! Give us 'The Banks', Mick!"

The compere stepped in as Mick was about to launch into another rendition. "I now call to the stage Alex Matthews!" quickly adding, "Mick will come back at the end of the interval to sing us out, that's a promise. Thank you, Mick, that was great, beautiful."

A reluctant Mick left the stage to be replaced by the pipe-smoking know-it-all Alex Matthews. He fumbled a bit with the mic, getting it to a higher position. Lanky Alex was a good ten inches taller than Mick. He tapped the mic with his pipe. That got a laugh.

"Testing, testing, aon, do, tri, cathar." More laughs, "Thank you, thank you," he said, hand extended in the direction of the departing singer. He put the pipe away. "A hard act to follow." Paying tribute to the talented Mick, he gently clapping his hands together.

"I wish you would follow him," came a voice from the crowd. "Off the fuckin' stage."

Amid the laughs and the "Give him a chance!" comments, Alex smiled, unperturbed. He paused and waited for them to quieten down.

Most of them knew what to expect for the multi-talented Alex could whistle like Ronnie Ronald, make a noise like a trumpet and do farmyard impressions.

"He can play the mouth organ with his nose," someone was heard to say.

"If I were a blackbird, I'd whistle and sing, I'd follow the boat that my true love sailed in," Alex sang and then satisfied his waiting fans with a shrill whistling the equal of any dawn chorus.

Claps and cheers and blackbird whistles from the audience greeted Alex as he went through his repertoire.

A few more acts followed, all greeted with enthusiasm. Mick Moroney returned to the stage, dragging Addie along with him. Roy proudly applauded. She could carry a tune OK.

"When Irish eyes are smiling—" all joined in, any excuse for a singsong "—sure, it's like a morn in spring..."

Eventually the Rhythm Kings were allowed back on the stage and the dancing recommenced until the countdown to twelve o'clock brought midnight and cries of "Happy New Year! Happy New Year!" and lipstick kisses everywhere.

"I love you, Addie." Roy took his beloved wife in his arms. "Happy New Year."

A giant circle formed, hands held, arms crossing and Auld Lang Syne rang out, in and out the line of dancers weaving back and forth.

A great net in the ceiling released a cascade of multicoloured balloons that came down upon the dancers. Amidst the balloons were many novelty toys and gifts, colourful paper hats, noise-makers and toy bugles—presents for all. There was a good-natured scramble.

What a night! After Auld Lang Syne came more dancing, the Hokey Cokey—"Put your left arm in, your left arm out, your left arm in and shake it all about..." The party continued to the early hours of the morning, and the hangers-on had a great singsong after the National Anthem was played.

As Roy and Adelaide arrived home to Ivy Lodge, the sun was rising on a new year.

Chapter 3

IVY LODGE BOASTED A GOOD bit of ground. To one side, spanning the long front garden and the full length of the house, was a large orchard. Originally a classic Victorian design, a high, ivy-covered wall bordered the orchard on three sides with many little pathways between the apple, pear and plum trees, potatoes, carrots and all variety of vegetables and fruit bushes.

Some time had passed since the great New Year's Eve Celebration. The seasons were changing and there was a hint of spring in the air.

The smart red MG sports car rounded the corner at the crossroads and passed by Harkness's shop. Big, brown eyes checked the rear-view mirror through stylish designer sunglasses. Slim, gloved hands on the wheel turned the car onto the country road, passing the little grocery store, then coasting to a stop at the open door in the high garden wall of Ivy Lodge.

"So, this is where Ian Jeffries lives." Laura Anne Robinson peered through the opening at the home of her son's school friend.

A dapper-looking man in his seventies appeared on the pathway leading from the house. Spotting the car, he approached curiously.

Deciding an encounter at this time would not fit with her plans, Laura Anne gunned the engine and sped away along the country road.

Grandad Hugh reached the entrance and stared after the fast- moving sports car.

"The idle rich nosing around, looking into people's gardens and driving open cars without a crash helmet. Whatever next?"

It did not cross his mind that such a person would ever come knocking at the Jeffries' door.

Chapter 4

THE HEAVY SPADE PLUNGED INTO the hard earth, dislodging a large sod loaded with weeds and the white roots of last year's potato crop. An expert lift and a twist turned the sod, and the spade moved on to repeat the action.

Roy and the kids worked methodically, preparing the ground for a new crop of potatoes, cabbages, onions, beetroot, lettuce plants and even turnips. All the produce of the garden patch would be consumed during the summer months with a fair quantity going to the grocery shop in the village. Some money could be made to supplement Roy's income; fresh vegetables were always on demand, but Marty Hartigan, the grocer, drove a fairly hard bargain.

Ian, the youngest, had his own spade. The handle was a bit shorter than the others, a real digging tool cut down to size and quite heavy. A sturdy lad, he worked with a dedicated enthusiasm that belied his years. In went the spade under the weight of a foot driven by a grubby knee. The handle pressed down, and the sod turned, then *bash, bash* with the side of the spade to break it up.

"Here's the robin, look at him." Always when they worked in the garden the tame robin came down to avail of the turned sod and the feast of worms.

Debbie was not working quite so enthusiastically for her mind was elsewhere.

"Hey, Pop, I'm thinking of changing my comic." Eyes squinting against the sunlight, she peered up at Roy as she stooped to pull at a large dandelion root. "You know I get *The Beano* comic on Tuesdays? I want to get the *Bunty*. It's for girls, and I'm eleven. It's better. *The Beano* is a bit young."

Roy loved Saturday. Half-day holiday with no work until Monday morning, time to be with the family, his turn with the kids. He drove the spade into the soil and rested on the long handle. Looking at his daughter's earnest, upturned, freckled face, he considered the problem, aware of the importance of a weekly comic. She waited for a reply, gangly legs bent, motionless with expectation.

"Well, that seems all right. Are they the same price?"

She looked back to her task, standing up as the big dandelion root came free of the soil.

"Well, that's the problem, Pop. *The Beano* is 2d and the *Bunty* is 3d. And I share with Ian," she said, throwing the weed to one side.

"Well, I suppose if *The Beano*'s too young it's no use to you. I'd say it'd be OK." He smiled kindly.

"Thanks, Pop." She beamed with pleasure, driving her spade in with a renewed gusto.

"That's not fair!" Ian's spade was propelled across the patch with some force. The robin took refuge in one of the large apple trees. "The *Bunty*'s for girls! It's all stories and no pictures! I want my own *Beano* then!"

Before Roy or the older ones could respond, Ian was on his way, heading for the house in a rage. At the gate, he turned and shouted, "And that's all there is to it!" Some years younger than the other two, the young lad was learning to fight his corner.

"Come back here, you!" Roy commanded, but Ian was gone through the gate and around the side of the house. Roy stuck the spade in the ground and turned a sod. "I can do without this," he complained. "It's a nice Saturday afternoon. I've been on the bike all morning. I could do with a bit of peace and quiet." They started digging again.

"He's a little brat," said James.

Debbie nodded her head.

Roy stopped digging and leaned his brown, folded arms on the handle of the spade turning his head to look at Debbie and James.

"You know, the young lad has a point," he said. "Debbie, if *The Beano* is no good to you then the *Bunty* is no good to him. Did you discuss this with your mother?"

Debbie looked a bit abashed and reluctantly said, "Yes, Pop."

"And what did your mother say?"

"She said I couldn't have it."

Roy couldn't help a little smile. "Sure, maybe we'll manage to get both comics." He put down the spade. "I'm not saying definitely," he quickly added. "I'll have to talk to your mother."

He stretched his back and stood for a minute, contemplating the work achieved. Quite a large part of the potato patch had been turned. The rest could be completed tomorrow if the rain held off. He looked at the darkening sky. "Let's call it a day." Putting his hand in his pocket, he counted out six pennies. "Here, James, run out to the shop and get some slab toffee. I'd better have a word with that young lad."

Standing wide-legged, in the middle of the orchard, rolled-up shirt-sleeved arms folded, Roy smiled as he watched the two dash off to the shop, James, tall and lanky in long corduroy trousers jostling through the garden gateway with the fleet-footed Debbie, skinny white elbows held high, giving as good as she got.

With a sigh, Roy headed in pursuit of the fiery Ian, Through the garden gate and across the little yard, through another small gate, around to the back of the house and past the shed with its rusted galvanised roof. In front of him was Grandad Hugh's chicken run leading up to the top road. He stopped to check the wire-mesh fence that ran the width of the run. Rhode Island Reds and Pullets crowded at the fence expecting to be fed. He *cluck-clucked* at them and walked on around the back of the shed heading to the 'paddock'.

The paddock—a large piece of untilled ground where nature had its way—was a riot of long grass and meadow growth.

Two lines of tall pine trees bordered the area. Stopping, Roy looked up at the lofty treetops waving back and forth in the light breeze. *Time they were topped. They're getting high and they're very close to the house,* he thought to himself. *Now where's that young lad?*

Halfway along the line of tall trees running parallel to the house there was a gap that led into the paddock. Here, Roy stopped, hands on hips.

"Hopalong Cassidy always gets his man!" he stated loudly looking around. "Show yourself or I'll start shootin'!"

The base of the pine tree nearest to him was sloped and wide with large branches spanning out on either side. Other branches had been cut away to create the gap, making perfect hand and footholds for climbing. Silence greeted the challenge.

"All right, you asked for it!" He strode out into the paddock and swivelled. Crouching, he drew an imaginary six-gun and began to shoot up into the branches of the tree. Dar! dar! dar!"

"Gotcha!" The Red Indian came out of the long grass behind him in a rush. Roy let himself collapse to the ground on his back, the hysterically laughing Ian astride him delivering imaginary tomahawk blows to his chest. Roy could see the tear smears on the laughing face and knew the little chap had been crying.

"Ya got me! Ya got me! Ya dirty rat!" He clutched his chest and closed his eyes.

Ian jumped up, rubbing his face with a grubby hand, half laughing and half crying. "It's still not fair!" he said.

Roy, from his position on the ground, looked up into the defiant, tear-stained face. "Well, sure, maybe we'll get the two comics," he said, stiffly getting to his feet.

"Yahoo! Thanks! Thanks! Thanks, Pop!" Ian galloped a lap of the paddock whooping and yelling, slapping his backside.

"Now, mind you, I'll have to check with your ma!" Roy shouted.

"My own *Beano* every week." Ian couldn't believe his ears. "Maybe I'll get the *Dandy* some weeks. It's the same price, Pop," he quickly added, out of breath.

They headed back through the gap and down the lane at the side of the house. The big iron gate let them out onto the road.

Ian let go his dad's hand and ran to meet the other two as they came down the road from Billy's shop. "We're getting a comic each! We're getting a comic each!" he chanted.

"We've got Cleeve's Toffee," came the reply.

As they stood at the step to the green door in the high wall near the big iron gates, without warning, it began to rain heavily. Under the arch of the laurel hedge inside the door, they paused to shelter.

"Let's run for it, it's a race!" They dashed up the path to the Virginia-creeper-covered house, James first, then Debbie, closely followed by Ian. Roy wasn't quite so quick off the mark. Reaching the front door, they entered the porch.

"C'mon, Paddy Last." The heavy rain bounced off the glass roof making a din. The excited kids were laughing, gasping, rubbing wet faces and hair. "I'm soaked."

"Quiet now." Roy put his finger to his lips. "Your ma's in bed with one of her migraines, shhh."

They tiptoed down the hall, passing the slightly open door of the darkened bedroom and into the short passageway that led to the big kitchen at the back of the house.

Three pairs of eyes watched as Roy carefully unwrapped the waxy paper revealing the large slab of Cleeve's Toffee with its twelve sections: three each.

"None for Ian," joked James, winking at his dad. He got a punch in the arm from the young lad for his trouble.

"None for you, you mean."

The large slab of dark toffee was laid out on the kitchen table. Debbie retrieved a knife from a drawer in the big country dresser and handed it to her dad. They watched in admiration as Roy, with a skill only possessed by fathers, made four indented lines on the back of the brittle toffee. Then *rap, rap, rap*, some sharp taps with the back of the blade and four pieces, slightly irregular, appeared. They were quickly doled out before comparisons in size and shape could be made, Roy taking what he considered the smallest.

This was a treat reserved for Saturday afternoons made all the more wonderful because of the presence of their dad. Sometimes there was a small tin of condensed milk. This would be shared too, four ways, a small amount each in a cup, none the less sweet for the minute quantity.

Today, the toffee was enough. Cheeks bulging, they sat at the table in contented silence, savouring the treat.

Roy enjoyed the weekend as much as the kids did. He looked out through the kitchen window at the rain teeming down. *Plitt! Plitt! Plitt!*

"Get some saucepans, kids!" The rain was coming in at several places in the hall. *Plitt! Plitt!* it went. *Splash, Splash* on the lino.

"James! Check the dining room!"

They all knew the drill. Get a towel or any piece of cloth. Put the pot, saucepan, bucket—any utensil that would hold water—under the drip and put the cloth in it. The noisy *plitt, plitt* on the lino became a much quieter *putt, putt, putt* into a container where the water was trapped, eventually to be emptied.

Roy looked up to the ceiling in the long hallway. There were two fanlights. The water was dripping down from both and also at the beginning of the passage to the kitchen. There was a pretty big watermark at each location where the rain had come in many times before. The wallpaper was slightly coming away from the wall high up at the ceiling.

"It's coming in bad in the dining room, Pop!" James shouted. "I'm running out of pots."

Off the kitchen was the dining room with its white-painted wood-panelled ceiling. James had positioned a series of pots but was losing the battle.

"Stand back! Stand back, Ma to the rescue." Holding the large ornate china chamber pot before her, Addie came marching into the room, fully recovered from her migraine.

"No, Ma, not the piss pot!"

She plonked the utensil on the dining room table under a pretty significant drip that was coming from the middle of the ceiling.

"I've seen everything now," said Roy. "Now all we need is an umbrella and we can have our tea."

The shower soon passed, and the rain, eventually, stopped coming in.

"It's whatever way the wind is blowing," Addie explained. "During the week, it rained and not a drop came in."

"I'll get up on the roof tomorrow and see what I can do," Roy declared. "How is the head? I'm glad to see you're looking better." He put his arms around Addie, who snuggled into his large frame. James smiled, Debbie smiled.

"Kiss her!" said Ian. "She doesn't have any lipstick on."

"It's stopped raining! Get the rugby ball!" James looked out the window. "I kicked one during the week, right through the gap, honestly!"

Debbie jumped off her chair. "No one saw you do it, so it doesn't count." She ran out of the room and came back with the ball.

They headed out the door and around to the paddock and 'the gap', Debbie leading the way, kicking the ball from foot to hand three times before it skewed to one side into the long grass to be retrieved by Ian.

"Girls are no good at rugby. Watch this." He stylishly attempted a drop kick, missing the ball completely. Not deterred, he attempted it a second time with a similar result. "Rugby's stupid! Anyway, I prefer soccer," he said, walking away from the ball.

Roy picked it up, jogged a few paces and threw it to James. Addie trotted alongside, and James threw the ball to her.

"Catch!" She threw the ball, and Debbie caught it. They played 'Catch' until they reached the line of pine trees. Tall, reaching high into the sky before them, their tops swayed slightly in the breeze. Two trees slightly further apart than the others created the gap high up near their tops where the branches did not meet. Ian had the ball. He threw it to James.

"Dad's the only one who can do it. Go on, smarty boots."

James took the ball. "I had a few goes before I succeeded."

"Go on, son, keep your head down over the ball and follow through," Roy encouraged. "Then Ian can have a go."

James looked up at the gap and threw the ball to Roy.

"You first—show us how it's done."

Converting the ball between the treetops was Roy's specialty. He didn't make it every time. All comers would make the attempt, none succeeding except for that Scottish fellow, on holiday, who had come out to visit with some of the lads from Roy's work. They said he had played rugby for Scotland.

Roy's first attempt fell short. Ian quickly retrieved the ball.

At the second attempt, the ball made it high and true, into the sky.

Ian watched it sail straight between the treetops. "Wow!" His eyes were bright with admiration for the dad that could do anything. "The Champion! Roy Jeffries scores for Ireland." He commentated as he ran to retrieve the ball from the middle of the paddock.

James had a few tries but fell a little bit short. It was generally accepted that girls couldn't kick a ball, but Debbie wasn't that far off. Addie pleaded the wrong shoes and claimed an injured toe when her stocking-footed shot didn't leave the ground. Ian, retrieving the ball on every occasion, panting and red-faced from the continuous exertion, made twice as many attempts as everyone else.

Chapter 5

SUNDAY WAS ONE OF THOSE days when you just knew that the blue sky was going to stay like that: blue all day. There was a slightly chilly east wind. Myriad birds chirped and hopped around the garden. *Click, click.* A thrush expertly tapped a snail's shell on a rock. Addie opened the back door that led into the little yard to let Mac, the black Labrador, out for a run. Across the small yard he charged, nose to the ground, out the small gateway and into the large orchard.

Addie looked up at the sky and then watched the dog for a while as he snuffled and explored the trails left by small creatures of the previous night, leaving his own mark where he thought appropriate.

Deciding to leave the kitchen door open to allow the early morning spring air to invade the big old kitchen, Addie noticed the horseshoe hanging on the door was upside down, held by a solitary nail. Many a door in rural Ireland boasted a horseshoe to bring luck to the house, but an upside-down horseshoe allows all the luck to fall out. Addie swivelled it around and upright again, holding it in place with her finger. *I must get a nail and fix it.*

The sound of Roy playing with the children drifted to her ears, along with the splutter of sausages, reminding her of breakfast and the porridge needing a stir. Turning, she hurried across the kitchen to the large stove. The horseshoe swivelled upside down again as soon as she took her finger away.

"Nine o'clock! nine o'clock! Get up, you lazy heads, there's work to be done!"

The three kids slept in the same room. Every coat in the house had been used on top of the blankets to keep the cold at bay. They felt cosy and warm and not inclined to get up.

"There's sausages for breakfast, and if you don't get up you won't get any!" Roy went from bed to bed, prodding and playfully punching the odd cocked bum in the air. Giggles came from under the blankets. "I warned you once—if you're not out of bed and at the table in ten minutes, there'll be war."

He picked up a grey woolly sock from the floor. "Whose is this?" He held it up, gave it a good sniff—"Agh! It's James's. Ten minutes or there'll be war!"—and marched out the door, but the promise of sausages rendered the threat unnecessary.

A short while later, at breakfast, Ian contemplated his porridge with an eye across the table at Debbie and James, their spoons working as they headed for the reward. Porridge consumed, there would be sausages. He looked at the melting sugar on top of the hot porridge, knowing the part would be nice. It was the middle down that caused the problem. If he could get halfway and add more sugar, then there was a chance of finishing and getting the sausages. Putting the spoon in—not too deep—he rapidly completed the first part of his plan, getting down to halfway without too much trouble.

"Can I have more sugar, Ma? I've nearly finished."

Debbie glanced across the table at her little brother. "That's cheating!" Indignantly, she held up her empty bowl to show that she had finished.

"No, it's not! You like porridge, it's easy for you!" Ian bristled.

Addie shot a warning glance at Debbie and then looked across at Roy, sensing the possibility of a row starting between the two children. Ian—a street angel and a house devil, as the saying goes—had a great capacity to charm and be highly amusing and was, in fact, by and large a well-behaved, good-natured boy, but volatile too. The most innocent situation could cause the holocaust to break out. Doors would get slammed, words of indignation would be bawled, and tears shed.

Many a wonderful day could be spoiled at the drop of a hat, and the warning signals were flashing.

Addie's tactic was deflection: spot the danger and deflect.

"How much would it cost to buy a gas fridge, Roy?" she asked, saying the first thing that came into her head as she sprinkled some sugar over Ian's porridge.

Oblivious to the impending danger, Roy looked blankly at her. A fridge was the furthest thing from his mind. The rain coming in from the porous roof and having to take refuge under an umbrella to have his tea was far more important.

"We can't afford to have the roof fixed. What's all this talk about buying a fridge?"

"Ice pops!" she said, cocking a head in Ian's direction. "Ice pops," she repeated. "There are these moulds in the fridge. You can put orange cordial and water in them—you can even get lollipop sticks. When they freeze, you've got an ice pop on a stick just like you buy in the shops."

Roy looked at his wife in bemusement and then around the table at the expectant faces.

"Oh, yes," he agreed vaguely and returned to his morning paper without a further word, the trials and tribulations of Dagwood and Blondie on the cartoon page of his Sunday paper offering him some sanctuary.

James speared a sausage. "The O'Neills have one, but Mrs. O'Neill doesn't let them have ice pops."

"Well, I'd let you make ice pops," declared Addie.

"When are we getting the fridge, Ma?"

Addie noted her youngest son had nearly finished his porridge.

"Ask your father," she said flicking the newspaper with the sugar spoon.

***

After breakfast in the kitchen, Addie was peeling the potatoes, slim hands moving expertly and quickly, her thoughts sometimes provoking a smile but more often a frown, causing her to pause in her work as her agile mind came to grips with the various household problems. Inevitably, all the paths of her mind led to the grey clouds of bills to be paid, school fees, electricity, gas, food—the endless problem of making ends meet. *The mortgage, the mortgage, the mortgage, the house falling apart.* She looked up at the paint flaking from the ceiling high above, the ancient taps over the big old-fashioned kitchen sink. *It's going to get worse.*

Monica Tracey's house with its lovely carpets and modern kitchen, semi-detached and new, swooped into her mind. Immediately, the counter argument came. *Semi-detached! How could you live sharing a wall with someone else? It would be like living with strangers, and those low ceilings and tiny gardens. No, No, never,* she consoled herself, a little smile tugging at the corners of her mouth.

Slowly coming out of her reverie, she looked around the kitchen, but she was not reassured. If only Roy was more ambitious. There was still no word about the inspector's job. Mr. Blackwell as good as said it was Roy's. She became more convinced as she thought about it, of course, the chairman himself had said it. How could she have been so foolish as to worry?

Sure, the job is Roy's for the asking, and Bradley, he told Roy last week that a decision on the inspector's job had been put on hold for a few weeks. Now why did he tell Roy that? Why tell Roy and nobody else? Because the job is his, she reasoned to herself. *Roy asked the other collectors if they'd heard anything, and all said no.* Feeling a bit better about things, she finished off peeling the potatoes.

Clump, clump! The noise was coming from above her head. They were up on the roof looking for leaks to plug. *Clump, clump!* She could just about make out the sound of their voices. Addie always felt a bit apprehensive when they went up there armed with spreading knives and yellow tubs of *Righto*: a black, waterproof, tarry substance guaranteed to weather all holes and cracks.

***

There were three gable ends to Ivy Lodge. The roof was high, as high as a two-storey house. In the old tradition of Victorian buildings, large tiles covered the roof, with a fancy ridge tile running along the width of the house at the top of each apex. The valleys in between were where the trouble lay, lined with one-hundred-year-old lead. The Irish weather had taken its toll, and the lead had become porous in places.

They worked, identifying trouble spots from their memory of where the drips came in. Old dried 'Righto marks' had become porous again.

"Over here, here's a bad one!" James crouched and, with a brush, began to clean away the gathered moss and bits of grit, exposing a crack in the lead flashing.

Debbie scrambled down the slope of the roof to join him. "That's the one over the hall."

Meanwhile, Roy worked at another place further along the valley, aware that their repair work could only be a temporary solution. Every visit to the roof disclosed more and more problems. Nearly all the old repair marks were leaking again and there were plenty of new ones. The whole lot would have to be replaced.

Alone in the yard, Ian played with a football. Being younger than the others had its disadvantages. They were up on the roof. He could hear them, and he wanted to be up there too. *It's not fair! Sunday is special!* On Sundays, they did things with their dad and ma. They looked for mushrooms in the fields opposite to the house, worked in the garden, played Cowboys and Indians or went out on the road playing with other boys and girls, or went to the beach on bicycles. Sometimes the O'Neills invited him to go for a Sunday drive in their car. Sundays, especially when the weather was good, were packed with lots to do, but not today because of the stupid roof. Ian listened to them laughing and joking and having a great time.

The kitchen door was open. The ball was at his feet.

"Stanley Matthews has the ball, he beats one player and another, he swerves to the right, he swerves to the left..." Ian commentated, dribbling the ball around the yard, "He turns and he shoots!" He kicked the ball through the inviting open doorway. "It's a goal!"

Addie was about to place the pot of potatoes on the stove when the ball came through the doorway, driven with all the force fuelled by the young lad's frustration. *Crash!* It bounced off the big dresser, rattling the row of willow-pattern plates, and landed on the kitchen table where Addie had laid out the ingredients for bread baking. A bag of flour exploded on impact with quite spectacular results. The cat, taking a direct hit, scampered out into the yard with a simultaneous howl and a sneeze, its coat instantly transformed from glossy black to snow white, leaving a trail of flour in its wake.

"Ian!" Addie surveyed the damage and strode purposefully out into the yard, but Stanley Matthews had beaten a hasty retreat and was nowhere to be seen. Deciding to deal with the fleet-footed Ian later, Addie returned to the kitchen with a sigh.

***

The ladder leaned against the shed wall. *You're too small to go on the roof.* Ian could hear his dad's voice in his head. His eyes travelled up the beckoning ladder to where it met the galvanise roof. Forbidden fruit. No sign of his ma coming in pursuit.

If I can climb a tree, I can climb a ladder. It's easy-peasy. "Somebody must always hold the ladder in case it slips. That's the rule." Debbie is allowed up the ladder and she's a girl. I often see people climbing ladders without people holding them.

He reached up to grip one of the wooden rungs and took the first step. It would be great to see the top of the galvanised roof. Up he went quickly. At the top of the ladder, he looked around and down. Excited by the height, his heart beat faster as he stepped onto the rusty, sloping roof. *Creak, creak.* He stopped and dropped to his knees.

The shed roof, at its highest point, was attached to the house. On hands and knees, Ian scaled the rusty galvanised slope to the tiles of the house. They reached away from him even higher. Looking around again, he could see the O'Neills' house below, about 100 yards away, Gerard O'Neill, his friend, in the garden with his pop. Ian waved. Gerard waved back, pointing, getting his father to look.

"Look at me! Look, at me!" Ian shouted and scampered up the sloping tiles of the house.

Paddy O'Neill felt the tug on his jacket and looked where his son was pointing. At first, he noticed nothing unusual, but then he saw Ian, on hands and knees, climbing up the high sloping roof, perilously close to the edge.

The fancy tiling at the top of the apex was almost in reach. Ian crawled higher, his feet slipping on the moss- covered tiles. He slid back and scrambled frantically, grazing his knee, momentarily panicked. Gasping with the effort, he just managed to grab the terracotta ridge tile and held on with both hands, lying on the sloping roof, afraid to move in case he lost his grip.

They're going to be mad at me if I fall. Gradually getting his breath back, and realising he was not about to die, he managed to gain a kneeling position. He got one grubby leg over and sat proudly astride the ridge. An old scab on his knee had been dislodged by the climb, and a bright-red trickle of blood meandered its way down a grubby leg to disappear into his sock. He examined it and then gave it a rub with an equally grubby knuckle, watching the blood as it oozed again from the wound.

The warrior in a high place looking out for the enemy from a vantage point higher than he had ever been before—higher than Jack when he climbed the beanstalk. He could see across the fields to the mountains in the distance; nearby, the road that passed the house, leading to the roof of Billy's shop at the fork where it joined the main road; the forge and the row of workers' cottages; the pub at the crossroads, on to the council estate and beyond to the dairy; people coming from Mass wearing their Sunday best; children playing.

Ian gazed at the view, heady with power. A car turning at the crossroads became an enemy tank and he riddled it with his machine gun. "*Ra! Tatt! Tatt!*"

"Stay where you are! Don't move!" his dad shouted in alarm.

Ian looked down into the valley where the next roof met with the tiles that sloped away from his outstretched legs.

Roy shouted again, his hand raised, fingers splayed in warning. "Don't move! I'll get you!"

"*Bang! Bang!* You're all dead!" Ian shouted in his excitement. With a last admiring look around, he cried, "Coming down! Make way for the champion!"

Before anyone could move, Ian had brought his other leg over the ridge and was sliding on his backside down the steep roof, his feet out in front of him to slow him down.

"See that, Pop!" he cried in excitement as he arrived in the leaded valley. "Do you want a hand?"

Roy looked at the boy in shocked surprise. "How did you get up here?"

Ian jumped up and headed at a run along the valley towards the edge of the roof. Roy was far too slow, and Debbie and James were the other side of him. Roy knew he could not catch the excited Ian before he reached the edge. "Stop, Ian! Stop!" He scrambled after the fast-moving lad.

Ian had never been so high up before in his life. "Yahoo!" At the edge, he dropped to his knees and looked down into the yard far below.

"Hulloo, hulloo!" he called, using his best funny voice, and grinned down at the upturned anxious faces of Ma and Mr. O'Neill, then startled in surprise when his dad's strong hands grabbed him from behind.

"I've got him!" Roy called in relief.

***

"Thanks, Paddy." Addie turned to the out of breath Paddy O'Neill at her side.

Paddy looked disapprovingly. "How did he get up there in the first place? He's only a young lad. He shouldn't be allowed up there at his age." The neighbour was enjoying the moral high ground. "Gerry is the same age, and I'd never let him up on the roof. Ian could have fallen and badly injured himself and then you'd be sorry." His expression showed his distaste for all irresponsible parents and their behaviour.

Knowing only too well what might have happened and feeling upset from the experience, Addie was angered by the neighbour's smugness. "Your Gerry wouldn't be able to climb up on the roof in the first place. Don't lecture me, Paddy O'Neill, and anyway, how would you know what your kids would be up to when you spend so much time in the pub?" Leaving Paddy no opportunity to reply, she marched off into the kitchen closing the door behind her.

Paddy O'Neill was still standing there, contemplating the back door and a possible retort, when Roy and the children came around into the yard.

"Hello, Paddy." Roy smiled a greeting to his neighbour.

"Abuse—that's all you get from the Jeffries. Abuse! Do a good deed and what do you get? Abuse!" The red-faced Paddy gave the unfortunate and confused Roy both barrels. "That young lad of yours is more trouble than he's worth."

"What's the problem, Paddy? Here, come in and have a cup of tea." Roy put out a conciliatory hand.

"No, thank you very much," came the lofty reply from the miffed neighbour. "I don't want your tea." He turned and headed for the garden gate, straight-backed and indignant. "Just because Addie is an attractive woman, it doesn't mean she can treat people like dirt," was his parting shot.

Not one to enjoy angry confrontation, Roy stood for a moment, amused by the incident and Paddy's indignation but at the same time upset at the unpleasantness.

"C'mon, you, let's see what's for dinner." He led the kids through the back door and into the kitchen, where the lovely smell of baking bread greeted them.

"Ian, come here you little brat!" Addie grabbed her son's arm, turned him around and delivered three hefty smacks to his backside. "I'm very cross with you! Don't *ever* go up on that roof again! And don't disobey instructions." She delivered another smack and released a tearful Ian.

"I'm sorry," said the dejected young lad, looking at his ma with tear-filled eyes. "I won't do it again. Anyway," he added with a tentative smile, "the slaps didn't hurt."

"Well, maybe I'll get a switch like Mrs. O'Neill, or I'll get your da to give you a good hard one." With a grip on the child's arm, she looked across the kitchen. "Your da's a lot stronger than me."

Roy was busy washing his hands at the big old sink and showed little interest in the invitation. "What's for dinner Addie?" he asked without turning around.

But the threat of a switch had the required effect on Ian. He'd been witness to Paddy O'Neill doling out punishment on the odd occasion and had no wish to receive the same.

"I'll be good, I promise." He put his arms up to receive a slightly tearful hug from his relieved ma.

"Do I smell stew?" Roy dried his hands and lifted the lid of the pot simmering on the stove. He looked at Addie. "All's well that ends well. Sure, nobody was hurt."

Addie was about to make a retort but thought better of it and said, "The dinner will be ready at one o'clock."

"We'll set the table." Roy replaced the lid carefully and headed for the dining room with Debbie and Ian, leaving James and his mother in the big kitchen.

Addie held her wrist and flexed the fingers of her right hand.

"Did you hurt your hand, Ma?" James noticed his mother's discomfort as she prepared the dinner. "Why do you always have to do the scolding? The other dads whack their kids when they're bold. You're not going to get a switch, are you, Ma?" The thirteen-year-old stood in the kitchen, looking earnestly at his mother. She looked back, their eyes at a level.

"No, I'm not going to get a switch, but don't tell the other two. You're a good lad, James." *How grown up he has become, how like his dad—curly, dark hair, grey eyes, tall, the same sense of humour, a handsome boy.* Instinctively, she reached out and put a gentle hand on his sleeve. "Your da is not an aggressive person. He's kind and thoughtful. Maybe he should be more assertive sometimes, but I love him the way he is. If you grow up to be half the man your dad is, you'll be all right." Her words, with the familiarity of repetition, tripped from her lips with ease.

James nodded, happy at his ma's confidential tone. "Yes, I know, Ma. He's the greatest dad in the world. I'll help them at the table." Turning, he left his mother behind in the big old ramshackle kitchen.

Addie's words still echoed in her head as she paused in thought. "No, I don't want him to grow up *exactly* like his da. I want him to have ambition and strength and conviction. I want him to get somewhere in the world."

She pulled out a chair and sat down at the kitchen table. The chair rocked on the uneven floor, and she gripped the table to steady herself, tears welling up in her eyes—tears of anger and frustration. "Damn the chair! Damn the bills."

A slight twinge in her wrist reinforced her feeling of helplessness. "I can't even discipline my own kids," she whispered fiercely. *Roy, everyone's friend. Handsome Roy. How lucky you are to have such a wonderful husband. Roy, Roy, Roy... If only people knew, beautiful, everybody's friend, Roy. Niceness, beauty and goodness doesn't pay the bills. A bit of drive and ambition would help.*

She went to the kitchen cupboard and pulled down the pile of bills all skewered together on a wire hook. The laughter coming from the dining room didn't improve her mood as she checked the latest demands on their meagre resources.

***

The modern house on Avondale Road boasted a very nice pebble drive, manicured lawn and a circular flowerbed. Outside, the red sports car was parked alongside a large saloon car.

Inside, Mr. Gordon Robinson of Robinson Decorating Products was home after a particularly gruelling board meeting. The day had not gone well, and he was in no mood to listen to Laura Anne's tales of their son Christopher's latest bad behaviour.

"Domestic affairs! That's your domain. I look after the business, you look after the home. And that includes Christopher's carryings on. Deal with it! I know he's an only child, I know he's spoilt, I know we can't have more children. Do what you have to do—adopt, get help. If you can't cope, employ someone who can. Whatever it costs, I'll pay.

"Now, I need a gin and tonic. Do you want one?" At the door, he turned with a resigned gesture, arms outstretched to drop at his sides. "I know Christopher is a problem child. I'm sure it would have been different had he had a brother or sister. Do what you have to do," he repeated in a more conciliatory tone.

Laura Anne followed him into the other room to organise the gin and tonic.

Chapter 6

SPRING RECEDING INTO SUMMER DAYS, the rain, less frequent now, came from a different direction and penetrated the leaky roof but not to quite the same extent. The daylight hours stretching, the clocks changed to accommodate the hour. The community had shed winter clothes and spent more time outdoors.

Weekends were best. Across the road and down to the left, a five-barred gate gave access to the fields of the farm owned by the Christian brothers. Divided by ditches and hedges, the fields—to a young lad like Ian—were vast areas inhabited by big cows and a bull and not to be ventured into alone.

Looking for mushrooms at weekends was great, Ian's dad leading the way through the gate and along the edge of the first field. The grazing cows turned their heads, curiously, before wandering in the direction of the five intruders. Ian bravely marched ahead, the grass in the meadow long and full of intrigue, daisies, cowslips, buttercups and, if you were lucky, buried in the lush grass you might find a clump of mushrooms. Debbie held her dad's hand as if her life depended on it, looking up into his face as she strode beside him, then hugging his arm tight as he swung her in a circle, her feet off the ground, *wheeeeee!* to land on the soft grass. He let her go and strode on. Jumping to her feet, she ran to catch up.

"Me now!" Ian ran back for his turn in the glorious game. James, too big for the game, walked beside Addie, taking up the rear with head bent, scanning for mushrooms, aware that this was not the best field to find them but just in case, their progress slower because of the blackberries to be collected on the way. The next field was the mushroom field.

"Watch me! I'm the champ!" Ian charged ahead towards the high hedge and another five-barred gate. "I can get over it a special way!" His foot hit the bottom rung of the gate. In one movement, he chested the top bar and swung his legs over and down to land on the other side.

"See that?" he cried triumphantly, looking back to receive his applause.

"Gotcha!"

Ian whirled in panic at the sound of the voice. Concealed from the others view stood Peter Mulligan, the man who patrolled the fields during the weekdays, keeping kids out, giving chase, waving a stick, threatening and shouting. Peter Mulligan was the most frightening person in the eight-year-old's world. "Don't get caught by Peter Mulligan," all the kids warned.

"Dad! Dad! Da..." Ian frantically tried to scramble back over the gate.

"Afternoon, folks," Peter Mulligan greeted, stepping out from behind the hedge and opening the gate with a big grin on his stubbly face as Ian retreated behind his dad. "There's a good few mushrooms over by the brook on the bank." He pointed with his big knobbly hawthorn stick.

Ian's eyes locked on the terrifying weapon, the stuff of nightmares. Debbie held her Dad's hand a little tighter.

"There's no need to be afraid of me." The big head turned and the half-closed eyes fixed on Ian. "Ye're welcome in the fields as long as you don't do damage. If you do any damage, ye'll get the stick," he growled and then, with a wink at Roy and a tip of his hat to Addie, he strode off.

The 'river' bordered one side of the mushroom field, its sloping bank a nice place to sit. Chopped egg and tomato sandwiches, with a little bit of onion and some salad cream, wrapped in the waxy paper of a large sliced pan and corned beef slices: a picnic on a riverbank.

Addie, in a candy-striped red and white dress, sat and handed out the precious sandwiches, tea in a flask for the adults, milk for the kids and a bottle of orange cordial, followed by a ginger-nut biscuit and some apples and pears from the garden. The stream and its banks were an adventure playground of frogs, grasshoppers, ladybirds, dandelions to blow, *one o'clock, two o'clock*, and the little seed parachutes flew away on the soft breeze. Daisies for daisy chains, cowslips to be gathered, and bobbing twigs floating in a race on the water. Pinkeens in the stream, a jam jar with string tied around the rim lowered into the slow-moving water—silently without the slightest movement, watch and wait, then whip the jar out for a quick examination, expectant eyes and nose close to the glass to peer into the muddy water, hoping to see the little eyes of a pinkeen looking back at you.

The little fish that inhabited the stream were quick and hard to catch. "Got one!" James was always first. He transferred the water and the little fish into the 2lb sweet jar brought for the purpose.

Debbie quickly followed. "Two!" She excitedly held up her jar for all to see and exclaim.

Ian sat looking at his jar in the water. Not leaving it in long enough, impatiently he had pulled it out seven times without catching anything.

Debbie proudly transferred the great catch into the large glass jar and returned to quickly cry out again at her good fortune. More fish were transferred to the large jar.

Ian jerked his jar out and peered into the muddy water. "Three!" he shouted and quickly emptied the water into the large jar before it could be checked.

"Fibber!" James started counting the fish.

"Good man, Ian." Roy looked into the jar. "Sure, we've got loads." He lay back on the soft grass while Addie busied herself putting away the picnic things.

"I hope the grass isn't damp." She checked with her hand before lying down beside him. For a few minutes, they lay and listened to the children.

"I hope that young lad catches a fish soon or there'll be war." She laughed. "We should have called him Dennis after Dennis the Menace in *The Beano*."

Roy glanced at her. "Sure, he's only fighting his corner, I suppose." The comment hung in the air. Addie propped herself up on one elbow.

"But is it fair on the other two. You're always making them step down, especially James."

Roy sat up straight. "You do it too."

"Not as much as you. You're too soft, Roy. James was only counting the fish. Debbie caught the most. Ian didn't catch any." She sat up angrily. "When you said, 'Well done, Ian,' it took the good out of it for Debs."

Roy stretched out his hands, palms up. "We all know Ian was only pretending, and Debbie knows we know. I'll say something to her on the quiet." He lay back on the grass.

Addie remained on one elbow. "It's all right for you," she whispered fiercely. "You only have to put up with it one day in the week. I have it from morning to night every day."

Roy sighed and remained silent. Addie watched the kids. James had abandoned his own efforts and was helping Ian, his hand on the string to Ian's jar. He jerked it out of the water, and Ian stood up. James let the string go at the same time, leaving the younger boy holding the jar aloft, peering expectantly into the muddy water.

"I caught one!" he exclaimed. "It's the biggest!"

Addie lay back and looked at the sky as Ian clambered up the bank to show off his catch.

"Look at what Ian caught—it's the biggest!" James informed them as he followed. "Good man, Ian!"

Roy helped him empty the catch into the big jar. "Addie, did you see what Ian caught?"

"Wonderful" she replied, without a glance, her voice displaying disinterest as she studied the sky.

The afternoon was closing in, and a chill breeze ruffled the long grass at the water's edge, the incident forgotten.

"C'mon, you lot, time to make tracks." Roy levered himself up from his sitting position. Pretending he couldn't stand up, he flopped backwards, reaching out. Debbie was first to grab the outstretched hand, and Ian ran behind him to help with a push. James busied himself with the picnic bag, and Addie folded away the tablecloth.

There wasn't much to carry as everything had been consumed. The picnic utensils fitted into the bottom of the rucksack now hanging limply from James's shoulders. Roy carefully took control of the large sweet jar with the controversial catch of the day. Addie had two bags: one with mushrooms and one with blackberries. The trip back through the fields was uneventful save for the occasions when Addie spotted a particularly laden blackberry bush. With everyone gathering, the bag was becoming quite full.

"There'll be a good few jars of blackberry jam in this lot," she exclaimed with satisfaction.

Roy walked ahead with Debbie holding his hand. Both of them were laughing—a beautiful sound that drifted back to Addie on the slight breeze. Ian, as usual, was racing ahead, slapping his backside and shooting imaginary Indians. Debbie laughed again, and Roy lifted the gangly girl onto his hip. She put her skinny arms around his neck and snuggled her freckled face into his shoulder.

Ian turned and looked, quietly waiting, sturdy legs apart, hands on his hips, face upturned with a slight furrow in his brow. He put up his arms to Roy as they drew level. "My turn."

Addie recognised the tone; the time bomb was primed. Remembering Addie's earlier criticism, Roy decided to make a stance.

"Do you think I'm Superman?" He laughingly indicated the girl on his arm and the heavy fish jar held by the knotted twine handle dangling from his other hand.

"I want to carry the jar." Ian grabbed the handle.

"It's too heavy for you." Roy strode on.

Ian tightened his grip, now with two hands. "But I want to. It's not!" He trotted alongside. The jar tilted, and some water spilled.

"No, don't be bold!" Roy admonished with a glance back at Addie, who remained silent.

Ian, tearful and defiant, dug in his feet and pulled backwards with all his strength. "Let it go!" he shouted. The string broke, and as Roy lost his grip, the big jar tilted upside down, emptying the precious catch to the ground. Tiny silver fish wriggled, mouths agape, as the water sank into the soft earth. Addie walked on while Roy and a tearful Debbie stood helplessly by, unable to save the little creatures in their struggle to survive. Ian stood defiantly, looking at his dad's face, unsure of what was going to happen next. The large empty sweet jar still held by the string lay on its side. Roy's expression surpassed any words as he glared at Ian, who stubbornly held his ground.

"You always spoil everything," Roy said with a sad shake of his head. "Here, Debs." He knelt down beside the distraught girl, who was trying to transfer the little silver fish to the jar with its remaining half inch of water. Ian tearfully watched the big brown fingers, clumsy in their attempt to gently disentangle the little silver bodies from the grass. He stepped forward to help but was stopped by Roy's hand.

"You've done enough damage."

Ian stood back, hurt, upset and at the same time indignant at the rejection of his small attempt to make amends.

"I didn't mean to kill them. Anyway, they're not dead and I don't care." Ian *did* care but didn't have the words. He walked away to follow his mother at a safe distance, who, by the look of her straight back and long stride, would be in no mood to comfort him. The little convoy made its way homeward.

With dusk not far off, they stopped to watch a lark rise. Addie and James looked and listened as the little bird with the sweet voice rose and hovered to rise again, hover and rise, the song more beautiful the higher it soared.

Ian, not wanting to catch up with his ma, stopped alone to watch the lark. He looked back at his dad and Debbie; she was pointing at the sky.

"Ian!" Roy called. "Do you see the lark?"

Ian wanted to run back and join them but couldn't bring himself to do it. Instead, he made two fists on his hips and kicked the ground to demonstrate his displeasure with them and his disinterest in larks. The little bird reached the zenith of its rise and hovered in a solo performance of sweetest birdsong. They stood, Debbie and Roy, Addie and James, for the finale, Ian alone looking at the ground.

He would not join them for mushrooms that evening—mushrooms in their black gorgeous juice with fresh buttered bread. He would reject any approach to join in for the rest of the day. There would be a funeral in the garden, and the little fish would be placed in a Swan Vestas matchbox to be laid to rest under one of the apple trees. Debbie would probably say the Lord's Prayer, and Ian would slam the bedroom door, the loud bang symbolising the extent of his anger. Then he would throw himself onto the bed and sob as he listened to the sound of their enjoyment, the precious Sunday evening passing by. Any olive branch offered he would reject with fury.

Later, when Ian lay tired from weeping, Roy, having judged the moment, quietly opened the door and came in with lovely mushrooms and a glass of milk, knowing that words would be met with the back of a curly head and a muffled rejection into a pillow. Roy placed the tray on the bed and quietly withdrew, knowing the little boy would wait until he heard the door close and then he would sit up, tearful and alone, to eat the feast.

In the living room, the fire crackled to the sound of the radio. James and Debbie played at the big table scattered with comics and a jigsaw puzzle. Addie busied herself with clothes for the morning, her splayed hand inside a woolly sock as she repaired a spud hole.

"I'll give it ten minutes and then I'll go in to him." She raised her head as Roy returned from his peace mission.

"How was he?" she asked, aware of the unpredictability of her youngest son's mood.

Roy sighed. "Still defiant, but crying. He didn't want me to see."

"He's a little brat," James stated from the table. "Why does he always spoil everything?"

"I know," said Addie. "It's hard to understand—I don't understand him myself." She put down the darning and stood at the table.

"I'm going in now to try to get him to join us." She held up a warning finger. "Now, if he comes out, not a word about pinkeens or skylarks or arguments. Just carry on as if nothing has happened. I know he could do with a good kick in the backside, but that would only make things worse." She smiled.

"World War Three," said Roy with a chuckle. "They should have sent him to fight the Germans."

Debbie laughed out loud. James grinned and put his fingers to his lips, trying to contain his laughter.

"Shh, don't let him hear you."

Ian was sitting on the side of the bed. He didn't look up. Addie stood.

"I'd better settle the bedclothes," she said briskly.

He stood up and moved away from the bed. The pillow was crumpled and the bedspread was half on the floor.

"Give me a hand."

They fixed up the bed together, not looking at each other. Ian sat down again, staring at the floor. She sat beside him, her hands in her lap. She was surprised when he leaned against her in an obvious appeal for comfort.

"You know, you're your own worst enemy," she said. Her hands parted but remained in her lap. He leaned away.

Knowing she should take control and give him a comforting hug, she couldn't bring herself to do it. Instead, she moved her hand to rest it on the bedspread behind him.

"We're going to toast mallows at the fire," she said in the same brisk voice, standing up. "And we're going to play cards." She stepped towards the door and put out her hand. "C'mon."

He would have liked it if she had put her arm around him when he'd leaned against her, but the offer of the open hand would not be repeated, so he rose from the bed. The son and the mother stood face-to-face. He longed to take her hand but instead continued staring at the floor, his jaw set. She dropped her hand to her side, and he followed her out the door and along the dark, cold hall to the lighted doorway of the warm living room. He could now make a dignified return to the family group. The four-hour fight was over and it would not be referred to again.

The doorbell rang.

"I'll get it." Addie continued along the hall to the porch. Peering through the rain-speckled glass, it took her a moment to recognise the two smiling faces. Her heart sank.

"What a nice surprise! It's the Blackwells," she called down the hall in a loud, cheerful voice belying the expression of desperation on her face. *I don't have a toilet roll in the lav. What if they want to use the bathroom? I don't have any biscuits, and there's only a drain of whiskey in that bottle.*

"I'll put them in the front room," she whispered.

"You can't. Grandad Hugh is in there," Roy shot back as he passed her in the hall on the way to greet the chairman of the gas company and his wife. "Hello, hello, welcome." He wrestled with the stubborn lock on the front door.

Addie quickly returned to the living-room. "Debs, get that table cleaned up. James, go out the back way to the shop and get a Baby Powers and three bottles of stout and some ginger-nut biscuits. Ian, get rid of that sulky look and go and wash your face we have important visitors. NOW!"

James was the first to react. He put out his hand. "Money!"

Addie hesitated only for a second then, taking a small tin box from the mantelshelf, extracted one shilling and sixpence. "Pay with that and put the rest on the bill—say it's an emergency."

James rushed out into the hall and down to the big kitchen at the back of the house and the back door.

With just enough time to push her hair around and check her face in the big mirror over the mantelshelf, Addie strode out into the hall to greet the Blackwells and usher them into the warm living room with its big fire and large dining table.

"I'll be with you in just a moment if you'll excuse me." She headed for the kitchen press where she kept the toilet roll used for guests and special occasions. This replaced the squares of newspaper hanging on a string in the toilet.

"Hello." Roger Blackwell sat down at the table and began poking and peering at the jigsaw pieces. "I love jigsaws."

Doris Blackwell apologised for the intrusion. "I'm so sorry, Roy. It's just that we were passing by and..." She didn't finish the sentence as Addie re-joined them.

"Here, sit beside the fire. Roy, take Mrs. Blackwell's coat."

"Oh, we're not staying. It's just that I..." Again, Doris was interrupted mid-sentence, this time by her husband.

"We were passing by when Doris was short-taken. I recognised the green doorway in the wall with the high hedge. 'That's Roy's house,' I said to Doris, and pulled in." He put out his arms i n an expansive gesture, a beaming smile on his big, florid face. "A fine excuse for a visit." He looked at Ian. "Is that a side piece you've got there?"

But Ian was looking at Doris Blackwell. "I'll show you where the toilet is," he offered the embarrassed woman, placing the piece on the jigsaw. "I'll take your coat, Mrs. Blackwell and Ma will make you a cup of tea." He jumped up from the table and put out his arms to receive the massive fur coat before heading for the door. "It's this way."

"What a charming young boy," Doris said with a smile as she followed.

"He has his moments," Addie murmured.

"Ah, he's a good lad." Roy smiled proudly.

"Would you like a whiskey, Roger?" offered Addie, hearing the back-door latch announce James's return.

"Don't mind if I do."

"Or if you'd prefer a Guinness," she offered confidently, seeing James's smile and nod as he came through the door.

"Whiskey would be grand if you're having one yourself. So, this is the son and heir!" he exclaimed, seeing James. "Roy, he's a chip off the old block. Hello, lad."

James shook the big proffered hand. "Hello, Mr. Blackwell. Pleased to meet you."

Addie, thankful she'd had time to put the toilet roll in place, went to check on Doris Blackwell. Ian, she contemplated, was always the perfectly behaved child when they had visitors. Even the neighbours would comment on his manners. "You're very lucky to have such a good child."

James had left the Guinness and whiskey on the kitchen table beside the packet of ginger-nut biscuits. *The Guinness goes back tomorrow if we only use the whiskey*, Addie determined, ever conscious of the cost. She took down the Jameson bottle from the shelf where it had been since the previous Christmas and was about quarter full. Carefully, she poured the whiskey from the small-sized bottle James had bought into Jameson bottle and nodded in satisfaction. The amber liquid came up to a respectable half bottle.

Why this unscheduled visit? The Blackwells had never called before. *It's the job. He's here to tell Roy he's got the inspector's job.*

With a laden tray of the best willow-pattern crockery, glasses for the whiskey, ginger-nut biscuits arranged on a plate and the respectable bottle of whiskey, she joined the company in the living room.

"Time for bed," she announced to the children, finding a place to deposit the tray on the table. "Tidy up this table and off to bed.

"Come and sit by the fire," she invited, handing her smiling guest a good measure of whiskey, enquiring, "Would you like anything in that?"

"No, this is grand. I like it neat."

Meanwhile, Roy offered a drink to Doris, who declined, making some comment about her bowels. However, she agreed to a cup of tea. Roger settled back into the fireside chair and looked around the homely room, the whiskey cradled in his hands. "Fine house, this." He peered up at the high ceiling, noting the water damage where the rain had penetrated, the wallpaper coming away at the corners, hairline cracks in the plaster. "Wonderful proportions to the rooms. You don't get high ceilings like that anymore, probably built at the same time as our head office." *The place needs a good bit of money spent on it*, he was thinking to himself.

"Say good night to our guests," Addie instructed the children, and James and Debbie smiled good-nights from the other side of the table.

"Come here, you beautiful boy!" The effusive Doris Blackwell beckoned to an outmanoeuvred Ian, caught on the wrong side of the table. Every fibre of his being shrieked, *Run! Run as you have never run before.* Bravely, he came and stood in front of the terrifying woman. He looked back at

James and Debbie with a defiant smile in response to their grins of pleasure at his discomfort.

"Good night, Mrs. Blackwell. It was nice meeting you." Ian beamed, his brown eyes sparkling in the firelight, full of mischief and life as he ran a grubby hand through his mass of black curls. It was a perfect performance.

Impulsively, the woman reached out and pulled him close. Ian's worst nightmare realised, he arched his back to avoid being engulfed by the soft, perfumed mass of intimacy. The powdered jowly face was close. He could smell the make-up. There was the flash of red lipstick and the kiss was planted. She released him to reach for the big cream and gold handbag, the matching purse in a chubby, red-nailed hand, the flash of a fortune in money and miraculously a ten-shilling note was produced and pressed into his hand.

"That's too much!" Addie was on her feet. "Really, Doris, that's far too much. Ian, give it back."

The impetuous Doris was not for turning. The big clasp snapped shut on the purse. Ian gripped the precious note tightly; it represented twenty weeks' pocket money, and he felt he had earned it.

"You'll have to share." Addie knew by Ian's expression that the note was not going to be released.

"Say thank you and give Mrs. Blackwell a good night kiss." She grimly trapped him.

Willing to pay the price, Ian put out his arms and delivered probably the first kiss of his life, avoiding the terrifying lips but having to settle for a revisit to the powdery cheek and the soft suffocating embrace. "Thank you."

Blessedly released, he stepped back, giving her the full benefit of his dimpled smile.

"Good night, you darling boy!"

Ian headed for bed. Wide-eyed and incredulous, James and Debbie followed, closing the door behind them. In the hall, the three children examined the precious note Ian spread out in all its glory.

"Ten shillings! You lucky sucker! Don't forget Ma said you have to share."

"It's mine. I kissed her. You were laughing at me. It was horrible." He scrubbed his mouth with the back of his hand. "Yuck! Yuck! I'm poisoned!"

They couldn't help laughing as Ian, clutching his chest, staggered down the hall to eventually collapse on the floor holding the note aloft. "But it was worth it!"

The grown-ups, unable to make out the words, smiled at the laughter coming from the hall.

"Such beautiful children and so well-mannered." Doris was reaching for her purse again, but Roy intervened.

"No, you've been more than generous. Addie will have a word with Ian. He understands about sharing."

The bulging purse was returned to the big bag.

Roger Blackwell swirled his whiskey and sipped, then spoke earnestly. "We feel we owe you a little...well, a lot more than ten shillings. I'm indebted to you." He raised his glass towards Roy. "My sister has been in touch. You remember our conversation at the New Year's celebration? I'll say no more." He smiled and raised his glass again. "To families," he toasted.

Addie, the inspector's job on her mind, raised her glass, her eyes on Roy. The unspoken words shrieked between them. Her expression said everything, but Roy gave no indication he understood.

Addie rose to her feet. "I'm going to say good night and tuck the kids in. Doris, would you like to come too?"

The older woman beamed in return. "I'd love to!" She reached for the big bag as she clambered to her feet. "It goes where I go." She chuckled as the two women left the room.

Addie turned at the door and fixed Roy with a fierce glare. *Ask him now!* she mouthed, nodding her head in the direction of their important visitor, who was contemplating his whiskey.

The children slept in one big room. Debbie had her own corner with a curtained partition separating her from the boys and allowing her some privacy. She called the corner 'Never Land'. On her last birthday, she had asked for the wallpaper with a big floral pattern that now surrounded the bed on two sides. Her pride and joy was a white painted locker beside the bed. It had a door with a key. Here, she kept her private possessions. Above the bedhead, there was a makeshift bookshelf, and on the bed, a multicoloured patchwork quilt she'd made herself. Debbie loved to collect Christmas and birthday cards, her favourites she had suspended over the bed on a string. The whole effect was startlingly colourful and reflected her cheerful disposition. Of course, the Never Land title referred to Peter Pan but also to the fact that the boys must never, ever, venture behind the curtain.

***

Ian lay on his back, minutely examining the precious ten-shilling note, James with the aid of his own angle-poise light, was reading the *Knockout* comic, and Debbie was fast asleep when the floorboard outside the bedroom door creaked. Swivelling in the bed and jamming the note under the pillow, Ian buried himself under the blankets, his back to the door and his breathing heavy in an exaggerated version of sleep, eyes closed, and fingers crossed, anticipating the approach and the dreaded lipstick kiss.

"They're asleep," he heard his mother whisper. Obviously, James had reacted as quickly as his younger brother. The light from the hall spilled into the room. The two whispering women crossed the floor to check on Debbie.

"The little darlings."

Ian heard the click of the clasp on the big bag and the half-hearted protest from his mother.

***

Shortly later, Addie and Roy watched the big silver Jaguar XJ6 pull away from their front gate. They waved and turned to walk up the narrow path to the lighted porch of Ivy Lodge.

"You didn't mention the inspector's job, did you?" Addie enquired, arms folded against the chill of the night. She sighed. "Did you see him looking around the house? He even noticed the wallpaper and the ceiling." She didn't give Roy a chance to answer. "I was ashamed at the state of the place."

Before he could form a retort, she walked on ahead quickly into the house. He followed. "Addie," he appealed to the ramrod straight back, hands out from his sides. She didn't answer.

Chapter 7

ROY'S WORKING DAY STARTED EARLY with the bus trip to the gas works to clock in and collect his bicycle. Hail, rain or snow, he would travel the suburbs of the capital, hands and face tanned brown by the weather.

At six feet two inches, he was lean and fit from the constant activity and hefting the big leather money bag heavy laden with pennies and shillings. Every hill was a challenge. The driving rain found its way through in spite of all precautions. The voluminous gas company waterproof cape offered some protection, though it proved a hindrance in the wind and impeded his momentum, sometimes forcing him to dismount and walk.

'Never go to bed on an argument', his mother had always said. Unfortunately, this had not been the case the previous night. Addie, angry at the missed opportunity of mentioning the inspector's job, had been merciless in her disappointment. After a very one-sided, heated exchange laying bare all Roy's shortcomings from lack of initiative to not caring about his family, she had flounced off to bed.

Exhausted from the confrontation, Roy had followed, but Addie was not to be humoured, presenting him with her back. He lay in wide-eyed silence, plans and counter-plans invading his mind, before eventually falling into a deep, weary sleep.

Head down, pumping his legs, straining to the brow of a hill, soaked by the splashing of a passing car, he caught a glimpse of the warm occupants. Everybody else seemed to be better off than him. Even the commuters waiting at the bus stop exposed to the elements. It would only be a temporary intrusion until they were aboard a warm bus, no doubt to spend the day indoors.

Hours on a bike gave a man plenty of time to think, and Roy took refuge in his imaginings. A resourceful positive person, in spite of all, he was happy with his lot and counted his blessings. The zenith of his ambition was a company van—*now, that would be grand, out of the rain, home for lunches and trips with the family to the beach at weekends.*

The image of his beautiful, ambitious wife interrupted the dream, and he sighed. *Addie, always wanting more, always pushing. "Ask about the inspector's job. Why don't you ask for a rise? Look at the O'Neills, they have a car. You're twice the man Paddy O'Neill is. Why don't you push yourself more? We need more money,"* and inevitably, *"The rain is coming through the roof again."* Roy reached the top of the hill.

Sure, we're all in the same boat. Everyone has problems. We'll get by. The O'Neills may have more money than us, but they're a miserable bunch and their kids are ugly. They're just jealous. He looked at his watch as he freewheeled down the hill. Four o'clock: just one more call and then the cycle back to the works, check in the money and get the bus home. Thursday, pay day, the kids would be waiting with smiling expectant faces for their sixpence pocket money, and his lovely Addie, smiling with a welcome kiss, the smell of fried sausages and a rasher. Maybe he'd get a couple of bottles of Guinness from the off-licence. What more could a man ask for? He pushed harder on the pedals, and the bike flew along the road.

***

The packed 46A pulled away from the city terminus, heading for the suburbs along the coast. Known to locals as The Mystery Tour, the double-decker bus travelled from the centre of the capital, serving the suburbs south of the city.

"Fares, please! Fares, please! Does anyone want to pay twice? There's the zoo! Stop here and visit the relatives, plenty of room on top." The Long-Nosed Bus Conductor entertained the commuters with his light-hearted banter. Nobody knew his real name but his nickname was well-earned; he really had a very long nose.

Upstairs, the air was laden with cigarette smoke, the tobacco smell mingling with the damp odour of wet overcoats, windows fogged by the breath of tired workers. Roy sat beside John, a co-worker, as they discussed everything except the inspector's job. Most of the surrounding seats were occupied by men, practically everyone smoking, heads turning and nodding as they chatted, many with newspapers, the *Evening Herald* and *The Press*. The job seekers' page was much in evidence, all glad to be in the warmth but impatient to reach their various destinations and waiting families, everyone a hero on pay day, but not all pay packets would find their way home intact. In many cases, the local pub would claim a considerable percentage before the missus got her hands on the reddies.

No such indulgence for the hardworking, conscientious Roy: every penny of his reddies had been accounted for.

Nearing home, Roy saw the lights of the pub at the crossroads ahead. The bus would slow at the crossroads and turn the corner, travelling another hundred yards before arriving at the bus stop. He joined a group on the platform for the hop-off at the corner as the bus slowed. The mood was boisterous, all anxious to avoid the extra hundred-yard walk. Having rounded the corner, the driver would gun the engine and pick up speed. Some of the more daring show-offs jumped before the bus had slowed, running alongside to keep their balance. One young lad, Jerry Fitzer, always jumped off first delivering a 'two-fingered salute'.

"He'll get a smack of a car one of these days, the little bollox," someone was heard to observe.

Roy hopped off the bus at its slowest, crossed the road and passed the inviting entrance to the pub.

"What about a quick one, Roy?" came the invitation from one or two at the doorway.

"No, you're grand." Roy hurried on past the row of cottages to Billy Harkness's shop on the corner at the fork in the road; the right-hand left the streetlights behind and led into darkness, the country road and Ivy Lodge.

Roy pushed the glass-panelled door to the tinkle of a bell. Billy's little shop, as usual, was crowded, six thirty on payday. Glass screw-top jars and open sweet boxes packed the shelves behind the high counter. Open boxes bulged with penny bars and wrapped sweets. Sugar sticks, Peggy's legs, liquorice pipes, Flash bars and lucky bags, Honey Bee Toffees, six a penny, Toffee Bars, Sailors Chew, Cough No More, Pixie and Gob Stoppers.

Billy himself was posed behind the high counter. Mrs. Harkness, as usual, sat perched on a high stool alongside her husband, her mottled jowly face inches away from the small wooden change tray as she poked the coins around with a fat, stubby index finger, presenting the customers with a view of the top of her grey, sparsely haired head. Short-sighted, she squinted as she identified the coins by feel. She loved the Scottish threepenny bits with all their corners; a silver two-shilling piece, though close to a penny in size, could be identified with a twist of the wrist to catch the light. She would sometimes make a mistake, uncannily always in her own favour.

Approaching his seventieth year, Billy was stocky with his brown shop coat and Buster Keaton face, always the comedian yet never known to smile. He moved at practised high speed, little shovels of bull's eyes, weighed on the counter scales with hardly a glance and deposited into small brown bags, evening newspapers folded and slapped onto the counter.

Billy knew what everyone wanted without having to ask. *Feel, twist, peer*, stubby fingers worked overtime as Mrs. Harkness did her best to keep up. The good-humoured crowd remained patient and expectant, the drill familiar; Billy's customers were his audience.

A diminutive figure stood beside Roy at the back of the shop.

"Yes, Sister," Billy addressed the nun in deference to her status, ignoring the men. "Can I help you?"

Sister Bridget looked around apologetically as the men shuffled to one side, turning their heads, some tipping their hats. The Little Sisters of the Poor at the convent were an important part of the local community. Few present had not benefitted from their help through the years.

On her way to the hospital, Sister Bridget had dropped in to buy a magazine. "Have you got a *Woman's Life*, Mr. Harkness?" she enquired with a glance at the magazines behind the counter.

Billy only hesitated for a moment. "No, Sister, I have a dog's life. If I had a woman's life, I'd be in heaven." Not a smile cracked the stony face, but the close observers detected a twinkle in the shrewd grey eyes.

Sister Bridget, unused to such familiarity, handed over the shilling and received her *Woman's Life* in some confusion, waiting patiently for her two-penny change to be identified and handed over.

The shilling found its way to the money tray to be prodded into position alongside the other silver ones. No new-fangled noisy cash register here; the money tray worked grand.

Chapter 8

No. 214, THE DRIVE; SHACKLETON: Roy checked the customer account card as he sat astride the big Rudge bicycle, his bare hands chilled by the east wind blowing off the Irish Sea. The account in the name of Gerald A. Shackleton was far from impressive—sporadic payment over the years, access had not been achieved on the two previous collector visits.

Some handwritten notations had been made by previous collectors, Roy noted. *'Edith, possible ME'*—man-eater, a code for 'watch your step'—*big dangerous dog*.

With a grim smile, Roy recalled Mick McCarthy returning ashen-faced to the collector's office, his trouser legs in tatters. Mick had described the Shackletons' hound as of massive proportions and vicious. He had put in a claim for a new pair of cavalry twills.

"I only just made it over the garden wall, but the beast had me by the trousers. I had the presence of mind to save my life by releasing me braces," Mick had explained. Number 214 the drive was an address to be avoided.

Roy replaced the card in the black folder and blew on his hands to warm them up. He leaned the bike against the low garden wall, removed his bicycle clips and hefted the big heavy leather money bag off the back carrier.

The gate was a simple affair about waist high with a press-down latch. A narrow, cracked, concrete path bordered by a weed-strewn flowerbed led to the blue faded front door, flanked by a rusted metal seat against the pebble-dashed wall of the three-bedroomed semi.

At the creak of the gate, a distant barking could be heard from behind the house, the deep, threatening sound of a big dog on the move becoming louder as the dread of all postmen, milkmen and delivery men alike came at speed along the side passage.

Having closed the gate, Roy was halfway up the short path when Brutus exploded from the side of the house, in a frenzy of snarling fangs, black hackles raised. Spying Roy, the dog adjusted his headlong charge and attacked in a swerving run, head down, powerful hind legs ripping at the weeds and long grass of the unkempt garden.

The big leather money bag, heavy with the morning's takings—all in pennies and shillings—had reached the zenith of its backswing, and the pendulum was making its return driven with all the force of Roy's lean six-foot-two-inch frame. A step forward to increase the momentum, judged to perfection, the heavy money bag caught the unfortunate animal mid-leap.

Transformed into a frantically scrambling black bundle of legs and wide-eyed confusion, Brutus travelled a good ten feet through the air to land on his back against the pebble-dashed wall while Roy, carried by the weight of the bag and the sheer force of the swing, spun in a circle with the balance of an Olympic discus thrower. Dazed, the mighty Brutus rose to his feet and, with a whimper and his tail between his legs, made his unsteady way along the side of the house.

Roy felt sorry for the poor beast and crouched, calling in a gentle voice, "Here, boy, good boy." He clicked his fingers. Brutus looked back with baleful eyes and made a feeble attempt to wag his tail before continuing on his way to the safety of the back garden.

Roy placed the bag on the doorstep and adjusted his tie before scanning the door: no bell, just some screw holes and a discoloured patch where it should have been. In similar fashion, the doorknocker had been removed. Someone had gone to considerable pains to avoid access. Stepping back, he was considering going around to the back of the house when a slight movement, the twitch of a net curtain in an upstairs window, caught his eye. Giving no evidence of the discovery, he stepped forward to the door.

***

Mrs. Edith Shackleton squinted, one eye against the spiral of smoke from the lipstick-stained cigarette trapped between her pursed lips and peered down at the head of wavy black hair. *It's the good-looking one.*

Having spotted the gas man at the gate, she had hurried upstairs to watch Brutus do his work. Expecting to see the man scrambling for his life over the wall—a sight that always amused her. She was too late to see exactly what had happened but quickly realised from the sounds that the big dog had lost the contest.

Craning her neck, she adjusted her position for a better view. The gas man was too close to the door, but as he bent down to peer through the letterbox, he presented a new aspect of his physique to the observer above.

"Mrs. Shackleton, it's City Gas!" The voice through the letterbox reached to the upstairs bedroom. Edith Shackleton took a drag on her cigarette, deciding not to answer the door.

"Mrs. Shackleton," the tone of the voice was considerate and reasonable, polite, "my information is that you've had a break-in and the money from your gas meter has been stolen. There could be damage to the gas supply pipe and there may be some danger. Please answer the door."

The gas man stood upright and stepped back into full view of the upstairs window, giving her a good look at his profile, the brown hands and the breadth of his shoulders.

"I'm on my way, baby," Edith murmured, moving away from the window to study her image in the full-length mirror. With quick deft actions, she removed the curlers, releasing her ash-blonde hair, her pride and joy. Her tired, drab, terry-towel housecoat dropped to the floor. A last quick glance reassured her that, in spite of the obvious sagging here and there, her ample figure more than compensated. With a grind and jiggle for further reassurance, donning her red and black silk housecoat and applying a quick touch of lipstick, she headed for the stairs. In the hallway, she checked her hair again in the mirror, pushing and prodding it expertly into the Doris Day tousled look.

***

Roy shifted from foot to foot and blew on cupped hands, pausing to check the time on his watch: 1.30.

Shepherd's pie with soup to start, apple tart with custard and a cup of tea to finish in the warm canteen back at the works. His stomach rumbled. If he rushed back to town, he'd be in time to catch the kitchen staff before they finished serving lunch. The handlebars of the bicycle jutted temptingly above the garden wall. *Leave Mrs. Shackleton to another day. The dog will be no problem.* He was saved from having to make a decision by the hall door suddenly opening.

"Come in." She stepped back, still holding the door, leaning forward to give him the benefit of her full but far from firm cleavage. "Come in," she repeated, looking up at him with an inviting smile.

"Thank you, Mrs. Shackleton."

She stepped back, barely giving him enough room to enter the narrow hallway and wipe his feet on the mat inside the door. The waft of Irish stew permeated from the warm kitchen to the end of the hall, assailing his nostrils as they manoeuvred past each other, she as close as possible, he trying unsuccessfully to avoid body contact.

"The meter?" he enquired. "Where's the gas meter?" The rich aroma of the stew mingled with the strong scent of her cheap perfume.

She raised her arm, limp-wristed, and lazily pointed to an area under the stairs, the action causing the exotic silk gown to open sufficiently for him to see that she had nothing on underneath.

Reaching with her other hand, she cut off his retreat by firmly closing the front door.

Amidst the clutter of Wellington boots, coats, a vacuum cleaner and brimming cardboard boxes, Roy could see the meter attached to the wall. It was obvious it had been tampered with. The broken lock was still attached to the money drawer, which lay on its side on the floor. He was glad to let the lamb stew aroma take over as he crouched down to examine the damage, but the perfume caught up quickly as she closed in behind.

"There was no one here when they broke in. I came home and found it like that with the lock broken and the money box pulled out." She was very close. "There was a good few quid in it—it hadn't been collected for four months. Just as well I didn't arrive home sooner. Who knows what might have happened? I might have been killed." She spoke rapidly and breathlessly, giving a reasonable display of being distressed by the affair.

Roy did not reply.

"Or raped," she added.

The space under the stairs offered Roy very little room for manoeuvre, but he had to read the information on the meter and enter the readings on the customer sheet.

In the empty space where the money drawer should have been he found a single shilling. Obviously, the same shilling had been used several times, as the readings on the meter indicated a liberal use of gas as recently as that morning. Still crouched in the cramped space with his back to the now overheated Edith, Roy began to fill the details into appropriate columns, pretty sure that the broken lock had nothing to do with a break-in. Everything indicated the Shackletons had broken the lock and were helping themselves to free gas.

"I'll have to report this to the police," he said, examining the broken lock. "You realise, of course, that break-in or no break-in, you are responsible for the deficit which, unfortunately, you'll have to pay. Are you sure there was a break-in? Maybe..."

He turned in the cramped space to look up at her. The housecoat was fully open.

She fixed him with her version of a seductive look.

"Are you sure you have to call the police?" she murmured. He tried to retreat, but there was no room. He couldn't stand up and going forward was not an option. She swayed closer, presenting at his eye level a close-up display of mottled pink and white flesh that framed a luxuriant V of greyish-black curly hair.

Roy looked down at the gas meter. "I think your slot is broken," he said, unable to resist the pun. Humour was always a good weapon in his arsenal.

But Edith Shackleton was past caring, Roy's proximity seemingly prompting a total loss of restraint. He was trapped, and she knew it. Holding onto the bannister with both hands, she impetuously straddled his shoulder and began to thrust herself against the side of his head.

Somehow, he managed to disentangle himself and retreat further into the limited space. She dropped to her knees and came in after him. He now had a slight advantage. They knelt facing each other, red-faced and panting, the gas meter between them.

The passion subsiding in the desperate housewife, the humour of the situation began to take over. The broken slot comment hung in the air.

Edith Shackleton was the first to break, the beginning of a smile tugging at the corners of her ruby-red lips. She backed out of the tight space on hands and knees and buried her face in the worn Axminster, consumed by uncontrollable laughter. Blessedly, Roy retrieved the precious customer cards that had been scattered during the struggle.

"I'm sure it's a grand slot, Mrs. Shackleton, but I have one of my own at home," he said with mock gravity sitting down beside her.

"What the fuck is goin' on here!" Mr. Shackleton came through the kitchen door, home for his dinner.

Roy scrambled to his feet but was off-balance.

"That's my missus!" The smaller man, full of righteous indignation, fists clenched, was ready for a fight but stopped short as Roy stood upright.

Mrs. Shackleton, wrapping her housecoat tightly around her, ascended the stairs at full speed.

"Nothing, Mr. Shackleton, not a thing." Roy stood wide-legged, hands outstretched. "Your wife slipped, and I was helping her up."

Gerry Shackleton squared up to Roy, sure he had the gas man at a disadvantage. Aware that he was in trouble over the meter, he spotted the bargaining opportunity. "That's not what I saw. You were maulin' her, and I caught you in the act. I'm going to report you, and you needn't think I'm going to pay the gas bill until I get compensation."

Uttering the compensation word prompted the man to grab his chest dramatically and stagger into the kitchen where he collapsed into a chair at the kitchen table, mumbling and gasping.

Edith, now back in an ordinary terry towel housecoat, returned from upstairs and followed her husband, clucking and solicitous to administer affectionate caresses.

"It's his heart, you know. He has a bad heart." She looked accusingly at Roy.

Gerry raised his head. "Yes, and I'm going to report you!" He pointed an accusing finger. "Trying to rape my wife!" His nose twitched. "Is that lamb stew?"

Roy stood in the doorway, surveying the scene. "Don't worry, Mr. Shackleton, you can report the attempted rape to the police when they get here to make their enquiries about the break-in and the stealing of the money from the gas meter. An inspector and a fitter will be here to cut off the gas until the matter is settled. I suggest you report the rape to them as well. Of course, you are responsible and will have to pay your gas bill whether you've been burgled or not."

The accusing finger wavered as this information found its way into the Shackleton compensation-fuelled mind, transforming his attitude swiftly from aggression to puzzled incredulity, the injured party.

"A burglar robs the meter and we have to pay? That's bleedin' stupid!"

"'Fraid so." Roy shook his head with a sympathetic look. "And if the police discover there was no break-in, they may decide you raided the meter yourself and bring charges. I'll see myself out." Roy adjusted his tie and lifted up the heavy bag.

"Hold you horses!" Gerry was on his feet. "There's no need to be hasty. Have some stew." He looked across at the gas cooker. "Are the potatoes ready, Edie? Get the man a plate."

Edith hurried to the dresser, took down some plates and began to lay the table. "Sure, there's plenty to go around. Sit down, sit down."

Roy hesitated for only a moment. The lid was off the pot, and Edith was ladling meat and vegetables onto a plate.

He sat down.

"Thanks very much, Mr. Shackleton."

"Gerry, it's Gerry, and Edie. Get the man a glass of milk, Edie. Get stuck in, boy. There's apple tart and custard for dessert." Gerry Shackleton had obviously decided to cut his losses. "Look, you're a reasonable man. I know by the look of you." His tone was conspiratorial as he leaned forward, knife and fork poised. "We were stuck for a bit of cash over the Christmas," he explained, "for Santy things for the kids and the aul' turkey. Edie suggested I should break the lock on the meter." He glanced quickly at his wife, who showed her support by concentrating fully on her plate of Irish stew. "Then, once it was done...well, you know just after Christmas, New Year's Eve an' all that. Sure, the one-shilling trick in the slot was a bit of a temptation. I'll pay every penny back," he hastily added. "I have a fair bit of overtime comin' up and we're goin' to rent the oldest lad's room and take a lodger."

Edie's head shot up and her mouth opened, but no words came out.

Gerry kept looking at Roy. "You understand, don't you?" He had punctuated the admission with frequent visits to the plate and most of the time with his mouth full, but Roy got the idea.

"I'm sure we'll be able to work something out, Gerry. You may have to commit that overtime. I'll talk to the accounts inspector and see if there's a way around the problem. There's a scheme you might qualify for," he explained. "You see, what happens is, you get less gas for your money for a period of time until the backlog is made up. It means that you're not cut off. It'll be up to the inspector to decide. I'll put in a word for you. But for God's sake, don't set the dog on him when he comes."

Having consumed a very nice dinner with dessert, Roy pleaded further collections to be made that afternoon and took his leave to the strains of *The Kennedys of Castleross* coming from the radio in the kitchen. The Shackletons seemed at peace with each other.

The wind off the sea had increased in strength and was driving a light misty rain into Roy's face as he mounted the big gas company bike and pedalled away from no. 214. There was more activity on the road now, and a bus pulled up at the stop further along the road. Schoolkids hurried past, faces flushed. A big lad dragged a stumbling young girl by the hand, her giant schoolbag swinging from side to side and throwing her off-balance as they crossed the road. Two other lads ran ahead.

Roy looked back, turning his head against the rain, to see the Shackleton kids open the gate of 214. He looked ahead again and pedalled the last fifty yards to no. 254, resolving to see what he could do to help the beleaguered family and feeling a bit guilty at the realisation that he had probably eaten the kids' dinner.

Chapter 9

FINANCIALLY, THINGS HAD NOT IMPROVED greatly in the Jeffries household. Roy had received some nominal increases in his salary, Addie got some part-time work in the local chemist, but the small rise in income was quickly absorbed by the usual household expenses. The inspector's job had not materialised, and the roof still leaked when it rained.

It was the beginning of Ian's first year in senior school, and when Addie was putting his lunch box into his schoolbag, she made an unexpected find. Amongst the tatty, dog-eared, exercise books and well-thumbed, hand-me-down textbooks, there it was, shining and new: a book with a gleaming yellow hardcover. There was a full-colour picture of a man clothed in animal skins crouched, looking at a footprint in the sand of an island beach. *Robinson Crusoe* by Alexander Selkirk. Addie withdrew the brand-new volume with a feeling of unease.

"Ian, where did you get this?"

"It's mine!" Ian, sitting at the dining room table, looked up. "I own it."

"Do you know anything about this?" Addie addressed James and Debbie, who shook their heads, eyes on the prized possession. A brand-new book was the reserve of Christmas and Birthdays, and even then, second-hand would be the norm.

"Well?" Addie fixed her youngest son with a determined look. "I'm waiting."

"It's a present. Christopher gave it to me."

"Oh?"

"Christopher Robinson—my friend at school. He's rich and he bought it for me as a present." Ian stood up and put out his hand. "It's mine, honestly." He nodded in assurance.

Feeling relieved that the precious book had not been stolen and at the same time feeling a bit guilty for suspecting the worst and for doubting her son, Addie stood her ground. "Ian, you're a good boy, and it's a beautiful book, but you can't accept such an expensive gift." She spoke quietly and reasonably.

Ian's fits of anger had diminished significantly, but if there was to be an outburst, Addie was prepared to meet fire with fire.

Ian weighed up the situation and came to the conclusion that he was not going to win this one. "He's my friend, and he's English and posh, and I look after him. Miss Markham asked me to."

Addie laid the book on the table and gently opened the cover.

"It's still mine until we give it back, isn't it?" Ian rested his elbows on the table and they all looked at the book.

"Five shillings?!" Debbie put a hand to her mouth and pointed at the flyleaf. "It cost five shillings!"

"I'll talk to your dad and we'll decide what's best to do. In the meantime, there's nothing to stop you from looking at it, but be very careful and don't get any marks on it."

"Am I in charge of it?" Ian put a protective hand on the cover.

Addie looked at the intelligent bright face. "Yes, you're in charge. I'll give you twenty minutes and then it goes up on the top shelf until we return it."

***

Kingsbridge Grammar School, with an attendance of seventy-eight boys and forty-two girls, occupied two buildings. The senior school, a one-storeyed, lofty, high-ceilinged building with five big Georgian windows, had a small car park and lawn to the front. The junior school was a lower, more modern building to one side with a separate small-gated entrance. Behind the two buildings was the playground, concrete covered, flanked by the boys' and girls' toilets and a long bicycle shed, all contained within an area bordered by a ten-foot wall.

All teachers in this private co-educational school wore a mortarboard and black gown.

The headmaster, Mr. Henry Edward Turner—*Henno*—was a tall, strutting authoritarian and scholar who had been educated in England's public-school system. He prided himself in the standards achieved at his school, basing its structures on the system he knew best. Navy blue caps with wide circular white bands, blazers with half-inch-wide white piping and a large intricate crest on the breast pocket, grey trousers and stockings to the knee with black shoes completed the boys' uniform. Girls wore similar with long, well-below-the-knee skirts.

It was a struggle for Addie and Roy to pay the fees. This was Addie's one indulgence, having her children in a posh school and giving them the benefits she had never experienced. Somehow, she managed to scrimp and save enough to pay the fees, although she fell short on the official uniform, improvising ingeniously with Woolworth's-bought white piping on hand-me-down blazers and shorts from the charity thrift shop where she helped out once a week.

The Jeffries kids were popular and well-behaved, most of the teachers recognising their down-to-earth qualities, some secretly preferring them to some of the better-off kids, as all types attended Kingsbridge Grammar School from the very well-healed to the not so well off.

Head of the junior school, Miss Emily Markham, spinster, certainly did not suffer fools gladly. Considering most of her peers at Kingsbridge School to be somewhat foolish, she presented a severe exterior. This was easily achieved, being a small slight woman with a drab sense of fashion, a penchant for sensible shoes and a lined face with small jutting chin. What she lacked in stature she made up for with a sharp and quick wit and an acerbic tongue. Not a woman to be taken lightly even Henno would think twice before confrontation. After moving from junior school to senior school, pupils remained under her jurisdiction for one year or until Miss Markham felt they no longer needed her support. This rule she had introduced herself and followed it to the letter.

Addie, prompted by Ian's explanation about the *Robinson Crusoe* book, especially the reference to Christopher Robinson, had decided to visit the school. She had not talked with Laura Anne Robinson since they'd met at the school sports day. They'd seen each other at the occasional school function since, and Laura Anne had seemed anxious to talk., but Addie had avoided getting into conversation. The incident of the silk scarf and the lipstick stains still lingered unhappily in her mind.

She cycled through the gates of the senior school, aware of heads turning to gaze at her through the high windows but unaware that cycling was prohibited on the short drive.

"Eyes front!" In Senior Form Five, nearest to the drive, Mr. Mitchell, Latin teacher, barked, showing his disapproval as he glared over the heads of the seated students. James Jeffries' face reddened as he realised his mother was the cause of the disturbance.

The bicycle shed or the car park? Addie was unsure as she neared the end of the drive. 'JUNIOR SCHOOL', the sign indicated, so she swung around the side of the building and out of sight of her relieved eldest son.

Finding a groove to hold the front wheel, Addie parked her bike in the bicycle shed along with all the others, retrieved the *Robinson Crusoe* book from the front basket and hurried along the path and through a small gateway in the hedge to the junior school.

The sound of children chanting times tables could be heard as she neared the glass door to the reception of the modern, low-structured building. The memories flooded back as she opened the door, prompted by the familiar smell: pencils, chalk and damp coats. The chanting was now louder.

"Seven ones are seven, seven twos are fourteen, seven threes are..."

There was no one in the reception area. A door to the right, slightly open, bore the sign 'Secretary' in neat letters. A double door facing led straight through to the classrooms and the chanting voices. Addie tapped on the 'Secretary' door and tentatively waited before pushing it gently open. There were two women in the room; the younger had arisen from the small desk.

"Can I help you?" She approached Addie with a bright smile.

"I'm Ian Jeffries' mother, and I'd like to see Miss Markham if she's available."

The young woman continued to smile. "Have you got an appointment?" she enquired.

It had not occurred to Addie. Slightly taken aback, she hesitated. "I'm afraid not. I never thought—"

"Hello, Mrs. Jeffries." The older woman stepped forward, and in some confusion, Addie recognised the headmistress of the junior school.

Miss Markham may have been the terror of the senior school, however, she was adored by the junior children.

"It's all right, you caught me on my break." She extended a delicate-looking slim hand. The strength of her handshake took Addie by surprise. "Your children are a credit to you, Mrs. Jeffries, and I am pleased to see you. Not that I would be with every one of my parents," she added with a forthright smile and conspiratorial laugh. "What can I do for you?" She glanced at the book in Addie's hand. "Ah, yes, the *Robinson Crusoe* book! Christopher Robinson...you want to return it," she anticipated.

Addie, who hadn't spoken a word, nodded as the cultured precise voice continued.

"I can explain. Ian is a bright boy, Mrs. Jeffries. Thoughtful, popular and well-behaved. Christopher Robinson is an only child, and his parents are English. They enrolled Christopher in our junior school three years ago. He is a quiet boy, not a very good mixer, but does not appear to me to be unduly unhappy. Last year, the Robinsons wanted to remove him from the school. I persuaded them to leave him here for another term to see what we could do to rectify things." She smiled and paused.

"Ian turned out to be the key. I had noticed how the two boys seemed to get along, so I suggested to your son that he might watch out for Christopher. I put them sitting together. It worked very well. The Robinsons were obviously grateful, and Christopher turned up in class with the book as a present for Ian."

She looked at Addie. "It all seems reasonable to me. I think it would be unfair to keep the book from Ian—he earned it." The quick-talking efficient Miss Markham was meanwhile leading Addie back into the reception area. She paused at the main doorway and took Addie's elbow, speaking in a low voice.

"There is something else, Mrs. Jeffries." She smiled. "Now that Ian has moved from the junior school into first year of the senior school, I will be recommending him for the McConnell prize. It is a cup awarded to a child who has performed most favourably in all aspects of Kingsbridge expectations and being exceptional in a given year. The award can only be made to members of the senior school, and I feel he is eminently qualified. Now, if that will be all, Mrs. Jeffries, my coffee break is over, duty calls." She shook hands briskly with Addie, smiled her lovely smile, all sparkling eyes and creases, and headed back to her beloved students.

It was a whirlwind experience that had only taken a couple of minutes, but the redoubtable Miss Markham had given all the answers without Addie asking a question. Back in the bicycle shed, her head in a spin, Addie retrieved her bike and headed for home.

Mainly uphill, as the school was on the coast near the seaside town, it took about twenty minutes to get home, and Ian occupied her thoughts all the way. *Why has he never said a word about the Robinsons?* She leaned forward and pushed hard on the pedals. *You'd imagine he would have told us.*

She felt a bit bemused—proud of the fact that everybody else heralded Ian as the wonder child and happy about the McDowell prize, but it was hard to equate this with the monster that could take over behind the closed doors of Ivy Lodge. Of course, for the most part, he would be their loveable fun-loving boy, but given certain circumstances, the red mist would descend and all hell would break loose. Sulks and slammed doors would ensue, and no amount of humouring or cajoling would restore normality until Ian decided to end the disorder. Though, she had to admit, he had improved greatly in recent times, and his outbreaks were less often and less intense.

Of course, Addie could see the child others saw. *Maybe it's me.* Tears welled up in her eyes, and she pedalled harder up to the crest of the long hill. *Maybe I don't really love my own child. I seem always to be in confrontation with him while everybody else loves him. Maybe it's me who has the problem.*

Reaching the top of the hill, the thought was soon dismissed as Addie swiftly freewheeled down to the pub at the crossroads around the corner and past Billy's shop, where the road divided into a perfect V. Checking behind, she stuck out an authoritative right hand and swerved across the road without slackening her speed.

Now in the countryside with fields on her right-hand side, she sped along, her red and white candy-striped skirt swirling around her legs, shining curling chestnut hair streaming and bouncing, highlights catching the sunlight all along the country road towards Hartigan's shop next door to the high hedge showing above the wall and the little gate that fronted the orchard and the garden of Ivy Lodge. She passed Mick Costigan and Alex Smart making their way from the next group of houses a mile further down the road. They acknowledged her passing with the simplest gesture of a raised index finger as they hurried to the pub with the intention of unloading what was left of their dole money.

***

Mick stopped and stood looking after Addie. "There are few sights better than a good-lookin' woman ridin' a bike," he announced. "Did you see the flash of a suspender as she passed?"

Alex was more interested in the promise of a pint of Guinness and strode on while Mick stood, craggy, unshaven chin cradled in his grimy fingers.

"I'm sure I saw suspenders and a flash of white flesh," he muttered to himself, storing the memory to fuel his fantasies for his next bout with Mrs. Costigan.

"Would you com'on an' hurry up?" Alex called, increasing his pace as if there was a real possibility of the pub running out of Guinness before he got there.

Mick turned and hurried after the impatient Alex. "Definitely I saw her knickers." The images multiplied in his mind, in time to be related, no doubt, as the day he saw Addie Jeffries naked on a bicycle.

***

As Addie arrived on her bike, a small group of local people were standing around a beautiful MG sports car parked on the road at the gate of Ivy Lodge, amongst them Brenda O'Neill, Declan Doyle, Sheila Boylan, a pram with a baby and some little ones too young to be in school.

"Hello, Addie, you have a visitor. You'd better hurry in and get the toilet roll out." Brenda, the joker, arms folded beneath her floral-patterned ample bosom, looked for the grinning approval of the others. She was rewarded by Declan Doyle's rejoinder.

"People who own cars like this don't wipe their arses."

Addie bumped the wheel of her bike up onto the step without comment. Anxious to see who had come visiting, she hurried through the entrance and up the gravel path.

The door into the porch stood open. *Grandad Hugh has let the owner of the car in*, was her first thought. *What's he saying to them?* the second, followed by, *I hope it's not someone important from the gas company. The beds aren't made and the hall carpet's still rolled to one side because of the leaks.* She quickly pushed the bike up the gravel path and leaned it against the windowsill beside the door.

"Hello?" she called as she entered the house. Checking Grandad Hugh's room first, thankful to find it empty, she closed the door and hurried down the hallway, checking the dining room on her way, aware of the damp smell and the brimming pots with cloths and rainwater as she scurried along the dark passage leading to the big old ramshackle kitchen at the back of the house. Nobody answered to her call.

"Hello?" The kitchen was empty, but the back door was open. Puffing slightly from the exertion and anxiety over the state of the house, she continued out to the little yard.

There were voices. She could hear voices. Addie stopped in the middle of the yard and took a deep breath, composing herself before following the sound. She could distinguish the cultured tones of a woman's voice and the sound of laughter as Grandad Hugh's voice joined in. Out of the yard and around the back of the shed, she found them beside the chicken run.

Grandad Hugh was in entertainment mode, loud and projecting in his poshest voice. Addie took in the scene. The slim-figured woman in a spectacular yellow Dior suit with wide black belt and matching Gucci handbag was looking up at him, laughing, a tinkling sound that somehow irritated the already agitated Addie. She buttoned the centre button of her tweed jacket and smoothed down her skirt, noting with some satisfaction the elegant visitor's high-heeled fashion shoes were half buried in the muddy soil at the wire fence of the chicken run.

"Hello?" She greeted them with the widest smile she could muster.

"My daughter," Grandad Hugh proclaimed grandly "Adelaide Jeffries."

"Sorry about your shoes." Addie stepped forward confidently in her stout Dubarrys.

"Adelaide." The Audrey Hepburn face followed the perfect profile as Laura Anne Robinson turned to Addie. Arms wide, ignoring Addie's outstretched hand, she stepped forward and embraced the surprised woman. Addie had no option other than to respond, though hesitantly. Overt demonstrations of affection were not part of Addie's repertoire.

"Please forgive me for arriving unannounced." Laura Anne thrust Addie to arm's length and looked candidly into her eyes, the gentle fragrance of expensive perfume lingering. "You really are so beautiful." She smiled. "I'm sure we can be friends."

Addie felt far from beautiful as she looked into the perfectly made-up face, searching for some sign of insincerity, but she could only detect candid admiration. *God*, she thought to herself with some cynicism, *beautiful, rich and a nice person too.*

"Your father was showing me the hens." Laura Anne glanced at the beaming Grandad Hugh. "And he's promised me some eggs."

His smile widened. "It's a pleasure, my dear."

"I'm so sorry for arriving out of the blue, but it was an impulse as I passed the end of your road, and I did so much want to see Ian's mother again."

Laura Ann put her hand on Addie's arm. It was a friendly gesture, and Addie was not displeased at the familiarity and attention of this sophisticated, well-heeled woman, who obviously accepted her on equal terms.

"You must be so proud of him. He's such a lovely boy." She linked Addie's arm as the trio made their way back to the house, Laura Ann somewhat unsteady in her stiletto heels on the uneven ground.

"What a beautiful place!" she exclaimed, looking across at the orchard, taking in everything as she wobbled, waving her free arm to regain her balance. "You are so lucky to live in the country. I believe you grow your own vegetables and potatoes, and the house is spectacular—so much room. Our place in London is so much smaller." She stopped and took a deep breath, looking at the tops of the pine trees showing behind and above the roof of the house. "Your father was telling me that there is a paddock around there." She waved a hand in the direction of the trees. "Do you have horses? I do envy you your life. It must be so fulfilling."

"No." Addie laughed. "We don't have horses.

Laura Ann Robinson leaned heavily on the arm that steadied her as they passed the back door of the house, crossed the small yard and went through the orchard gate. She openly admired Addie, showering her with compliments about strength, her flawless, healthy complexion without a hint of make-up and her full curvaceous figure. Even her hair, which Addie confirmed, with its wave and chestnut colour, was perfectly natural.

They strolled along the side path of the large orchard. Strangely, Addie did not feel uncomfortable at the proximity of her new 'friend'. The expensive perfume lingered, and Laura Ann's stilettoes were coping better with the more even ground. She admired the rows of vegetables—"Potatoes, cabbage plants, lettuce, onions even beetroot!" she exclaimed. "And the apple, plum and pear trees—your gardener must be very hard-working."

Addie smiled and waved a casual hand in an expansive gesture, letting the comment pass. "I love your car. It's an MG midget, isn't it? Gorgeous red. Every sports car should be red, don't you think?"

Laura Ann stopped. "That's what I think too. Gordon wanted me to get racing green, but that's macho men for you." The two women made their way around to the front garden, sharing a quiet giggle at the expense of their men.

"Would you like to come in for a cup of tea?" Addie offered, quickly adding, "I'm afraid the house is in a bit of a mess at the moment."

"No, thanks." Laura Ann shook her head. "Maybe next time. I know what it's like when you're getting work done, and I must be off to collect Christopher from the school."

Slightly relieved at the refusal of tea, Addie was surprised at the 'Having work done' comment.

"Maybe I'll sit just for a minute." Laura Ann changed her mind, indicating the two-seater garden chair. They both sat down and chatted for a while before Laura Anne broached the real reason for her visit.

"When I'm collecting Christopher from school, why don't I collect Ian as well?" she asked, looking intently at Addie with a hopeful little smile. I could drop him on the way home, we practically pass your door. "Better still—" she put her hand on Addie's arm as if the idea had just occurred to her "—Christopher has been asking if Ian could come for tea someday. He's always talking about his friend Ian Jeffries." Laura Ann paused and looked down at her hands. "Addie..." She looked up. "That's why I'm here."

The emotion showed. Addie was about to protest but hesitated at the look in the other woman's eyes. She waited.

"It's the first time Christopher has ever had a friend and talked to me about it." She hesitated and looked at her hands again. When she looked up, her eyes were moist, and she spoke quickly. "When Christopher was little, he was unwell. Gordon, that's my husband, he's very busy always with his work and away a lot. I was modelling in London, leading the high life." She smiled with a slightly rueful shrug. "We left most of Christopher's upbringing to our housekeeper.

"I'm sure you've heard of Robinson's Paint & Decorating Products. That's my husband—we own it."

Robinson's Economy Paint covered most of Ivy Lodge's walls and had been applied with Robinson's *Professional Quality* paintbrushes. Of course Addie had heard of it.

"Well, that's why we're in Ireland. Gordon is building a distribution centre here. He's busier than ever, and we only see him at the weekends." She looked appealingly at Addie. A slightly wistful smile trembled on her perfectly shaped lips.

"So, you see how important Christopher's friendship with Ian is. His upbringing is left to me. Modelling is a thing of the past. I'm struggling to cope. It's so difficult to step into a boy's life as a mother." She sighed.

"Christopher is a different person when he's with Ian. I would so like to have him come today. I can collect him and deliver him back to you at about seven o'clock. It's Friday, so there's no homework to be done. I've talked to Ian several times at the school, and we're friends. He's an extraordinary boy, so mature for his age yet so full of innocent fun."

Addie could hardly take in all that Laura Anne had said. She spoke so quickly and her accent was unfamiliar, but there was no doubting the sincerity of this very unusual woman.

"OK," she heard herself say. "Just make sure the school knows that he's going with you."

"Thank you so much." The model's slim arms were around Addie's neck, and she felt the soft cheek against hers. Laura Anne drew back. "Please give me your phone number just in case we need to be in contact."

The finances in the Jeffries' household didn't stretch to the luxury of a phone, so Addie gave her the phone number of Hartigan's shop, banking on the fact that it would not be needed. The phone box at the pub was another option but further away.

Producing a beautiful embossed notebook from her very spectacular designer handbag, Laura Anne carefully noted the number, then handed Addie a business card. "This has our home number. Now, I really must go." She rose to her feet, wriggling her hips as she smoothed down the figure-hugging pencil skirt. "I'll have him back about eight o'clock—we must do coffee some morning soon." Addie received an air kiss to the side of her cheek and with a "Thanks a million, you're a pet," Laura Anne was on her way, stilettos just about coping with the gravel path.

The bike leaned against the windowsill, the *Robinson Crusoe* book in the basket. Addie smiled to herself. *Well, that's for Ian to keep. He earned it.*

As she pushed the bicycle through the gateway into the orchard, she heard the open sports car's engine fade in the distance. *I hope Ian remembers his manners.* The thought popped into her mind to be disregarded almost instantly. *Of course he will. Street angel and house devil—Ian will love every moment of it.* She looked at the business card, *Robinson's* with an embossed gold crown on the 'I' and underneath, in smaller letters, *Paint & Decorating Products. Gordon H. Robinson, Chairman and Managing Director.*

They must be rolling in money, and we can't even afford to have the roof fixed. Addie sighed as she pushed the bike into the small yard and stood surveying the back door with its peeling green paint, and the cracked plasterwork of the kitchen wall.

"Paint and Decorating Products, my eye!" she muttered, pushing the bike over the cracked concrete of the yard and into the dirt-floored shed. She mimicked Laura Anne's voice: "Oh, you're so beautiful, and your house is so spacious, I do envy you."

Her mood was not improved as she entered the old kitchen. Everything looked shabby, even the new curtains she'd made and had been so proud of. Everything was diminished in comparison to the image of the wealthy Laura Anne.

Grandad Hugh stood in the entrance to the passageway off the kitchen, now wearing his best tweed jacket, sparse grey hair slicked down. The turned-back hall carpet with its array of pots and rain-catching utensils stretched out behind him.

"Has she gone?" he asked with a disappointed look. "She forgot her eggs."

With a derisive laugh, Addie pushed past him. "I think Laura Anne will be able to manage without your eggs, and take off your good jacket! Go and help the imaginary workmen who aren't fixing our roof!"

The heavy sarcasm left Grandad Hugh looking bewildered.

Chapter 10

BEAKY WANTS YA!" THE SECURITY man shouted.

Roy bent to remove his bicycle clips. He wasn't fond of Jimmy Furlong; few of the collectors were. He approached the security shack located at the gate to the big yard, passing a line of orange gas company vans on his way. "What?"

"You heard!" Officiously, he scanned his clipboard, casually flipping pages. Furlong wasn't fond of anyone. *Security men can't afford to be anyone's friend.*

Roy waited. *Beaky—the inspector's job*, he speculated. The job hadn't been filled, and everyone was more or less agreed that it never would be. Beaky had treated Roy with a reluctant deference ever since the New Year's Eve dance, from time to time passing a pleasantry.

The collector's office was not that often frequented by senior management, and collectors seldom had occasion to go to the main building. *No way, it's got to be something else.* But Roy couldn't think what.

"Two fifteen at head office, his secretary rang."

"Thanks." Roy looked at his watch; he'd just have time for lunch.

"Wait, sign this!" Furlong slapped the clipboard down on the window counter and, with a nicotine-stained finger, indicated the spot. He then dropped the bombshell.

"Some lead piping has gone missin' from the yard and you're a suspect."

Roy looked up into the deadpan face. Expressionless, unsympathetic eyes looked back.

"What?"

"You heard!" The expression on Furlong's face didn't alter as he savoured Roy's discomfort. He pulled the clipboard away and slammed the window shut, leaving a bewildered and worried Roy alone to cope with the unexpected news.

Chapter 11

To her friends and family, Mary Keating was recognised as good-natured, affable and generous of spirit. Within the office environment, as office manager of City Gas, 'Bloody Mary' as she was known, was recognised as a hard-faced spinster and an intimidating, demanding taskmaster. The office girls, twenty-three of them, went about their duties, heads bent and eyes averted, when addressed responding with, "Yes, Miss Keating, no, Miss Keating, Miss Keating, if you please."

The general office occupied the second floor of a three-storey terraced Georgian building. High windows stretched the full length of the street-side wall. The other walls were mainly wood panelled with some areas painted gloss green punctuated with groups of metal filing cabinets. Desks stretched the length of the long room in three rows to a doorway set into the dark wood panelling; white, bright, neon strip lights glared from the high ceiling.

From her desk, located on a slightly raised vantage point, Bloody Mary could observe every inch of the austere surroundings. Beyond a door at the end of the area in a small, windowless, box-like room, Beaky's secretary guarded the entrance to his palatial office.

The parquet flooring of the general office rendered it impossible to move without 'clacking', so high heels were prohibited, soft soles being mandatory. The secretaries to management did not come under the jurisdiction of Bloody Mary. They clacked in their stilettoes. Normally, the quietness of a library prevailed, to be broken only when Bloody Mary was not present.

"My office, if you please, Miss Keating," Beaky Bradley commanded without breaking stride as he passed by the office manager's desk, heading for his lair at the end of the long room.

His gait slowed as he moved between the rows of bent heads. Not one would choose to catch his eye. This accorded him the opportunity to study a shapely leg, cleavage, slope of a young neck, head tilted with a pearl earring, demure downcast eyelashes, delicate complexion and pouting red lips. The girl in row two never disappointed. Nine from the front, her name escaped him. He could feast lecherously and feed his fantasies, safe in the knowledge that she would never look up.

Bloody Mary observed the erratic passage of her boss, noting the points at which he slowed and once came to a stop. After he had passed through the door to his office, she waited a further five minutes before following.

Beaky arranged himself behind the huge desk, shooting his cuffs and opening a folder, posing at an angle so the light from the large window would present his profile to the best advantage for a person entering through the door opposite. The knock came exactly when expected.

"Come!" he summoned, presenting his profile, waiting until she had entered and was correctly positioned before turning to face her. Eyes down with pursed lips, he perused a sheaf of papers, selecting and examining, tapping his teeth from time to time, brow furrowed in concentration, the great intellect coping with the problems of distributing gas to the nation.

She waited patiently until he addressed her.

"Naked paper, Miss Keating!" He looked up. "Naked paper!" he repeated his expression, resigned and despairing as he shook his head to emphasise the gravity of his words.

"When? Where? Who?" Bloody Mary looked incredulous.

"Your department, I'm afraid. That blonde girl, the new one." Grim-faced, he continued, "She walked the entire length of the accounts department with two sheets of A4 paper not encased in an appropriate folder. She actually passed me with the documents in her hand!" Beaky, now incensed, slammed a fist onto his desktop. "How many times?!" Enraged, the bully roared.

Now in full flow, the familiar tirade ran its course. Bloody Mary, knowing better than to interrupt, waited until he paused for breath then spoke in a quiet voice, looking at the floor. "I apologise for the transgression, Mr. Bradley. I'll speak to the girl again."

"No, you will not speak to her! You will chastise her!" His indignation had driven him to his feet. He sat down again and raised his hand, his eyes now returning to the paper shuffling. "It's obvious that you are incapable of proper control of the staff, Miss Keating." He now spoke in a quiet, resigned manner. "Send her to me directly. I'll deal with her myself. You can go." He made a shooing-away gesture with the back of his hand, and the loyal servant of twenty-five years left the office, brushing away a tear of frustration lest her tormentor's secretary in the small outer office see.

"Miss Furlong." Beaky summoned his secretary with his very best attempt at a genial smile. "Would you come to my office, please?"

The leggy Miss Furlong rose from her desk, overhearing the muttered, "I'll swing for that little fucker one of these days," as the red-faced and furious Bloody Mary passed.

"Yes, Mr. Bradley," Miss Furlong observed the wolfish grin with distaste as she entered the room, closing the door behind her.

"Roy Jeffries is coming to see me at a quarter past two. Please remember he is a collector and not management. Treat him accordingly. He has a reputation for charm, which may be misunderstood. You get my meaning?" Beaky repeated his wolfish smile.

The secretary, having no idea what Beaky meant, offered a customary, "Yes, Mr. Bradley," returned to her office.

"Good girl." Beaky's eyes stayed with her legs all the way.

***

The silence that normally prevailed in the big office had succumbed to the din of twenty-seven girls taking advantage of the absence of Bloody Mary, who had decided to take a late lunch. With eyes on the doors of the large office, they exchanged views on every topic from pop music to movies, to make-up, to men... mostly to men.

Roy had run the gauntlet of the long office on two other occasions and knew what to expect. He opened the door to a deafening silence as every head turned. A daunting prospect, the door to management at the other end of the long room could only be reached through the corridor of desks, and it seemed a very long way away. This was their domain, their hunting ground, and a man was a man and fair game.

"Six foot two, eyes of blue..." the chant began, at first just a murmur.

"Who's that smasher?"

Blondie leaned back in her chair, queen of the predators, hands reaching up and behind her to readjust her perfect hair, the action stretching her blouse and showing off her figure. The already-stressed cross-your-heart bra taking the strain wasn't coping very well. The collective office took up the chant, "Has anybody seen my man..." They sang as Roy walked the gauntlet.

"Nice lips, big boy—" giggles, catcalls "—all I want is loving you and music, music, music, closer, my dear, come closer..." They chanted the words of the hit song, some with stretched-out arms, some making kissing noises as he made his way between the desks. Obstacles seemed to appear from nowhere, impeding his progress.

"Hi, gorgeous." Blondie was off her chair and linking his arm. There was nothing else for it. Roy hugged her close and danced her the rest of the way to the door, which suddenly opened.

"Mr. Jeffries!" Beaky's secretary stood to one side. Roy tried to release himself from Blondie's arms, but she wasn't letting him go till he kissed her. He obliged and skipped through the doorway to a crescendo of laughter, *oooohs!* and *ahhhhs!*

"My! Aren't you the popular one? Take a seat and I'll tell Mr. Bradley you're here."

Roy sat down and, producing a handkerchief, tried to remove the evidence of Blondie's bright-red lipstick. The secretary returned and took her place at the small desk.

"He's busy at the moment," she said quietly with an apologetic smile.

"I'm not looking forward to the return journey." Roy glanced ruefully at the lipstick-stained handkerchief before returning it to his pocket. "Is there another way out of here?"

"I'm sure you'll cope," came the reply as busy fingers now typed vigorously.

The completely wood-panelled, windowless room was like a square box and very warm.

"God, it's hot in here." Unused to such a confined space, Roy was beginning to sweat; the big office gauntlet-run hadn't helped. He ran his fingers across his brown, aware of the beads of perspiration, the unaccustomed tightness of the tie around his neck. He longed to remove his jacket. He loosened the tie and opened the top button of his shirt. The clacking of the typewriter hesitated for a second. Long eyelashes fluttered.

Gillian Furlong had seen many a lamb to slaughter sit in this same chair. *But not this one*, she concluded, *a most unlikely looking lamb.*

"Do you feel hot too?" he enquired with a smile. She had no way of knowing that in Roy's world, this was just an innocent remark and a genuine enquiry. Her fingers flew faster with no immediate reply presenting itself.

The condemned man examined his cell.

As Roy looked around, he speculated as to why he had been summoned. The inspector's job seemed the obvious reason. The reference to stolen lead had been eliminated by colleagues who were more in tune with the gateman's sense of humour.

"Smoke?" He proffered his cigarette case. The eyelashes fluttered, fingers poised.

"No, thanks. Not allowed, Mr. Bradley does not allow smoking in the office."

"Why the ashtray?" Roy nodded towards the ash-stained piece of cut glass on the desk.

"Management," came the curt reply. "You're not management."

"Oh!" Roy leaned back and stretched his long legs out in front of him, studying the clock on the wall above the girl's head.

"Twenty minutes...does he always leave people waiting for twenty minutes or is that a management thing too?"

The eyelashes remained lowered, and the typing didn't falter.

Roy closed his eyes. *It's got to be the inspector's job, probably to tell me I haven't got it. Addie is going to be disappointed. Maybe it's good news, a rise in pay. Young Ian could do with a bike—time he was going to school on a bike with the others, save a few shillings in bus fares.* He smiled. *He's a great young lad, full of spirit and fun, always laughing and doing funny stuff. Ah, the temper tantrums...* Ian's tantrums were less frequent these days, but to Roy, his youngest son was just a spirited kid with an enquiring mind who wanted to know about everything. He smiled again, letting his mind wander, and in the warm room with the opportunity to relax, he began to drift off. *A ring for Addie, a diamond to replace the garnet stone she's worn since we got engaged. A silk scarf, a new handbag, breakfast at Tiffany's. She's like a film star—Jane Russell's hair and Ingrid Bergman's face, a beauty. She should have nice*

things, designer clothes instead of second-hand from the thrift shop.
He sighed deeply.

The typing stopped.

Gillian Furlong scanned the stretched-out figure, black
hair greying at the temples, tanned handsome face in repose,
eyes closed, smiling in his sleep, the lines of his face softening,
kind and thoughtful, strong and steadfast. *Why are all
the best ones married?*

Roy stirred and sighed as thoughts cascaded into his mind
disturbing the reverie. *Keeping pace with the mortgage, roof
deteriorating every winter, school fees. Addie finding fault all the
time, nonstop, nonstop.* He snorted a loud snore, and his eyes
flew open.

The illusion shattered, eyelashes dropped to reddening cheeks
and the typing commenced. *Men! They're all the same, pigs!*

The phone on the desk tinkled twice.

"Mr. Bradley will see you now." She stood up, opening the
door to Beaky's office. Roy jumped to his feet, confused.

"Where, what time is it?" He pushed the knot of his tie
into place, two-handed. Miss Furlong guided him into the
accountant's impressive quarters, to the huge mahogany desk
and Beaky's profile silhouetted against the light from the high
Georgian window. By the time Beaky had completed his posing
and paper-shuffling ritual, Roy had composed himself and stood
tall and calm with a friendly smile.

"Hello, Mr. Bradley."

"Sit!"

To redress the height advantage, Beaky quickly rose to his
feet, indicating a chair. Roy sat down and so did Beaky. Roy could
hardly make out the other man's features silhouetted against
the blinding low sunlight, so he stood up again and, to Beaky's
dismay, committed the most outrageous transgression by sitting
on the edge of his shiny mahogany desk.

"Nice piece of wood." Roy ran his hand appreciatively over
the polished surface. The outraged accountant glared, words

refusing to form into a sentence. Mr. Blackwell had indicated to him that Roy was favoured and not to be offended by antagonism from management. He wanted to scream, *"Get off the surface of my beautiful expensive desk you pathetic underling!"* Instead, he covered his annoyance by striding across the room to take up his favourite position. The huge Georgian room boasted a magnificent marble fireplace with a golden eagle framed mirror; this was where he headed to confront the object of his outrage. Roy hadn't moved.

"Jeffries, Roy, you have not been successful in your application for the inspector's job." The blunt statement provoked the reaction he'd sought. Roy looked disappointed, shrugging his shoulders, palms held out in a resigned gesture.

"To tell you the truth, I didn't really expect to get the job. Thanks for telling me." Roy slid from the desk, about to head for the door.

"I haven't dismissed you!" Beaky barked testily. Roy returned to his position on the desk.

"I have...the board has decided, some time ago, not to fill the position." Beaky began a tour of the room striding slowly, presenting his profile to add gravity to his words. "The workload has been shared successfully amongst the other inspectors. So, the position never materialised." Spinning on his heel, he strode back to Roy, stopping some yards short. The sitting Roy was still too tall for comfort. Beaky smiled his wolfish smile.

"Mr. Blackwell, in his wisdom, has requested me to offer you an experimental and unique position."

Roy looked down from his perch enquiringly and the uncomfortable Beaky returned to his striding.

"There is a shortfall in the shortage department in the collection of poor payments and bad debts. Mr. Blackwell feels that someone like you—" Beaky grimaced uncomfortably "—someone with your unique charm and personality may be well employed in this area."

He continued briskly, returning to his desk without looking at the other man.

"I have drawn up an outline of your duties." He brandished a folder. "Basically, it would involve travelling with a technician to bad debts, using company motorised transport, of course. Your collection duties will be taken over by other staff. You will negotiate consumer payment terms, and where necessary, you may have to instruct discontinuing supply. You will report to the head of Shortage Collection. If Mr. Blackwell's idea works, you may be offered this as a permanent position, at which time we will consider increasing your remuneration."

The chairman had left the matter of a pay increase up to the accountant, fully expecting Bradley to increase Roy's income from day one. But Beaky had decided against it, feeling that he had the measure of his man.

Off the bike, a company van. Roy tried not to smile too broadly. Addie would not be totally happy. He could hear her questioning voice: *Why didn't you ask for more money?*

"You say there'll be more money?"

"Of course...eventually."

Chapter 12

T HE SCHOOL CLOCK HIGH ON the wall at the end of the corridor could be viewed through the upper half of the glass and wood-panelled partitions that separated the classrooms. The hands moved agonisingly slowly towards three o'clock and escape for the silent head-bent pupils of Kingsbridge Grammar School, Preparatory A. The high Georgian window offered another temptation: the invitation of a summer's day and the playing fields or whatever took an eleven-year-old's fancy.

Twenty-four in the class, eight girls and sixteen boys, the girls packed in the centre, two to a desk. A favourite punishment for reasonably fair-minded teachers would be to place a boy who had misbehaved amongst the girls or, indeed, the other way around. In either case, the victim would suffer mortification, normally evidenced by a bright-red face.

No such namby-pamby measures for Mr. Bruce Medford. At a beefy six foot two, an ex-heavyweight boxer of no great achievement with bulky shoulders and large hands, he outweighed the average twelve-year-old by a good two hundred pounds. He was a man of beaming geniality, with a jowly, florid face and a very short temper. In the blink of an eye, Medford's geniality could transform into violent enragement. With cane or a ruler and sadistic accuracy, he would deliver six of the best, his big face reddening at each stroke, shoulders hunched for maximum impact. Or the short hairs on the back of a scrawny neck could receive the attention of a big finger and thumb to lift a boy from his seat, stumbling to keep up with the jerking motion of a powerful arm, designed to keep the child off-balance as he was propelled to the door and out into the corridor, often with the assistance of the toe of a size eleven, handmade Italian loafer. Medford was a civilised man who liked his fashion.

Preparatory A served a specific function as preparation year for secondary education, housed in the senior school building and still under the influence of Miss Markham. Unfortunately for the pupils, its location accorded the punitive Medford the opportunity to practise his particular method of education without fear of interruption. His genial manner, reserved for the headmaster and other teachers, especially Miss Markham, belied his real temper and cruel nature. And, being the only classroom without a glass partition, Preparatory A guaranteed him privacy.

The room had a heavy oak door, two-foot solid walls and its own clock, on the back wall behind the children. For a large part of the time, Medford behaved in keeping with his reputation—genial and pleasant and possessing a good sense of humour. His unexpected outbursts of aggression and uncontrollable rage could be attributed to the fact that he had received a few too many blows to the head in his boxing days.

Anticipating the weekend, Medford was in a favourable mood this afternoon. Ian and Christopher occupied a double desk to one side, halfway along one wall. Every so often, one or the other chanced a glance back at the clock, which moved at snail's pace while the summer's day beckoned through the high window and Medford, with back to the class, boomed the dates, the battles, the kings. The chalk screeched across the blackboard, all heads bent to the task of copying down the facts into exercise books.

Not long to go, maybe ten minutes to escape, Christopher nudged Ian, showing him his finger below the level of the desktop.

"Look at my poor finger," he whispered. "There's a nail stuck right through it."

"Wow!" Ian eyed the trick finger with white gauze wrapped around it and a very realistic plastic nail apparently sticking in one side and out the other. False blood spattered the bandage. For a moment he was fooled. "That's terrific."

The wooden-backed chalk duster exploded between them, bouncing off the desk and engulfing the two boys in a cloud of white dust. It was hurled with such force that it continued its flight against the wall to land somewhere at the back of the classroom.

"Out here, both of you!"

Christopher, ashen-faced and terrified, froze wide-eyed, staring at the desktop.

Knowing what would happen next if the bellowed instruction was not obeyed, Ian manhandled his friend out of the desk to stand before the terrifying Mr. Medford. The joke nail and bandage fell to the floor.

"What have we here?" The toe of a highly polished loafer nudged the offending object, the voice calm quiet, over-polite and full of deadly intent. "Robinson, an...swer...me." The big head lowered close to the stunned, terrified boy as Medford slowly reached for the ruler with a beefy hand. The entire class waited, but Christopher remained silent. His lips fluttered but no words came out.

"Well, if you can't speak..." Bruce Medford gently tapped the ashen-faced boy on the nose with the deadly instrument carefully enunciating each word. "Perhaps you would hold out your hand."

"It's mine!"

Medford heard Ian but was reluctant to turn from his game.

"It's mine. It's a joke—he's not to blame," the voice quietly persisted. The big head turned.

"You like jokes, Jeffries?" The ruler slammed down on the desk. Ian stood his ground.

"Yes, Sir," he whispered.

"Perhaps you would like to tell us all a joke, then?"

A meaty hand grabbed Ian by the back of his neck and forced him to the front of the class to stand behind the teacher's desk.

Medford strode back to sit on the edge of a desk halfway down the classroom, folding his arms as he savoured the boys' discomfort.

"Go on, Jeffries, tell us all a joke. Entertain us." The sickly smile was back in place.

There were one or two titters around the class. Ian's face reddened, he stood at a loss.

"I don't know a joke, Sir," he muttered.

"Speak up, we can't hear you, Jeffries. Can you hear him, girls? Come on, Jeffries, tell us a joke...or do you want me to give Robinson six of the best?"

Ian glanced at his terrified friend and in a quiet voice said, "Why did the chicken cross the road?"

Medford stood up and took a step towards the boy. "No, no, no. You'll have to do better than that, I'm afraid." He shook his big, jowly, red-faced head, his voice threatening.

"A man in a French restaurant..." Ian started to say, remembering his dad telling a joke—a joke that he didn't understand.

"Yes?" Bruce stopped mid-stride, arms still folded, the ruler twitching as it was gripped tighter. "Go on?" He looked down at Ian enquiringly.

"The man said to the waiter, 'Have you got frogs legs?' The waiter said, 'Wee, wee.' The man said, 'Hop over to the counter and get me a ham sandwich.'" The remembered words tumbled out in a rush.

The joke hit a bulls-eye on Bruce Medford's funny bone, transforming the threatening, fierce expression.

It started as a quiet rumble and built as his big frame shook with mirth to explode in a bellow of laughter.

At that moment, the hands of the school clock reached twelve and three, and the school bell rang. Astounded, the pupils of Preparatory A watched as Bruce Medford, still chuckling, waved his big hands to indicate the end of class for that day. Ian and Christopher took their chance with the rest of them in the general melee out the door to join the throng heading for happy release.

In the corridor, the two boys looked at each other in disbelief at their narrow escape. Christopher grabbed Ian by the arm and they moved as quickly as they could with a glance back to make sure that 'Bruiser Bruce' was not following.

"Thanks! Thanks! You saved my life!" There were tears of relief in Christopher's eyes. Ian was afraid he was going to start crying, so he made a funny face.

"I hope old Bruiser dies laughing," he said.

At the school entrance, Laura Anne stood waiting. She saw the two boys approach down the corridor amongst all the other children. Christopher was laughing and had a hold of Ian's arm, both boys making funny faces. Laura Anne smiled, her resolve to complete her plan now stronger than ever—a plan that was going to change all their lives forever.

Ian stood back, slightly embarrassed, as Laura Anne greeted Christopher with a customary hug and a kiss on his cheek.

"Hello, Ian." She stepped forward and, to his astonishment, greeted him in a like manner. She smelled nice, and her arms were light on his shoulders. For a moment her soft cheek was on his, and he felt her hold him close. His face reddened for the second time that day, and he glanced around in embarrassment in case some of the 'hard lads' had seen.

"You're coming home with us for tea. I was talking to your mum and she said it's OK. The car is parked outside. Would you like to sit in the back or the front, Ian?"

Her voice sounded soft and posh, and her expression was inviting and kind. Ian smiled back, happy at the prospect. She linked the two boys by the arms, and they headed for the school gate and the sports car parked outside.

"This is great! I can show Ian my electric trains and my new bike—can we have ice cream?" Christopher talked all the way to the gate. Ian remained silent, aware of the arm linking his and the intimacy and closeness of Laura Anne. He glanced sideways at the beautiful film-star profile as she listened to Christopher. She turned her head at that moment and smiled at him.

"I'm so glad you two are friends," she said and pulled him closer. He didn't resist, instead letting his head fall against her shoulder just for a moment. He was a good bit taller than Christopher, and when he looked at her face, their eyes were almost on a level.

"We're going to be such good friends." She smiled again as they reached the car.

"I usually sit in the front, but you can if you like," Christopher offered generously as he climbed over the side of the open car and sat into the small seat behind the driver.

Ian threw his schoolbag in beside Christopher and pressed down on the shiny door handle. The door opened, and he stood looking in admiration. "I was never in a sports car before!"

"Hop in," Laura Anne said, already behind the steering wheel. "Hold my hat, please!"

Ian slipped onto the soft leather passenger seat as the engine burst into life and the wide-brimmed hat was placed in his lap. "Can she do a hundred?" He looked at the speedometer.

"One-twenty!" Christopher shouted from the back as they took off under the admiring glances of all and sped past bicycles and the crowd at the bus stop. The car picked up speed, and the wind blew Ian's hair. He looked to the left and the right and waved at familiar faces; you had to shout to be heard.

Up the hill from the school, the traffic lights were green. The car bounced on its suspension. Ian wanted to go faster.

"Do a hundred!"

Laura Anne laughed as they went through the traffic lights and gunned the car when they reached the next turn.

"We're doing fifty!" Ian looked at the dial and watched the needle creep up. "Sixty!" he shouted, looking at Laura Anne. She looked back, keeping her foot on the pedal.

He turned to beam at Christopher. "We're doing sixty!"

Christopher was clutching the back of the driver's seat. "Slow down, Mum, slow down!" he yelled, but she didn't seem to hear him. Christopher screamed in panic, and Ian could see he was crying. "Slow down!"

This time, at his cry, she slowed the speed of the sports car. Christopher's mouth made a quivering line; he was breathing sporadically through his nose.

"Don't worry, Ian. Yesterday, he wanted to do sixty, today he has a panic attack." Laura Anne flashed a conspiratorial smile at Ian, who, feeling very grown up, acknowledged with a nod of understanding. "He'll be fine in a minute. All right now, darling, do you want to stop for ice cream?"

Christopher instantly stopped crying. "Yes, please."

Ian, bemused, watched him wipe away his tears.

"It's only a game," Christopher protested with a sniff and a half smile. "I was only pretending."

Laura Anne glanced from the road to Ian. "Of course, you were," she murmured. "Ian, do you like homemade ice cream?"

"Yes, please, thank you very much."

"With ripple—raspberry ripple!" Christopher leaned forward on the back seat.

The drive to the Robinsons' home lasted twenty minutes. On the way, they passed by the pub near Ian's house. The usual group of local men propped up the wall.

"There's Paddy Boylan and the Gimlet," Ian said as they pulled up at the stop sign. "Hiya, Paddy, Hiya, Gimlet!"

Heads turned to survey the sleek sports car, eyes scanning the occupants and coming to rest on the familiar, grinning face of Ian Jeffries. "How'ya, Curly?" A couple of caps were doffed in deference to Laura Anne and the car.

"Is that your girlfriend?" The Gimlet winked at his cronies and laughed. Fortunately, there were no cars approaching from either direction, so Ian was saved further banter. The locals' eyes followed.

***

"Did ya see that bit of leg showing, with your woman sittin' like that? Ya could see right up her skirt. Ya know, there's no sight better than a good-looking woman in a short skirt drivin' a sports car." The Gimlet nodded vigorously.

"Or Addie Jeffries on a bike."

"Or Addie Jeffries on a bike," they repeated in unison as they watched the car disappear around a bend, each conjuring up his own individual imaginings and speculation.

"I saw that car outside Jeffries' gate on the way up. That Ian is a nice lad. I call him Curly. They're a bit snobby, them Jeffries, with the posh school and that."

"They're Prods. What do ya expect? All Protestants are a bit posh."

"They only think they are…"

"Well, I never saw a poor one…"

"The Aul lad, Hugh, he has a few reddies. I'd say, he's a bit of a gent."

"Ah! Sure, I suppose they're all right. That Addie one's a bit of all right."

The Gimlet coughed and laughed. "Don't let yer man Roy hear ya say that. He'd knock ya into the middle of next week."

"Roy Jeffries—now there's a gentleman for you. He's a decent man."

The heads nodded in collective agreement. "A decent man," they repeated.

"Still, I wouldn't kick your woman out of the scratcher." The Gimlet wheezed a laugh and spat into the gutter.

***

"Who were those men at the crossroads?" Laura Anne glanced at Ian.

"They're my friends. Well, the Gimlet is, anyway."

"They were dirty," Christopher joined in from the back. "Their clothes were dirty."

"Well, I like the Gimlet," Ian defended. "He calls me Curly."

"Why is he called the Gimlet?" Laura Anne skilfully deflected, but she was also curious about Ian's association with the locals.

"I don't know. Everyone calls him that. I think it's something to do with his eyes."

"Are they friendly with your parents? Do they come to your house?"

The questions puzzled Ian, who had never thought about the local people as anything other than friends.

"They never come to the house. Ma and Da talk to them on the road, and sometimes the Gimlet helps in the garden."

For the remainder of the four-mile trip to the Robinson home, Laura Anne concentrated on her driving, letting the two boys interact without interruption, now and then glancing in the rear-view mirror, watching her normally petulant son enjoy Ian's company. She had never seen him so animated, his normally stern expression transformed.

"Can Ian stay in our house tonight, please?" The question came unexpectedly, and Laura Anne realised she'd been thinking the same thing herself.

"Nearly home," she said.

Chapter 13

WHAT IMPACTED IAN MOST AS he stood in the bright hallway of the Robinsons' house was the carpet, blue with a greenish pattern, stretching from wall to wall, drawing his attention to the uninterrupted white line of the pristine white skirting board, then the stairs with their shining, polished, wooden bannisters rising up towards the sunlight streaming through the landing window. There was a nice smell; no cracked lino, damp patches or dark cobwebby corners here.

A woman appeared at the top of the stairs, carrying a wash basket brimming with clothes. Her face was familiar to Ian, and after a moment he recognised her as Mrs. Smithers, the mother of a boy from the workers' cottages. If she recognised him, she gave no sign as she took the stairs down to the hall.

"Hello, Mrs. Robinson, there were two telephone calls. I wrote the names in the book." She spoke clearly and distinctly, pronouncing her words carefully. Ian wanted to laugh at her attempt to be posh, but her expression was so earnest he thought better of it.

"Thank you, Peggy. There'll be an extra one for dinner this evening, and I won't be needing you after seven o'clock"

"Thank you, Mrs. Robinson." She swept past and down the hall.

Ian was about to call 'Hello, Mrs. Smithers', but was distracted by the sight of Christopher removing his shiny black school uniform shoes, revealing his unblemished, ribbed, grey uniform socks.

Laura Anne stood on one leg with an outstretched hand on the bannister for balance, in the act of removing her high heels.

Ian looked down apprehensively at his brown sandals, knowing that the worn, creased leather with its pattern of air-holes concealed stockings that had been through the wars, probably too large and certainly darned in several places with thick wool. One, he knew, had a hole in it. A not-so-clean big toenail had been protruding for the last two days.

"Slippers on, Christopher!" Laura Anne called as Christopher skipped down the hall in his stocking feet. "Sandals don't count," she said in a quiet voice, aware of Ian's hesitation.

A much-relieved Ian rose to his feet and followed into the gleaming kitchen.

Christopher sat on a high stool at a silver topped counter. "Have a banana," he invited, gesturing to the huge glass bowl overflowing with oranges, apples, pears and even grapes, a bunch of bananas alongside.

Ian selected a high stool and studied the feast, wide-eyed. "Can we?"

Christopher casually snapped the stalk of a banana and quickly peeled it, popping half the precious fruit into his mouth. "Of course, silly," he said cheeks bulging. The rest of the banana quickly followed.

Pure extravagance! Ian had never seen a banana treated with such disrespect. He had never had control over an entire banana. In the Jeffries household, such a treasure would be carefully peeled by his mother, cut into even, round, slices and shared equally.

He looked at the bunch of bananas, contemplating the possibility of pocketing one to produce triumphantly at home for James and Debbie to share. Somehow it seemed wrong to keep a whole one to himself.

Incredibly, Christopher reached for another one. Ian watched in wonder as it received the same treatment as the first.

"Do you not like bananas?" Christopher enquired, cheeks bulging. "Let's play with my train set." He jumped from the stool and headed for the door without waiting for a reply, leaving Ian alone with the bananas, which beckoned in delicious silence. He quickly reached for one and gave it the Christopher treatment; another quickly followed into his pocket. He jumped from the stool but hesitated at the door. It seemed like stealing. Reluctantly, he returned it to its place with the other fruit in the bowl.

Just then, Mrs. Robinson came in and asked, "Would you care for some fruit, Ian?"

"No, thank you," Ian replied politely.

"Go on, put this in your pocket for later." She smiled and waved a banana temptingly.

He took the fruit. "Thank you, Mrs. Robinson."

"Are you going to play or not?" Christopher called impatiently from down the hall.

"Coming!" Ian headed out of the kitchen, following the sound of his friend's voice. Mrs. Smithers emerged from a doorway. Ian smiled a hello, but his greeting was returned with a disapproving glare.

"Put that back immediately!" she whispered, pointing at the banana sticking out of Ian's pocket. "That's stealing!" She grabbed his wrist in a strong reddened hand and thrust her face close to his.

He recoiled from the strength of her outrage. She smelled of lavender water and stale tobacco. To Mrs. Smithers, stealing a banana was tantamount to a major crime.

"I'm going to tell Mrs. Robinson!" Convinced she had caught the Jeffries boy red-handed, she was relishing the prospect.

"Mrs. Smithers! What *are* you doing?" Christopher's mother enquired in a concerned voice as she approached along the hall.

"He took a banana, I caught him. It's in his pocket!" The woman pointed triumphantly.

Laura Anne valued Mrs. Smithers as her housekeeper, but the Jeffries boy was far more important. She rested a firm hand on the housekeeper's wrist and spoke firmly and distinctly. "Ian's mother, Mrs. Jeffries, is my friend. Ian is a guest in this house, and there's no question of stealing. You are being quite ridiculous. You must apologise to Ian immediately. We hope to see a lot more of him in the future. He is like a brother to Christopher and must be treated accordingly."

Mrs. Smithers hesitated for a moment before releasing her grasp. "Sorry, I was only trying to help," she protested.

Ian felt embarrassed for the housekeeper. He and her kids, Joe and Martin, often played together, and he had been in their house.

"It's all right, Mrs. Robinson. Mrs. Smithers didn't know you gave me the banana."

"Are you playing or not?!"

At the sound of the now-exasperated Christopher's voice, Ian hurried away to the doorway down the hall.

A room just for toys greeted him. They were everywhere, shelves piled with them, boxes overflowing—Meccano, Monopoly, jigsaws and books. The doors of a floor-to-ceiling cupboard stood open revealing shelves packed with even more wonders. Open-mouthed, Ian stared, unable to believe what he was seeing. He reached up to touch the wing of a beautiful model Spitfire hanging from the ceiling; other fighter planes hung at varying angles in a fabulous dogfight.

"You lucky sucker!" he exclaimed.

"The Flying Scotsman is leaving the station!" Christopher's voice came from the other side of a spectacular landscaped train display.

Ian had seen an electric train set once before at Christmas, in Cleary's window. He, Debbie and James had watched the train going around and around, captivated by the spectacle as it stopped at the station and then disappeared into a tunnel to reappear, green and shining, with its carriages streaming behind. They had eventually left on threat of missing the bus home, but the train set had been the source of conversation for some time after that. Each of the children vowed to one day own such a wonderful treasure, all knowing it would be a very unlikely possibility.

The Cleary's train bore no comparison to this display. Ian watched Christopher working the controls, and the train left the station, snaking along the track into a tunnel in a mountainside with roads and grass and trees and little sheep grazing under the watchful eye of a shepherd. The train emerged from the tunnel, passing fields with cows, a road with crossing gates that lifted automatically, past a village with houses and people, and around to Ian's side of the display. He dropped to his knees to study the train at eye level as it passed and following its course as it rounded a wide bend to pass engine sheds and sidings with more engines and carriages, through the station for a repeat performance.

"How do you stop it?" Ian enquired, torn between the great train set and the vast amount of attractions surrounding him.

"Easy!" Christopher dropped a metal toy soldier across the tracks. To Ian's horror, the beautiful engine rounded a bend at speed, cannoned into the obstruction and derailed, dragging the beautiful coaches with it, dangling precariously off the edge of the table for a moment before, in spite of Ian's best efforts, the whole lot crashed to the wooden floorboards.

"You can have this Spitfire." With scarcely a glance at the engine and coaches, Christopher reached to drag the huge model plane from its mountings.

The horrified Ian on his knees tried to rescue the damaged model train.

"It's yours! It flies with remote control!" Christopher made a magnanimous gesture as he proffered the most wonderful toy of Ian's dreams. "You saved me from Brucie. You're my friend. Take it! I don't want it anymore!"

"Thanks" Ian said without looking up. He was still searching the floor for pieces of the train set. "But I can't take it. Me ma wouldn't let me."

"Take anything you want. You're my friend," Christopher put down the model plane and, with outstretched arms, expansively indicated the entire toy-stacked room.

"No, thanks." Ian stood up from his task.

"So! You don't want to be my friend then!" Christopher frowned, upset.

"Don't be silly." Ian laughed.

To his amazement, Christopher shouted, "I'm not silly!" and ran from the room.

Ian stood looking at the open doorway. He listened to the retreating footsteps and the sound of a door slamming somewhere in the house. Shaking his head, puzzled, he kneeled down to continue the rescue operation.

***

On hearing the commotion, Laura Anne had come to investigate. She leaned against the doorframe and studied the boy kneeling on the floor. *Hard to believe he and Christopher are the same age. So much taller, his limbs strong—the shoulders showing the promise of the man. He seems thoughtful and independent, and those rough edges could be easily smoothed out. He and Christopher get along so well...* It was all adding up—adding up to a decision, a resolve, to bring Ian back to England with them as a brother to Christopher.

He looked up, and she was struck by his expression: innocent, without guile. Strong eyebrows, black curling hair; brown eyes steadily gazed back.

"What happened?" she enquired, arms folded.

He stood up quickly, relieved to see she was smiling. "It crashed."

She looked at the broken pieces in his hand.

"I think it's badly damaged." He indicated the coaches on the floor.

Laura Anne eyed the toy soldier wedged in the train track. "How did that get there?" Having overheard the exchange, she was very well aware of what had happened.

"I couldn't say." Ian slowly shook his head from side to side.

"Did you do it, Ian?" She frowned sternly.

"I couldn't say, Mrs. Robinson." The boy looked her straight in the eye.

"Did Christopher do it?" she tested.

"I couldn't say, Mrs. Robinson," he repeated, adding, before she could ask any more questions, "I think it looks worse than it is. I'll be able to fix it."

"Don't worry, Ian." She stepped close and put her arms on his shoulders.

Ian stood still, rigid, as he felt her cheek against his and the gentle kiss, her perfume invading his senses. The most wondrous sensations. He returned the embrace, holding on clumsily, unaccustomed to such a gentle show of affection.

"I know it wasn't you." Standing back with her beautiful face close, she raised a slim hand and gently thumbed the lipstick mark away.

Debbie Reynolds, Tammy's in love. Embarrassed, unaccustomed feelings stirring, the sensations drove the colour to Ian's face. He could only stare into the wide brown eyes of the all-knowing Laura Anne.

"I *am* Christopher's friend. Do you want me to go after him?" He hoped she'd kiss him again.

"No, it's all right. I'll do it. You stay here and play with the toys." She smiled and went in search of her son.

Left alone in the room, Ian looked around. Suddenly toys didn't mean quite so much anymore. Well, maybe the big model Spitfire. Using both hands, he reverently lifted it into position on its mount, his fingers lightly touching the fuselage as he examined every detail. It even had a fighter pilot in the cockpit. The train engine and its carriages were soon returned to the table, carefully placed on the tracks and examined for damage. Satisfied with the result, he went to the doorway and looked up and down the hall.

Hearing muffled voices, he decided to head in the opposite direction, towards the front of the house and the large sitting room.

Heavy curtains draped at the big window, the carpet stretched floral and luxurious across the room, with deep-cushioned chairs and a big sofa. Here, he made himself comfortable to await the return of Christopher and his ma.

A television! He had never seen a real one close up, only pictures in magazines and in shop windows. It looked like a radio set only it had a big shiny glass panel in the middle. He was about to examine it more closely when he heard Laura Anne's voice coming from the hallway.

"There you are! Christopher wants to say something to you."

He came bounding into the room. "Soorry!" he singsonged in his best funny voice. "Do you want to watch television?"

"Yes, please!"

"*The Count of Monte Cristo* is on."

"Wow! Wait till I tell James and Debbie."

Standing at the door, Laura Anne watched the two boys settle down to watch the television, happy with her plans for Ian Jeffries and quite sure that she would have her own way in the end. Coming to a decision, she headed for the kitchen, her handbag and the phone number Addie had given her.

***

At the sound of the wooden gate to the road opening, Addie—on her hands and knees, weeding a flowerbed in the front garden—looked up. It was Gerry Hartigan, the young lad from the shop.

"You're wanted on the phone," he announced, slightly breathless and obviously under instructions from Mrs. Hartigan to hurry. Not waiting for a reply, he ran back out the gate.

Addie quickly followed, rubbing her hands on her apron. She was out onto the road when she remembered the two-pence for the phone call. Hesitating for a moment, she hurried on after the retreating figure, to the shop fifty yards away. She could give the two-pence to Mrs. Hartigan later.

The phone was positioned on the rear wall of the shop. "Hello, Adelaide Jeffries here." She spoke in a low voice, her back to the curious shoppers.

"Hello, Addie."

She was surprised to hear Laura Anne's voice and immediately enquired, "Is everything all right?"

"Of course!"

Slightly taken aback, she listened as Laura Anne explained the reason for the call. Apparently, there was something wrong with the sports car and it would not start—would it be all right for Ian to stay the night? They would bring him home the following day, Saturday. Laura Anne was very apologetic, explaining that her husband would not be home until after the children's bedtime. She spoke very rapidly, her voice merging with the crackle of interference on the phone.

Usually, a phone call to the shop carried bad news. Heads turned and necks craned; silence prevailed. All present wanted to hear.

Addie had two concerns. Maybe Ian did not want to stay with the Robinsons, and what about his underwear and the holes in his socks?

"I'd better have a word with Ian. If he's happy about it, it's OK, I suppose."

She heard talking in the background, Ian's voice animated, and then he came to the phone.

"Is that OK, Ma? They have a television! I'm watching *The Count of Monte Cristo*. They have pyjamas for me, and I can wear one of Mr. Robinson's pullovers. We're going to a hotel to have our dinner." He spoke rapidly, obviously excited about the idea. Addie could understand why.

"OK, OK, but be good and say 'please' and 'thank you', and don't get too excited."

"Thanks! Thanks!" The phone crackled as the receiver was dropped, and she heard in the background, "Ma said yes! I'm allowed!" as a laughing Laura Anne came on the phone.

"We'll take great care of him and deliver him home safely to you tomorrow evening."

"Well, if it's not too much trouble," Addie said.

"Not at all. We're delighted to have him, he's such good company for Christopher. We must do lunch sometime soon." They said their goodbyes, and Addie returned the phone to its cradle.

The shop became a hive of activity immediately the call ended. Addie looked around.

"For your information, that was my friend Laura Anne Robinson. Ian is going out to dinner with the Robinsons, to a hotel, and staying overnight in his new pyjamas." With a feeling of some satisfaction, she swept past the shoppers, head held high.

"Did you leave your two-pence for the phone?" Mrs. Hartigan sniped from behind the counter with a grim smile.

A slight straightening of an already rigid back and a tossing of the auburn hair were the only indications that the comment had hit home. Addie strode from the shop.

"That one's getting far too big for her boots."

Several heads nodded in agreement.

Chapter 14

Laura Anne replaced the phone on its cradle. The house was quiet. She glanced at the kitchen clock: four forty-five. Mrs. Smithers, in the hall, had removed her apron and was struggling into a big overcoat.

"I'm finishing now, if that's all right, Mrs. Robinson," she called.

Laura Anne, with some regrets for the earlier banana incident, decided to make amends. After all, Mrs. Smithers knew Ian's family and could prove to be a useful source of information.

"Would you like some biscuits this week? And I'm sure we can spare some potatoes and vegetables," she called back.

Mrs. Smithers appeared at the kitchen door. She always carried a large shopping bag, and often on a Friday, Laura Anne would allow her to take some groceries home for the weekend. The offer was always accompanied with an explanation, thus saving any embarrassment to the cleaning lady's pride.

"Help yourself to some things." Laura Anne gestured to the open larder door. "We seem to be very overstocked this week."

Mrs. Smithers scanned the shelves. "Well, I wouldn't mind some carrots for a stew, thank you." Her anxiety not to appear too grasping was doing battle with her desire to fill the shopping bag to brimming point. With six hungry children and a husband who needed to be dragged from the pub every pay day, the Robinson larder must have represented Mrs. Smithers' idea of heaven.

"Oh, we can do better than that." Laura Anne began to fill the bag: a head of cabbage, carrots, a turnip and tomatoes. She opened the door of the big fridge.

Anticipation overcame Mrs. Smithers' sense of pride, and she held the bag wide. "No! no! Thank you! That's too much!" she protested as rashers, half a dozen eggs and some sausages were transferred to the big shopping bag.

"Nonsense! We're eating out tonight and will probably do the same at the weekend." A friendly hand was placed on the grateful Mrs. Smithers' arm. "You are a trusted and valued asset to our home, and we're glad to have you. Here are some lamb chops for that hungry husband of yours." A wrapped butcher's package was placed on top of the laden bag.

Mrs. Smithers looked appealingly at her benefactor. "I'm sorry I said anything about the Jeffries boy."

"Think nothing of it—a perfectly understandable mistake. Do you know the Jeffries well?"

"They're very nice people, especially Roy...Mr. Jeffries," she corrected herself. "He's a gentleman, and the children are good, well-behaved. My Brian plays with them sometimes—he was at Ian's birthday party last year.

"And Mrs. Jeffries?"

Laura Anne waited as Mrs. Smithers' grasp tightened on the handles of the shopping bag, her eyes shifting to the side, face betraying uncertainty.

"Very nice too," she said without conviction.

"You're not very keen on Mrs. Jeffries, are you?" Laura Anne's smile was an invitation to say more.

"Well, I wouldn't like to say. You're her friend." Encouraged by Laura Anne's silence and open smile, she continued, "She's a bit full of herself, thinks she's beautiful and better than most. They act posh but don't have much money." When no contradiction was offered, Mrs. Smithers leaned towards Laura Anne and said in a confidential tone, "She's a Dipper, a Holy Dipper. So is the old fella, her father. And he's a bit of a toff as well. Butter wouldn't melt in his mouth."

"What's a Holy Dipper?" Laura Anne, matching the other woman's tone.

Sensing she was in unchartered territory, never having had to define the phrase, Mrs. Smithers threw caution to the wind.

"When Holy Dippers are baptised, they're dunked right under the water without a sign of the cross." She looked horrified at the thought. "And from that time on, they have to take lots of baths, not just once a week, like good God- fearing people, but every day.

"Well, at least she must be very clean." Laura Anne couldn't help it.

"Oh, no!" Mrs. Smithers shook her head knowledgably. "They're not allowed to use soap. They're Baptists!" She looked into the laden bag and then at Laura Anne, her normally stern features transformed into a smile of genuine gratitude. "You're very kind, Mrs. Robinson. Thank you very much. God bless you. Now, I must be off to catch the bus."

Hardly able to believe her good fortune, she left the kitchen and let herself out by the front door. It had been a long time since there were Donnelly's skinless sausages and lean back rashers in the Smithers household.

***

The Robinsons' house with its well-tended garden was set back from the road alongside similar detached homes. With a light step in spite of the heavy shopping bag, Mrs. Smithers made her way past the little red sports car to the gateway.

Expensive rashers, posh sausages, packets of chocolate biscuits and other expensive items could be exchanged in Hartigan's shop for a good supply of oats for porridge, flour and some stewing steak. The carrots and other vegetables would come in handy.

The Jeffries and the Robinsons, friends! Who would have thought it? Well, that's Protestants for you. Always sticking together and looking after their own. Maybe the Jeffries are better off than I thought.

Chapter 15

THOUGH IN HIS LATE FORTIES, Gordon Robinson considered himself fit and youthful for his age. Ex-army, active service, with a ramrod straight back and direct gaze, the chairman and managing director of Robinson's Paints and Decorating Products did not suffer fools gladly and possessed an inflated opinion of himself. He had attended public school and was a bully by choice. Always dressed appropriately in handmade suits and tailored shirts, he was not impressed by the sight of Christopher's friend wearing his brand-new golf sweater.

"So, this is your friend Ian," Gordon addressed Christopher, further annoyed to see that the sweater fitted the twelve-year-old boy perfectly. The irritation added an edge to his words and showed in his slightly bristling stance. "My golf sweater looks very nice on you." He stood for a moment at the door of the sitting room before briskly heading along the hallway into the kitchen.

Ian, who had stood up quickly when he heard the voice, sat down again. Christopher hadn't moved his attention from the Lone Ranger.

"I don't appreciate you letting that young fellow wear my new sweater."

At the kitchen counter, Laura Anne looked up calmly from the evening newspaper. "We're going to eat out tonight and he had nothing appropriate to wear. The table is booked for eight o'clock." Lowering her voice, she appealed, "This is the boy's first visit. Be nice—you know how important this is. He's staying tonight, and we're taking him home tomorrow." She shot him a warning glance. "Domestic matters are my domain, *my domain*! Use some of that charm you lavish on your customers."

None too pleased, he made a noncommittal kissing sound in her direction and headed for the bedroom and a shower. Friday night: casual dress, cavalry twills, casual shirt and a sweater... but the boy had his new one. His new golf sweater. Settling for a white shirt and Harris tweed jacket, Gordon returned downstairs in a disgruntled mood.

***

On the way to the hotel, Gordon studied the boy reflected in the car's rear-view mirror. Laura Anne's plan seemed to be coming together. While he agreed in principle—domestic matters, *Laura's domain*, did not impinge much on him—he still considered himself in control, but indulging her was always a worthwhile investment. After all, everything came with a price.

He glanced sideways at her profile; she was the perfect wife: beautiful, fashionable, a reflection of his success and the envy of all his business associates, male and female alike.

"I believe you're a great sportsman, Ian."

Surprised, Ian looked back at the eyes in the mirror. It was the first time he had been addressed directly by Christopher's dad other than the sweater comment, and he was not sure what to say.

"Mrs. Robinson tells me you've been standing up for Christopher at school. We're grateful, aren't we, Chris?"

"Yes." Christopher made a face at Ian.

"Thanks for the loan of the sweater. It's very nice," Ian said. "I like this car. Does it come with the job? My dad wants a job with a car supplied."

Gordon glanced at the bright-red face in the mirror, highly amused by the comment. "Yes, Ian, it does come with the job."

"My father's getting an inspector's job with a van," Ian said, quickly adding, "I hope so, anyway."

"Your father is a fine man, Ian," Laura Anne said. "I'm sure he'll be successful." She glanced meaningfully at her husband.

Gordon, understanding, nodded agreement.

***

Table for four at the Gresham, white table cloth laden with cutlery, flowers in a vase, muted conversation and the clink of bone China, the occasional sound of a cork being popped...the well-heeled out for the evening.

Like a movie with Audrey Hepburn, Ian impulsively pulled out the chair for Laura Anne to sit down at the round table.

"Why, thank you, kind sir," she laughed.

Ian looked around at the surroundings in wide-eyed wonder. He felt very grown up as he scrutinised the menu, but nothing made any sense.

"What are you going to have?" he whispered to Christopher.

"Steak and chips. I don't want a starter," Christopher said without opening the menu.

"What would you like?" Gordon asked from across the table. "You can have anything you want."

"Steak and chips, please." Ian didn't hesitate.

"And for a starter?"

Ian didn't know what a starter was, but the word triggered a memory. He remembered his mum and dad discussing a starter and laughing.

"A prawn cocktail, please." At Gordon's surprise, he added, "If that's OK."

"I think it's on the menu," smiled Laura Anne, amused that Gordon's attempt to put the boy on the spot had failed.

"Perhaps you'd like to select the wine?" Gordon countered, handing over the menu with the word *Wine* gold embossed on the leather cover.

Ian opened it, but none of the words made any sense. At a loss, he said nothing.

"They always have a Chablis or a Beaujolais," Christopher said. "Can we have an orange drink, please?"

Laura Anne glowered at her husband. "We'll order the wine when we decide what we're going to have to eat," she said.

Gordon, his mood improving, ordered another gin and tonic.

Normally, the Robinsons didn't bother with a starter, so the waiter was somewhat surprised when three prawn cocktails were requested. Everyone was having steak. Ian following Gordon's example, said 'rare' when asked how he preferred his steak.

"Ugh!" Christopher made a face. "Blood! I hate rare steak. Well done, please."

"Are you sure you want a rare steak, Ian?" Laura Anne asked. "I like well done." She nodded encouragingly.

Gordon waved a dismissive hand. "Let the chap have his steak whatever way he wants. We men like our steak rare, don't we, Ian?"

Ian smiled happily. "Yes, Mr. Robinson. Rare, please."

The wine arrived, and the waiter poured a small amount into a glass. Fascinated, Ian watched Christopher's dad lift the glass and swirl the liquid around, holding it at an angle to examine it before tasting it and nodding to the waiter.

"Wine, Ian. The elixir of life." He held out the glass. "Here. Taste it."

"Gordon!" Laura Anne warned.

He ignored her, holding out the glass.

"It's yucky and you get drunk!" Christopher exclaimed.

The wine in the glass shimmered in the subdued lighting of the restaurant. Ian had tasted wine the previous Christmas, when he had been left alone with his mother's wine glass. It tasted bitter and he hadn't really liked it.

"Go on! It won't hurt you," Gordon encouraged.

Ian looked at Laura Anne, but she was glaring at Gordon.

"Domestic affairs! My territory," she snapped, but Gordon, wishing to assert himself, was not prepared to step down.

Ian did not understand the nature of the conflict. He took the glass. "I've had it before. It's nice." There was only a small amount.

To Gordon's amusement, Ian swirled it around and examined it before tasting it. He handed it back with a slight grimace.

"There!" Gordon exclaimed, clapping his hands together. "No harm done." "Pour a glass for Ian," he instructed the waiter with a warning glance at Laura Anne, who looked at the table and remained silent. "My son thinks wine is yucky." He shook his head with a resigned sigh and ordered another gin and tonic for himself.

Laura Anne knew the signs. Her belligerent husband needed to win a certain amount. She looked across at Ian, catching his eye, and winked.

Ian winked back, liking the idea of a conspiracy but not really understanding what was going on.

An apprehensive glance to the left confirmed, to Laura Anne's relief, Gordon had not noticed the exchange. "Christopher, show Ian the lobster tank while we're waiting for our starters." she suggested.

Christopher led the way over to the big tank the other side of the room. "They're huge with giant pincers. You pick one out and they cook it for you to eat—they're not red, they're black."

Back at the table, Laura Anne watched the boys' progress. "What do you think of Ian?"

Gordon nodded, knowing what she meant. "Yes, for once I think you've got it right."

"Well, don't spoil it, he likes us. And ease off on the gin and tonics. It's going really well."

Gordon sat back and folded his arms, pursed his lips and smiled to show how much in charge he was, aware that he could spoil it all if he so wished. In reality, the plan appealed to him, and Ian seemed the perfect candidate.

The waiter returned to the table to announce that unfortunately there were no prawn cocktails available and would they accept the chef's apologies.

"Perhaps we'll just have the main course, then, if that's OK?" Laura Anne looked across the table as the two boys returned.

"OK!" Ian nodded, relieved. He hadn't been looking forward to the mysterious prawn cocktail.

With an uncharacteristic show of humour, Gordon said, "I didn't want one, anyway. They're yucky."

Laura Anne put her hand on his arm, pure Audrey Hepburn, *Roman Holiday*, lush-lipped and beautiful. She smiled gently and gazed into his eyes. She had the chairman of the board where she wanted him.

The steaks arrived, and Laura Anna shared an understanding smile with the waiter that promised a healthy tip.

Ian lifted his knife and fork and speared a big fat potato chip, his eyes transfixed by Gordon's plate. Red oozed around the blade of the serrated knife as Gordon cut into his steak. Ian watched the bloody piece of meat travel to his mouth and disappear only to reappear again momentarily as he spoke.

"Beautiful!

The wine glass quickly followed, blood red in the subdued light, like a scene from a horror movie.

With a feeling of dread, knife and fork poised, Ian contemplated the big, juicy piece of meat on his plate. He looked across the table. Gordon was watching him. Laura Anne gave a slight nod of encouragement. Ian tentatively cut into his steak, waiting for the red ooze.

The concept of 'rare versus well done' became a reality. Immensely relieved, he was greeted by the sight of lovely, tender meat without a trace of red. Another conspiratorial wink from Laura Anne assured him she had tipped off the waiter. He looked at Christopher's plate: the same.

Cutting himself a generous piece, Ian reached for the tomato ketchup, aware of Gordon's disappointed look.

"I usually have rare, but I prefer a steak this size well done," he said.

For dessert, there were knickerbocker glories in the highest glasses Ian had ever seen, packed with fruit and ice cream, with a long spoon so you could get at every precious drop. He had never had a more delicious meal in his life—even on Christmas day.

Chapter 16

IAN SAT ON THE EDGE of the bed in the lovely guest room, alone, his head full of the strangeness of it all. *Clean.*

Clean walls were covered in wallpaper in straight lines, blue and gold. His image reflected in a tall mirror on the door of a shiny mahogany wardrobe with gold handles, polished to a beautiful sheen. His hands rested on the turned-down, crisp, whiter-than-snow sheet. His feet stuck out from the legs of the sweet-smelling, striped pyjamas, buried in the deep pile cream carpet that stretched to every corner of the room.

They'd had lovely cups of cocoa and some biscuits, after which Christopher had gone for a bath and then come, wrapped in fluffy white towels, to say good night.

"No, thank you!" Ian had replied when asked would he like to take a bath. He did not want them to see his once-white vest or his feet or the holes in his socks.

Should I climb in between these inviting white sheets? He hesitated. *What if I make a mark on them with my grubby feet? What if, in the morning, Mrs. Smithers comes to make the bed?* He put his school socks back on and slid down into the bed. Reaching out, he switched off the bedside light and lay in the darkness, aware of the murmur of voices from downstairs. *Christopher's a lucky sucker.* He yawned, closed his eyes and snuggled down in the most comfortable bed in the world, his mind full of the excitement of the day, anticipating tomorrow and wishing he could stay more than one night.

The sound of footsteps in the hall and murmuring voices...

Am I sleeping or awake?

He opened his eyes wide then closed them immediately as the guest room door slowly opened, the soft light from the landing reaching inside silhouetting the slim figure of Christopher's mother. Feigning sleep, eyes closed, Ian felt her lean over him, smelled the now-familiar scent of her perfume. Her touch was gentle on his forehead, brushing his curling hair.

"Such a beautiful boy." The words were whispered, and he opened his eyes. Still with gentle fingers on his forehead, she sat on the bed and smiled. Ian smiled back, enjoying the moment and her closeness.

"I didn't mean to wake you. I was going to leave this beside your bed for you to discover in the morning." She showed him a long, slim box tied with a ribbon. "It's a present for you because you are so good to Christopher. You can open it now if you like."

Digging his elbows into the deep pillows, he sat up, the action bringing them closer together. She didn't move away, and he found himself leaning against her, their heads close as he pulled the gold ribbon bow open. It was a nice feeling, private and intimate, something longed for but never admitted to himself. Demonstrations of affection were a scarce commodity in the Jeffries household.

Weir Jewellers: the gold letters and crest of Dublin's famous store were embossed on the lid; there was a small clasp holding it closed.

"Open it." She helped him prise open the spring-loaded, hinged box.

"A gold watch!"

It sparkled in the light filtering into the room, a white face with roman numerals and a gold wrist band.

"Is it mine?" Ian whispered in disbelief. "Can I keep it?"

"Of course, my beautiful boy," she replied, her voice smiling and low.

He looked at her, she with her Debbie Reynolds beautiful smile, he, dark eyes brimming with tears that overflowed and tumbled down his cheeks. A slim hand reached to gently brush away the tears, lingering for a moment. Unmoving, he waited, hoping for the kiss. It came just where the tears were.

"Thank you," he whispered, raising his arms to place them around her neck and burying his face into her shoulder. He sobbed softly for all the longed-for, intimate moments never realised.

Laura Anne, touched by the show of emotion, held the boy close. "There, there," she murmured.

Eventually, gently pushing him away, she bent to look into his tear-stained face. "Where did that come from?" she asked kindly.

"I don't know," he said with a rueful smile, keeping his head down, embarrassed by his feelings.

Cupping his chin, she tilted his face up to look into his eyes. "Tears are nothing to be ashamed of. All men cry at some time or another." She dabbed his face with a small handkerchief then handed it to him. "Here, blow your nose."

"I might blow a hole in it," he joked, taking the little hankie with its pink embroidered flowers.

She waited for him regain his composure, curious to understand this normally self-assured young man.

"Can I stay here a little bit longer?"

"I don't think so. We'd love you to stay, but your parents will be expecting you home tomorrow."

"Can I come again?"

"Whenever you want, and for longer if you wish, but it depends on your parents."

He rescued the watch from the folds of the bedspread and examined it again. The gold band stretched over his hand to fit snugly on his wrist. He twisted it around to face him. "Is that the right time?"

"Yes. I set it for you and it's wound. All you have to do is look at it."

"My own watch. I can't believe it." Impulsively, he kissed her cheek. "I love you," he said without looking at her.

"And I love you too. Now, snuggle down and I'll see you in the morning."

Sinking back onto the crisp, white pillows, Ian left his arm outside the covers so he might study his new watch.

She bent and kissed him on the forehead. "Good night, sweet boy."

Ian lay on his back in the darkness. "It's luminous!"

He studied it until, eventually sleep overtook him. His last thought as he drifted away was *Debbie Reynolds wasn't wearing lipstick.*

Chapter 17

Mathew Hennessy, or Henno, as he was known, Headmaster at Kingsbridge Grammar School, considered himself to be a fair man. A product of the English public school system, he was dedicated to the principles of teaching and discipline, the moulding of tomorrow's society in his hands. Being head of a co-educational school constituted some difficulties. Teaching boys posed no problems, but girls remained a mystery to him. The astute Miss Markham, head of the junior school, proved invaluable with her advice, on occasion.

During the course of each teaching day, he would stroll the corridors, observing and being seen by all, his expression intentionally grim and his stride purposeful. A child standing outside a classroom door evidenced a teacher had reached their limit, and Henno would mete out appropriate punishment, almost always a caning: six of the best administered to a young backside, grey trousers pulled tight by the position held as the poor unfortunate stretched across a chair. This would take place in the headmaster's study. On the occasions when one of the girls transgressed, he would have Miss Markham deal with it. Sometimes he wondered what punishment she meted out. He knew she did not possess a cane, but nonetheless her methods seemed effective, evidenced by the inevitable rueful expression on a child's face. Proportionately fewer girls than boys transgressed.

The ejection of a child from a class room was generally reserved for repeated offenders, so as he left his study, Henno was surprised to come across the well-behaved Jeffries boy, standing outside Preparatory A.

Ian watched the terrifying figure approach along the corridor. Bruce Medford had ejected him for no apparent reason. *Perhaps the frog's legs joke has not been forgotten.* Ian had witnessed many times a boy returning from a visit to the headmaster's study, moving and sitting down gently, tear-stained face ashen white with shock, having received six of the best. For Henno, as in all matters, administered the punishment thoroughly and with some vigour.

"Jeffries." Henno stopped, presenting the boy with a look of resigned disappointment shaking his head, tsk-tsking. "What have you to say for yourself? You are a disappointment to me. I would have thought better of you."

"I did nothing, Sir."

"Nothing? Mr. Medford put you out of the class for doing nothing?"

"Yes, Sir."

"You know what I have to do, Jeffries?"

"Yes, Sir."

"And what is that, Jeffries?"

"Hit me, Sir?" It was phrased hopefully as a question.

"Correct, Jeffries."

"You don't have to if you don't want to." The boy's look was steady.

Henno struggled to keep the amusement from showing on his severe headmaster's face. "That's very thoughtful of you, Jeffries." Ian's look didn't waver, but Henno detected a glimmer of hope. "Six of the best. An example has to be made." The severe face was back.

"You could pretend," Ian bargained

About to grab the boy by the ear and march him to his study but never before encountering such bravado, Henno enquired,

"And how would I pretend to give you six of the best, Jeffries?" He leaned forward closer to the boy. "Well?"

"You could take me to your study and not do it, and I would pretend to be crying, back in the classroom," Ian negotiated hopefully.

Stroking his chin, Henno considered his course of action. He was not a great fan of Bruce Medford's methods and suspected the boy may have been unfairly treated. "Jeffries, go to the girls' cloakroom and get one of Joan Forbes' gym shoes. Bring it to my study and wait there." He strode off along the corridor lest the Jeffries boy see his amused expression.

Ian immediately set off for the unfamiliar surroundings of the girls' cloakroom. It smelled different to the boys'. There were coat hangers with names in metal frames over long bench seats against each wall. There was no mistaking Joan Forbes' gym shoes; he could see them from the doorway protruding out from under the bench. Ian considered Jenny May's size-fours alongside but discarded the idea, sure that Henno would not be fooled. Joan Forbes, the biggest person in the school, was reputed to take size ten in shoes.

Ian headed for the headmasters' study, carrying the instrument of his downfall. The big, flat-soled gym shoe would hurt but not as much as the cane. Perhaps he could bargain further and escape with an even lesser punishment. His active imagination whirred with the possibilities. He knocked on the big wood-panelled door.

"Come!"

The room was darker than the rest of the school and did not smell like the cloakrooms, but Ian did not have time to look around. Henno was in a hurry.

"Place the shoe on the desk, pull up your blazer and lean over that chair."

No time for negotiation here. Ian did as he was bid. The chair seat was lower than he expected, his position awkward, his knees nearly touching the floor. The submissive position offended the boy's competitive spirit. With resentment and frustration, combined with an unexpected feeling of humiliation, he felt the sole of Joan Forbes' gym shoe caress his buttocks as Henno marked the spot.

"Do not move or you will get an extra one."

The experienced executioner spaced the words carefully and slowly with deadly intent.

Ian closed his eyes. The noise of the impact penetrated to the expectant ears in Preparatory A.

Medford, looking straight at Christopher Robinson, addressed the class. "Open you text books at page twenty-four," he commanded, his face showing no indication of his deep satisfaction.

Chapter 18

NOW PROMOTED TO THE EXPERIMENTAL position of shortage collector, Roy no longer pedalled through the streets and up and down the hills of Dublin's suburbia. The big orange Rudge bicycle had been replaced by a bright orange van with the big gas company logo on its side. Beaky had reluctantly agreed to a very small increase in Roy's remuneration with the promise of more to come, depending on Roy's performance and the success of the experiment. Somewhat appeased, Addie was glad Roy was no longer exposed to the elements, and the van, though she would have preferred one without the big logo, offered opportunities at the weekend—picnics and visits to the seaside.

Blackwell's judgement was not far off the mark. Roy conducted the handling of bad debts with honest compassion and sincerity, almost always, even in the worst cases, managing a solution that worked to the benefit of the consumer and the company. On the rare occasions when a supply had to be cut off, he would consider it a personal failure and would work tirelessly to resolve the case and have the power restored. He became known as the Gentle Terminator.

Roy was a kindly person by nature, and the job was taking its toll. He longed for weekends and Sunday mornings with Addie in the passenger seat, James, Debbie and Ian packed into the back of the little van with the inevitable salad sandwiches, sausages and ginger-nut biscuits, out along the Bray Road, hail, rain or snow. Glorious times at the foot of the sugar-loaf, Powerscourt Waterfall and the Rocky Valley made all the more wondrous with the addition of a primus stove. Sausages sizzling on a pan, mugs of tea, the little van with its precious cargo winding over the Featherbed and Lugnaquila, sunlight breaking through rain clouds, the hills converging in browns, greens and purples. The glimpse of a lake and little stone bridges over streams, each one hailed as the source of the River Liffey. Descending through the pine forest, stopping to stand outside the van to exclaim at the sight of Dublin City, evening lights beginning to flicker, greys and blues to the sea and the horizon—

"It's a long way to Tipperary...for my heart lies there. I love to go a-wandering...along the mountain track. She'll be comin' 'round the mountain when she comes..." Addie led the singing.

—to eventually arrive at Ivy Lodge.

A whole new world of possibilities had been released with the arrival of the gas company van.

Chapter 19

ADDIE, IN BILLY HARKNESS'S SHOP, flicked through the pages of *Woman's Life* magazine.

"Look at them! Skinny, not a pick on them! Lingerie for the discerning woman," she read aloud.

Roy looked over her shoulder. "Not a patch on you," he observed.

"They'd never get on the Silver Screen," Billy muttered from behind the high counter. "Jane Russell—now there's a real woman for you. Are you goin' to buy that magazine or are you goin' to wear it out lookin' at it?" He never took his eyes from the change tray as his wife short-sightedly poked and prodded the coins, rearranging them into a complex pattern to her own private liking.

Addie flicked a few more pages, the heading on a small advertisement catching her eye.

Modelling Classes for Women with the Fuller Figure.

About to return the magazine to its place on the shelf, she changed her mind.

"I'll take it." She handed it to a surprised Roy.

"Threepenny worth of boiled sweets, four aspirin and the magazine, please," Roy said, searching his pocket for some extra change.

"Jane Russell," Billy muttered, just loud enough to be heard as he reached for the sweet jar, unscrewed the lid and, with a little shovel, deposited the sweets into a small paper bag. "Jane Russell," he muttered again with a glance at his wife's chubby fingers still rearranging the money tray. "I wouldn't mind poking her threepenny bits."

He completed the transaction without change of expression or further comment, leaving Roy and Addie to exit from the shop.

"Did you hear what he said?" Addie laughed. "Is that Cockney rhyming slang?"

"Yes," said Roy, laughing. "Threepenny bits, tits. Apples and pears, stairs."

Arm in arm, they made the short walk along the country road to Ivy Lodge, Addie reading out the contents of the ad in the magazine to a disinterested but attentive Roy.

"For the fuller figure. That means curvaceous like Marilyn Monroe, or Jane Mansfield, Diana Dors...or Addie Jeffries. Why not? We could do with some extra money."

"Ten shillings is why not!" Roy stabbed the page with a finger. "It's a scam—you pay the money for a test. They say you fail the test and they keep the money."

That would have been the end of the matter but for Gladys Moroney, wife of Mick Moroney at the gas company...

***

Sometimes Addie helped at the local charity shop, where Gladys helped too. Blonde and busty, Gladys had decided to go for the modelling interview and was prepared to publicise the fact.

"My Mick says I've got what it takes," she announced to Addie. "I'm going to give it a go." She ran her fingers through her peroxide mop and made a pout with big red lips, hefting her ample bosom. "When you've got it flaunt it, that's what I say. It's on Tuesday night at the Shelbourne Hotel, interviews at eight. They're going to have a photographer. Why don't you come with me?" She looked Addie up and down. "You're not bad-lookin." She hefted her bosom again. "But maybe a bit skinny and not blonde."

Addie laughed and posed, running her hands over her curvaceous hips. "Skinny? You must be joking. Size thirty- six-B." She laughed again.

"Come with me," Gladys persisted. "Sure we'd have a bit of a laugh."

The next mention of the modelling interviews came from an unlikely source. At teatime the following day, Roy speared a sausage with his fork and said, "They're taking bets at work on Gladys Moroney being accepted as a photographic model. Mick is boasting about how beautiful she is." Roy raised his eyes to heaven, and Addie laughed.

"That's love for you."

Roy continued with an amused smile, "Alex Matthews said you should enter, and Mick said you weren't busty enough and that Gladys is better-looking. Imagine that!"

"And what did you say?" Addie put down her knife and fork.

"Nothing. I laughed, and that's all I said." Roy didn't notice the warning signal. He was concentrating on his fried egg.

"So! You think Gladys Moroney is better-looking than me and you let your buddies at work think the same?" Addie bristled.

"No..." Roy protested. "That's not what I said."

But Addie was not to be deterred. "They're saying I wouldn't be selected and they're taking bets on Gladys."

"No! you're far better-lookin'. Sure, everyone knows that"

"Not good-lookin' enough to be a model?" Addie lifted up her knife and vigorously buttered a piece of toast, indicating the end of the conversation.

Roy looked appealingly across the table. "Of course you're good looking enough! You'd pass the interview with flying colours!"

Addie remained silent, waiting for the concerned Roy to take the bait.

"I think you should go for the interview," Roy said, breaking the silence. Standing up from the table, he took the tin box from the mantelpiece. "There's ten shillings in this and we get paid on Thursday."

***

The Donnybrook Recruitment Agency ran their ship on very tight lines. Any illusions one might have about glamour, stardom and prestige were quickly dispelled. Having waited in a corridor along with about fifty other aspirants, Addie and Gladys were herded in single file through a room with two exits.

An elegant, superior-looking woman in her fifties stood in the centre of the room, quickly scrutinising and assessing, a tap on the shoulder and a pointing fingernail, polished ruby red, indicated acceptance or rejection. Addie and Gladys, along with ninety per cent of the girls, took the indicated door, entering a large room where they were requested to fill in a form and relieved of their ten shillings in exchange for a cloakroom ticket and an instruction to wait until their number was called. To the tune of 'Smoke Gets in Your Eyes' followed by 'Rock Around the Clock' they were all requested to parade in single file, moving to the rhythm of the music.

The Elegant One and an assistant with a clipboard patrolled the room blatantly assessing in an obvious selection process. Anxious to impress, the girls strutted their stuff until, eventually, they were allowed to take their seats. Gladys, rocking on the highest of high heels, flopped into a chair red-faced and breathing heavily. Addie, straight-backed, chin held high, presented her profile as often as possible.

"Well, we made it so far." Gladys drew deeply on a cigarette and slumped in her chair. "They'd better hurry up with the interviews." She looked at her watch. "Mick said he'd babysit until ten o'clock and then he wants to go to the pub. Look out, here comes your woman!" She hauled herself into an upright position and presented her abundant cleavage as the Elegant One hovered, clipboard poised. "Hey! D'ya think ya could speed things up a bit?" Gladys was getting impatient.

Elegant shoulders squared, elegant back straightened, she turned, and in the silence all eyes were on Addie and Gladys. The perfect Cupid's bow straightened into a thin line, but only momentarily.

"Number, please?"

"Twenty–Seven." Gladys held up the pink cloakroom ticket. "Do I win a prize?" She played to the gallery and was rewarded by a few nervous giggles from the other contestants.

"And you?" Long eyelashes and enormous brown eyes under arched pencil-line eyebrows dared Addie to be so adventurous.

"Thirty-three," she answered, matching the Elegant One's pose as best she could. "Blue."

The Elegant One tapped perfectly even white teeth with her silver Biro and scrutinised the clipboard.

"Gladys Moroney and Adelaide Jeffries, you have been selected. You are in the first group." Quickly turning to the rest of the room, she read another eight names from the list, informing them that they were also selected in the 'Fuller Figure Category'. "Please come with me, ladies." She strode through a doorway marked *Studio*.

With nervous, broad smiles and exclamations, the chosen ones followed, leaving what appeared to Addie to be the youngest, prettiest and thinnest ones behind. *Obviously another category*, she concluded.

More seats just inside the doorway faced the other end of a long room where the photographer waited, bright lights trained on a red chair centred on a small stage with a white backdrop.

"Ladies, this is Tony Jarvis. We are very privileged to have Mr. Jarvis here today. He is a renowned photographer with many awards for his work. *Vogue* magazine has featured several of his pieces." She clapped her hands and nodded her head, encouraging all to do the same.

Tony strutted around the large camera and took a bow. To Addie, the skinny, diminutive man sporting a cravat and a little beard seemed familiar, but he turned quickly to make some adjustments to the camera, and the moment was gone.

"Please walk to the camera position when your name is called. Three pictures will be taken: standing full figure, profile and full face. These will be the starter pictures to your modelling portfolio and will remain at the agency where they may be viewed by interested parties for ramp work and advertising exposure." The Elegant One spoke rapidly and efficiently. "No 24," she called, "Pamela James."

A good-looking girl, about Addie's age and very confident, stepped forward.

"That's me, girls." She shot a hip and sashayed the length of the room to take her place in front of the camera.

"Boop-oop-a-doop. My name's Marilyn, what's yours?" she mimicked.

"Beautiful, nice, beautiful," Tony muttered and peered through the lens. *Flash!* "Turn." *Flash!* "Stand. Good, good..." *Flash!* "Thank you."

Pamela stayed where she was and took up another pose.

"Next!" Tony's head popped up from behind the camera.

"Thank you, Pamela." the Elegant one intervened, and Pamela reluctantly gave up her position in front of the camera to strut her way back to the admiring group.

"I'm going home—we haven't got a chance, she's a professional." Gladys was having a confidence crisis.

"Well, what's she doing here at a beginner's class, then?" Addie flashed.

The entire performance had taken about four minutes. In quick succession, the wannabe fashion models had their turn with the photographer.

"That's it, beautiful, head back, turn, smile, don't smile, good."

Gladys had her turn, stumbling slightly on the long walk in her new six-inch-high stilettoes, her red dress bulging and straining to confine her voluptuousness. Making it to the little stage, she grabbed the back of the chair for support and faced the camera pouting and leaning forward, violently squeezing her arms each side of her oversized breasts to achieve a cleavage

of mighty proportions. The cheap material did its best. *Flash!*
"Turn. Pout." *Flash!* "Close up." *Flash!* "Next!"

With an earnest look of concentration, she made her way back
to Addie.

"How did I do?" she asked with a doubtful look.

"Great!" Addie laughed. "But you'd better do yourself up."
The dress, unable to cope with the strain, had split in the front.

"Jaysus, Addie! Have you got a safety pin?"

"Number thirty-seven, Addie Jeffries."

Addie made the walk. The photographer turned to face her,
and Addie remembered where she had seen him before: Bray sea
front, two summers previously, less fashionable clothes and no
beard; no mistaking the street photographer. Addie strode, tight-
lipped, to her position, fixing him with a fierce look.

"Now, Adelaide." The head disappeared behind the camera—
"Smile, please!"—but Addie wasn't in the mood. *Flash!* It was
a con. *Flash!* Roy was right. They took the money and that
was it. *Flash!*

"Next!"

Addie's number was pinned to the form by elegant fingers.
"We'll let you know, Adelaide."

Addie stood her ground. "He's a phony—a street photographer.
I want my money back."

Elegant eyebrows rose as the only indication that her words
had been heard. Addie was about to repeat her complaint but was
interrupted...

"Next, number seventeen—Joanne Grimes."

The Elegant One indicated for Addie to step to one side,
saying, "I assure you, this is not *a scam*, as you put it. Everyone
here on your behalf is a legitimate professional, including
Mr. Jarvis. If I return your ten shillings, you forsake all chance
of selection. There are many opportunities on our calendar
for ramp work in your class and indeed the possibility
of lucrative advertising work."

She handed Addie a sheet of paper. "This is a complaint form.
Post it to the address supplied and it will be assessed."

Addie took the form with a grim determination to expose the sham and get her money back.

***

A few days passed by, and Addie did not fill out the form. The story of Gladys's dress malfunction and the *Vogue* photographer were recounted much to the amusement of all. Gladys was not quite so confident of success, but Mick's loyalty never waned.

One week later, a cream manila envelope arrived in the post from the Berkley Model Agency.

> Dear Adelaide,
>
> It is with great pleasure that we inform you of your success in our recent recruitment venture...

Addie couldn't wait for Roy to come home.

"They want me to do a fashion show at Butlin's Holiday Camp next month, and I have to do a modelling course. They say Wednesday evenings for six classes. I will be paid five pounds for the fashion show at Butlin's and that will cover the price of classes."

"So! You don't actually get any money?" Roy looked sceptical.

Addie brandished the letter impatiently. "Don't you see? I get training as a model—there's plenty of work. The model agency supplies people all the time for shows. Two shows will pay for the classes and then it's profit from then on, and...I might even become famous. The Berkley Model Agency chose me!"

"I know." Still worried but unable to think of a further argument, Roy gave in to her enthusiasm and the sparkle in her eyes.

"You're a beautiful woman, Addie. Of course they chose you. You're made for something like this, and it's in the evenings, so it won't affect the kids."

"The Jeffries' luck is about to change, Roy. I have a great feeling about this. I wonder how Gladys did..."

Chapter 20

THE BERKLEY MODEL AGENCY, BRAINCHILD of Elizabeth Janet Berkley, occupied a stylish location in Essex Street just off Dublin's equally stylish Grafton Street.

Originally from Dublin, Liz had travelled to England in the early fifties seeking fame and fortune. An extremely stylish woman possessing great charm and wit and a calm grace, she was drawn to fashion but found it difficult to attain any standing mainly because of her lack of contacts in the very closed industry. She secured a job as a receptionist in one of London's prestigious agencies, dealing with advertising agencies, designers and photographers and developing her understanding of the business.

Liz also achieved some success as a ramp and photographic model but, seeing no future for herself in modelling, she turned her attention to Ireland, where the fashion industry had not yet taken off. At the time, Dublin had boasted only one agency, so Liz made her contacts and presented herself and one other girl. Fresh from London, nobody doubted her obvious credentials.

Casting the net through small adds in the newspapers and magazines offering modelling classes and a career in fashion, Liz exploited the natural, fresh beauty of Irish women, and within one year, the Berkley Model Agency was up and running with an impressive portfolio, Liz topping the list.

The industry was growing, attracting competition, but the Berkley Agency saw off all comers. Liz ensured she was seen at all the industry events, and she was ruthless in her dealings with any opposition. On the one-hand formidable and austere, she could also be charming and gracious. She attended all the training sessions personally, always on the watch out for that special face, that special figure.

Maria Barker, the 'Elegant One', had been discovered in those early days and become Liz's right hand. A clone of her mentor, she stalked the newcomers and calculated the profits.

Forty-five candidates, all paid up for their first session: Maria flicked through the photographs, matching numbers, forms and faces. Selecting four of the fuller-figured women, she set their information to one side.

"Tony!" she called as she busily attended to her filing system.

Freelance photographer, Tony Jarvis, put down his *Irish Times* and briskly got to his feet, stubbing out his cigarette in the onyx marble ashtray. The door to the Elegant One's office wide open, he rounded the low glass coffee table and strode across the plush modular carpet of the spacious reception area.

Grabbing work where he could, the evening sessions at the agency, using the on-premises studio facilities, were a reasonable earner and not particularly exacting on his photographic skills. The pictures were being used for reference only; making sure they were in focus was the main requirement. The arrival of Polaroid and instant pictures proved lucrative, especially for street photography, but Tony kept away from the Dublin streets, concentrating on the holiday spots down the coast. If Liz found out, she would be none too pleased.

"Yes, Maria?"

The Elegant One picked up one of the photographs from the selection table. "What happened here?" She held up a full-face picture of a girl with fire in her eyes. "Where's the smile?"

"No idea. Moody...probably fed up waiting for her turn."

"She's the feisty one who complained. Said you were a street photographer." Maria looked Tony straight in the eye. "I wonder where she got that idea."

"Some people are just natural complainers—you know the sort. Not bad-looking, though." Tony studied the picture. "Are you going to use her?"

"No way." Maria shook her head. "I've got enough problems. Maybe a bit of ramp work, that's all." Taking the three pictures of Addie, she stuck a statistics label on the back of each: *36, 22, 32, height 5' 10"*.

"This one goes in characters." She tossed the little bundle to the end of the table and looked at her watch. "I better show this lot to Liz." She arranged them in order and put them in a folder, quickly writing *Newcomers* and the date on the cover. The fuller-figure pictures went into a separate folder. "It will be interesting if she follows up that complaint," was her parting shot as she headed for the stairs and Liz's office, leaving Tony to ponder the possibilities.

***

Maria knocked on the pale wood door and entered without waiting for a reply.

"Oh! Sorry I didn't know you had company."

Three heads turned at the intrusion.

"No, you're fine." Liz beckoned from behind the long, curved desk, standing up, silhouetted against the big window with the Dublin skyline beyond. "You know Marcus and Jim?"

Marcus Deering and Jim Nolan of Fitzers Advertising, Marketing and Public Relations, Dublin's largest Agency, were excellent clients.

"Maria." Forever the gentleman, Jim, accounts director, stepped forward, hand out. Marcus Deering, creative director and not so outgoing remained seated.

"A new venture?" Jim indicated a seat. "The woman with the fuller figure. I believe you've made a start?" He glanced at the folder in Maria's hand.

She hesitated for a moment, but at an almost imperceptible signal from Liz, she opened the folder and began to spread the pictures out on the desktop.

Enthusiastically, Jim Nolan scanned the pictures. "What's the idea here, Liz? Some of these are quite fat."

Liz, not the slightest bit deterred, leaned forward. "I intend using some of these girls at our next fashion show. There are many women aspiring to the bustier figure, and we intend catering for them. Presented as a variety piece initially, I'm pretty sure it's the way to go."

"Well, makes a change from the usual titless wonders, I suppose," Marcus Deering said. "What about this one? She doesn't look particularly pleased with herself." He picked up the picture of Addie and, without looking at it, tossed it back onto the table.

"We haven't made our final selection yet," Maria quickly interjected.

***

After the meeting, the two ad men strode, side by side, back to the Fitzers Advertising Agency in Pearse Street—within walking distance of the Berkley.

Jim tried to match strides with the fast-moving energetic Marcus. "What's the rush?" He was losing the battle. "What did you think of Liz's idea?"

No answer.

Marcus strode on, preoccupied with his own thoughts. Liz's words echoed in his head; the image of Addie's angry face all he could see. He had the beginnings of an idea. *Independent woman, sex to sell cigarettes.* He stopped; Jim caught up.

"Cigarettes and women. All the cigarette advertising is directed at men—good-looking lads with a titless beauty alongside, both of them smoking or striking a light, looking into each other's eyes, cigarette pack in prominence with a tagline about satisfaction.

The man's always the hero in the ad and the woman's secondary. So, we reverse the roles. Give women their own cigarette, long and slim, elegant, gold, red lips, aggressive. *For the woman who knows what she wants.*

"That girl! Liz has her—what was her name? One shot. That's all we need. Set it up, Jim. Go back to the agency and tell them we want that woman. Shift your ass."

Knowing better than to argue with the volatile Marcus, Jim turned on his heel to retrace his steps.

Marcus strode on. By the time he reached the impressive entrance to the advertising agency, he had the basis of the campaign worked out in his mind.

Chapter 21

GRANDAD HUGH, STRAIGHT-BACKED, HANDS CLASPED behind him, stood on the doorstep and stared the two men up and down with obvious distaste. "What's your business?"

"We have some good news for Adelaide Jeffries." The sharp, tricky-looking one in the suit stepped forward, hand extended, beaming and confident, and proffered a business card.

The hand ignored, Grandad Hugh stepped back. "My daughter does not accept news from strangers, good or bad."

"I'm James Nolan, account director at Fitzers Advertising Agency, and this is Marcus Deering." He introduced the bearded, low-sized one with the quick eyes as if Grandad Hugh should know him.

With a conciliatory grunt, Grandad Hugh accepted the business card and searched his tweed waistcoat, pocket by pocket, for reading glasses. "And what is it that concerns my daughter?"

Marcus Deering, not one used to being questioned but so far resisting the temptation to walk away, was saved by the appearance of Addie in the porch behind the grumpy guardian.

"They say they're from an agency, Addie. We don't buy anything at the step. Goodbye!" He stepped back, about to close the front door.

Addie's expression transformed into a smile of greeting, but Marcus had enough time to catch the slightly irritated expression that preceded the transformation. The ad man had seen what he wanted.

"Come in!" Addie beamed. Grandad Hugh stood his ground for a moment and then thought better of it.

"I'll be across the hall if you need me." He beat a dignified retreat into his room.

'I love your home." Jim followed Addie into the front room.

"Would you like some tea?"

"No, thanks," Marcus declined for both of them.

"You're with the Berkley Model Agency," Jim began, making himself comfortable as Addie indicated for them to sit down.

Marcus remained standing and interrupted with, "Do you smoke?" He held out a long, slim, red pack of cigarettes. "Try one of these, they're American."

Irritated by his abrupt manner, Addie turned to Jim Nolan on the sofa. "Yes, I'm a model with the Berkley Agency" she said with a smile. "You caught me unawares. I'm afraid I look a fright." She pushed her hair about with a casual hand.

Marcus remained unmoving. Addie turned back with an *are you still here?* expression. He smiled slightly and shrugged, about as much of an apology as one was likely to get from Marcus Deering.

Addie took one of the cigarettes. It was much longer than an ordinary cigarette and very slim, red in colour with a gold band and a small gold crown. Addie had never seen a cigarette like it before.

Marcus flicked his Ronson and lit the king-size cork-tipped cigarette for Addie.

She sat back and inhaled, eyes half closed as she let the smoke trickle out between her full red lips.

Marcus made his decision.

"I want to use you in an advertising campaign for Gold Crest cigarettes. Jim here will contact Berkley's. You may keep the packet of cigarettes if you wish. Thank you and nice to meet you."

Addie stood up and accepted the handshake. Marcus nodded and, with a pursed-lipped smile, walked from the room.

"Don't mind Marcus." Jim was on his feet. "It's just his manner. He's really a nice person, when you get to know him."

Addie looked askance. "Thank him for the cigarettes. I really love them. The pack is beautiful."

"The agency will be in touch in the next few days to advise you on all the details. Thank you, Mrs. Jeffries. I know that this is the beginning of something great." He handed her two business cards and they shook hands.

Addie watched from the porch as the two men hurried down the path; there was the glimpse of a shiny car at the small doorway in the wall.

"What was that all about?" Grandad Hugh emerged from his room. "I didn't like the one with the scruffy blue jeans. I didn't like either of them."

"They want me to be in advertising. I'm going to star in a photoshoot. The model agency will be in touch with the details." Hardly able to believe what she was actually saying, Addie sat down on the hall chair and looked at her father. "Can you believe it?" she asked, lighting another long, slim, red cigarette with its gold band.

"Filthy habit, if you ask me." With a sigh, Grandad Hugh retired to his room.

***

The telegram arrived the following day:

> Congratulations. Please contact me right away.
> – Liz Berkley

Below the name was a phone number.

This would be one phone call from Hartigan's shop Addie would not mind people overhearing.

The photoshoot would take place the following week. There would be a fitting session in two days, hair and make-up tests and a crash course in photo modelling. The Berkley machine was on the move. Marcus Deering stepped in.

"No photo modelling crash course thank you." So that was cancelled. Marcus Deering was running the show.

A big Mercedes car came to Ivy Lodge to collect Addie for the photoshoot. She and Jim Nolan sat into the back seat. The usual bunch of neighbours came out to watch.

"She thinks she's a film star. It's the children I'd be worried about. They're goin' to be neglected, mark my words."

Addie waved from the window as the car surged away past Hartigan's shop.

"Y'd think it's the fuckin' coronation. Give us a couple of Aspros there, Mrs. Hartigan. I got a bleedin' headache. Did you see that fella beside her? He looked like Laurel without Hardy."

But there was no denying the Jeffries were moving up in the world.

"Ah, fair play to her. Sure, God loves a trier."

***

They arrived at the studio at ten thirty, and the Berkley team were waiting.

Addie had been well briefed. Jim Nolan had been in touch a few times, but she hadn't seen Marcus since the visit to Ivy Lodge.

Surprised at how confident she felt, she stepped from the car feeling very grand. Maria led her through the modern building to the studio, past a doorway with a glimpse of shadowy figures against bright lights and the sound of voices to a dressing room with a mirror surrounded by lights. Two smiling women greeted Addie with some deference and many compliments, inviting her to sit down. They chatted nonstop, removing Addie's jacket, and replacing it with a protective cape.

"Jane Russell, definitely Jane Russell." The older of the two women placed a photograph of the famous star on the dressing table. "Marcus Deering said to keep the hair full.

"Your hair is magnificent, lucky girl... No, we'd prefer if you didn't smoke. Just relax and we'll do the rest. Jane will give you beautiful nails. Head up, look into the mirror and try not to move too much."

Addie watched the transformation take place as the two beauty experts plied their trade. They chatted in a friendly manner, and she found herself relaxing, enjoying the attention and full-on compliments.

"Three children? Two boys and a girl? What ages? You don't look old enough!"

The transformation took about an hour. Eventually, Addie stood to admire herself in the full-length mirror. The most amazing red cocktail dress completed the picture, low cut tailored to her figure, gold stilettoes and accessories. Addie Jeffries looked and felt like Jane Russell, the resemblance astonishing.

"Do you like cats?"

The voice came from the doorway behind her. Reluctant to take her eyes from her image in the mirror, Addie turned, her profile following the turn of her body, her head coming slowly around to give the source of the voice the full benefit of the Jane Russell stare.

Marcus Deering, truly impressed with how Addie looked, had another agenda.

"Do you like cats?" he repeated without adding the obvious compliment Addie was expecting.

"A bit more than I like some people." The Jane Russell attitude remained intact as Addie demonstrated her dislike for the creative director's manner.

"You will need to stroke a cat. Have you any problem with that?"

"No, I do not have any problems with stroking a cat," she replied in a measured tone, eyes flashing.

"Good." He turned and left the room before she could catch his look of satisfaction.

"What a charmer," Addie remarked to the make-up ladies. "After all your wonderful work, a word of appreciation wouldn't have gone amiss."

The girls just smiled and exchanged a look not unnoticed by Addie.

The moment was broken by the arrival of Liz Berkley and Maria.

"You look amazing! Well done, girls."

Addie was scrutinised from her long ruby-red artificial fingernails to her beautiful gold stilettoes.

"Is Marcus happy?" Liz enquired, taking Addie's hand to examine her nails one by one, her touch matter-of-fact and impersonal.

"I don't know, he didn't say." Addie shrugged.

"He must be, then. You'd know if he wasn't. Right, see you later."

Maria took over guiding Addie along a passage to the photo studio she had passed earlier, the make-up girls following behind.

Everything was red, gold and black: red leather button-backed high stool with ornate gold arms; red drapes; black ebony curved bar. Shadowy silhouetted figures moved beyond the bright spotlights and the large camera.

"Hello, Addie." Another bearded one stepped into the brightly lit area. "I'm Jason." He smiled a greeting, his quick eyes examining, judging, assessing the lighting effect on Addie's face. "Tone down the cheeks, please."

One of the make-up girls stepped forward as the photographer indicated for Addie to take a seat and face the camera and busied himself, peering from every angle, adjusting lights, checking through the camera lens, studying his light meter, all the time humming the 'Black Hills of Dakota' interspersed with whistling through his teeth the same repetitive tune. Addie reacted to his instructions, taking the pack of cigarettes from the counter with her right hand, removing a cigarette, returning the pack to the counter and taking up the slim gold Calibri lighter to light the cigarette.

"Good. Nice. Hold—when I say hold, you stop the action and look at the camera." He smiled. "It's as simple as that, Addie. You're a natural and very beautiful. We will have some sensational shots. Just remember not to let your shoulders come forward, you must keep a straight back on a high stool." He smiled again and disappeared behind the camera. "Action!"

Addie reached for the pack and opened it.

"Hold. Smile...let me see the pack. Hold...hold...good. Excellent, beautiful. Shoulders back, more to me, hold...good. Hold...hold...smile. Another. Show your teeth. Hold..."

Just as Addie's back began to ache, the instruction to relax came.

"Thank you, Addie. You're doing really well. Take a rest for a few minutes."

Jason, Maria and the make-up girls became busy retouching make-up and adjusting lights. Jim Nolan stood to one side.

"You're doing great, Addie." He beckoned her from her perch on the stool and led her beyond the lights. She was surprised at the amount of people now gathered all looking at her admiringly.

"Meet Addie Jeffries, the Gold Crest Girl." A camera flashed as Addie was introduced to the cigarette manufacturers.

"Pleased to meet you." Addie had never had her hand kissed before.

"You are sensational!"

She beamed and posed.

"Can we have Sasha, please?"

A woman, obviously the big Persian cat's owner, appeared and placed Sasha in Addie's arms.

"She likes you. I can tell you're used to animals—I'm so glad." The woman backed slowly away as Addie stroked the cat and posed.

"Thank you, thank you, our star must get back to work." Marcus Deering clapped his hands together and ushered Addie back to her high stool to continue the session.

"Smile for the camera, Sasha," said Addie, flushed with success, holding the big Persian cat up close to her face and beaming into the camera, playing to her newfound audience. There were some amused sounds of approval.

Confidently, Addie began the second session, this time with the addition of Sasha.

"Take the pack, hold it as you light the cigarette…good. Stroke the cat, hold…good, nice. Light the cigarette, look at the camera…" Addie was finding it difficult to comply with the directions. The cat was sliding off her knees and her back was beginning to ache. Jason, about to suggest a break, was interrupted by an impatient voice.

"You're not holding the pack correctly. The name is not showing."

Addie tried to readjust her hold on the pack.

"Stroke the cat." Again the impatient voice.

Addie angrily reacted, eyes flashing.

"That's impossible! How can I stroke the cat and take a cigarette from the pack at the same time?"

"You're the model! Just do it!"

Furious at the tone but up to the challenge, Addie quipped, "I suppose you want me to smile as well?" Her expression showed her distaste for Marcus Deering.

"Sorry, sorry. In your own time," came the singsong voice from beyond the camera.

Beginning to regret the whole affair, Addie reached for the pack and stroked the cat while looking at the camera.

"The pack's not in the shot. Hold it closer to your face, stroke the cat."

Addie put down the pack and looked into the darkness. There was a pause as, eyes flashing, she confronted the shadowy figures.

"I don't think you like me very much." Marcus's amused voice broke the silence.

"Absolutely," Addie confirmed.

"Are you sure? Normally I have great success with the ladies."

"Well, not with this lady!" Addie dismounted from the high stool, took one step towards the camera and threw the cat, with all her force, straight at the voice.

With a howl and frantic scrambling of legs and black fur, Sasha landed amidst the figures the other side of the camera.

"The session's over. Thank you!"

Addie stormed out the door and down the corridor, Maria and the make-up girls quickly following.

In the dressing room, she contemplated her image in the big mirror, hair in disarray falling around her face in a halo of black curls, slightly out of breath, chest straining against the low-cut bodice.

"Well, that's that. So ends a wonderful modelling career, such a beautiful dress," She turned side on to admire her image.

Maria and the girls clucked their concern and muttered their disproval of Marcus Deering.

Addie made a serious face but couldn't help seeing the funny side of the situation.

"I've always wanted to throw a cat at someone." She bit her lip in mock mortification but couldn't help laughing. "Ever since I met that Marcus fella, I've wanted to put him in his place."

The laughter in the small dressing room was interrupted by the sound of a cough from the doorway. Unnoticed until that moment, Marcus Deering stood leaning against the door jamb, a smiling Jim Nolan alongside.

The make-up girls hastily busied themselves, fussing around with their beauty equipment.

Addie opened her mouth to speak but was silenced by a smile and a raised hand.

"Congratulations, Addie. We got some great pictures—exactly what's needed. You look terrific in that dress. Please keep it, as a gift from me." Without waiting for a comment, he turned on his heel and left the room.

"And that's the nearest thing to an apology you're ever going to get from Marcus," Jim said, amused by the women's looks of bemusement.

"But I threw the cat at him, and ruined the session, and how about the cat's owner? Is the cat all right?"

"Slow down, Addie. These matters are not for you to worry about. Everything has been taken care of. You're the Gold Crest Girl—all you have to do is get used to the idea. You were sensational!"

Addie sat down and reached for a cigarette.

Jim turned to Maria. "Addie will be needed for some public relations shots. We'll work out a programme for her. The cigarette company are very impressed. Don't forget the model release form. See you soon, ladies."

After he left, Addie and Maria discussed some details, and Maria handed over a model release form and a pen.

"What is it?" Addie asked. She had a suspicion of all forms and hesitated, pen poised.

Maria laughed. "After all sessions, the model signs the form. It simply allows the agency to use the pictures for advertising purposes."

Addie read the simple wording and turned over the single sheet. She laughed. "I was just checking for small print."

"You'll be signing lots of these—after the public relations sessions, whenever your picture is taken and you are paid a fee."

"How much do I get?" Addie asked.

From her briefcase, Maria took a folder with Addie's name on the cover. "That hasn't been settled yet—you'll have to talk to Liz. Don't forget, you're not a trained model yet. I would say about five pounds an hour, but don't quote me."

"Five pounds an hour!" Addie's eyes went wide. "Roy gets twelve pounds a week!"

"It might be more, or maybe a bit less. It depends on Liz—she's the boss. Now, as a model, you always have to look your best, so an account has been opened in your name at Switzer's and at Brown Thomas. All you have to do is sign for a purchase in the store. Of course, there will be special discounts for the Gold Crest Girl. Lucky you!"

Addie listened as Maria talked.

"Ramp work doesn't pay quite as well as photographic work, probably half, but you will get some travel expenses when needed. Don't forget the training session on Monday evening at eight o'clock. Can you come at seven? Liz wants to go over things with you. Today's photographs will go in your portfolio as samples of your work. Being the Gold Crest Girl is quite a start to your modelling career." Maria closed the folder.

Addie nodded, taken aback at the wonder of it all. She glanced at her watch. "Look at the time! I have to go!"

"Wait, are you not coming for a drink to celebrate? We always go to Madigan's after a shoot."

"Who?"

"Marcus, Jason, Jim Nolan, maybe Liz, some of the cigarette people."

"No, I'll have to rush. Roy will be home for his dinner! I'll catch the bus," Addie answered instinctively.

"No need!" Maria stood up. "The car you came in will still be here to take you home."

Downstairs in the reception, a man was waiting for them, the big car outside on the street. Addie was ushered into the back seat. The large designer bag with the beautiful red dress and a box with the gold shoes, plus a bottle of Champagne, which someone had left in the reception with her name on it, were placed beside her.

Maria said goodbye with a friendly hug. "See you Monday"

Addie sat back into the soft leather upholstery, unable to believe her good fortune as she was driven through the streets and out along the coast to Ivy Lodge and Roy's dinner. There was a card attached to the bottle of Champagne with a gold and red ribbon.

Well done!
Welcome to the Berkley Model Agency
Liz xx

Regretting not going for a celebratory drink with all these sophisticated people, Addie consoled herself with the thought that it would not be the same without Roy. *Maybe next time.*

***

"The Gold Crest Lady!" Roy sat at the dinner table. He picked up the red and gold pack, turning it in his big brown hand. "Very nice, very posh." He took out one of the long cigarettes with its little gold lion and gold band.

"Try it," Addie said, taking the slim gold Calibri lighter from her handbag and flicking the smooth action.

Roy's eyes opened wide. "Who owns that? It's a Calibri!"

"It's mine. Marcus gave it to me."

Roy drew on the cigarette and inhaled deeply, allowing a small trickle of smoke to escape as he savoured the American cigarette. "A bit mild for my taste, not a patch on a Major. Who's Marcus. Is he the fella that you don't like?" He took another drag on the cigarette and handed it to Addie. "Here, you finish it."

Addie took the cigarette, disappointed by his reaction.

"He must want something." Roy looked worried. "A Calibri, Addie! You shouldn't have taken it!"

Addie laughed and leaned forward, beaming with glee. "Wait till you hear the rest of it. The Calibri is nothing! I have had the best day of my life!"

Tentatively, Roy took in his wife's happy face as he sat back in his chair, arms folded, while Addie recounted every detail of her day, from the moment the neighbours watched her leave to the return trip along the coast in the big car.

Throughout, Roy's reaction varied from amusement to concern, attentive to amused to concerned, but mostly incredulous.

"Stay where you are!" Addie finished. Jumping up from her chair, she left the room.

Roy sat, his mind struggling with all the information, unsure how to feel.

"The Gold Crest Lady!" Addie was at the door in the low-cut, figure-hugging designer cocktail dress. She assumed the model stance, her spectacular hair tossed around her face, lips as red as the dress. Gold shoes and gold accessories sparkled. "The woman who knows what she wants. Have you got a cigarette, Roy?"

He jumped to his feet, tall and smiling. "Wow! You look sensational!"

Unexpectedly, Addie's lips began to tremble. She put her hands to her face as the tears came. Roy went to her, and she buried her face in his chest. Half laughing, half crying, the words tumbled out.

"We...can get the roof...fixed." Composing herself and dabbing her eyes with Roy's handkerchief, she looked earnestly into her husband's face. "I really do think we've cracked it. At last the Jeffries' luck has changed."

"Yes, it has. Our luck has changed." Roy repeated her words as she snuggled into his arms, unaware of the worried expression on his face. Free designer dresses, Calibri gold lighters, expense accounts in top-flight fashion stores—in Roy's world, there would have to be a catch. *If something seems too good to be true, then it probably is.* But when he looked into Addie's happy face, he could not spoil her enjoyment.

"Is there any sherry? I think there's a bottle of stout," he said. "We have to celebrate."

"We can do a bit better than a bottle of stout!"

Roy followed Addie out to the kitchen. She threw open the door of the high press over the sink. "Champagne!"

Roy took down the bottle and examined the label. "It's an expensive one too!"

"Of course!"

"Where are the kids? Wait till we tell them that their ma is famous?"

Addie had to think for a moment. "Ian is with the Robinsons, Debbie is at Guides, and James is out with some girl or other."

"I was wondering why it is so quiet."

The happy Addie watched as Roy, beginning to enjoy the feeling of success, expertly popped the cork without spilling a drop.

They sat at the big kitchen table and drank the Champagne.

"I could get used to this," Roy said. "I can't believe you threw the cat at yer man and then he gave you all that stuff. What did they say? Five pounds an hour? I hope you didn't sign anything.

"Just a model release form allowing them to use the pictures for advertising purposes. There was no small print." Addie quickly added, "All the models have to sign after a shoot. They can't use the pictures unless you let them."

Roy put down his glass, looking sceptical.

"They gave me a copy." Addie took the form from her handbag and showed it to him.

He read it carefully: just two sentences stating that Addie Jeffries of Ivy Lodge gave her consent for the pictures taken at the photo session for Gold Crest cigarettes to be used for advertising purposes. Addie's signature was on the document, and Maria Barker signed on behalf of the Berkley Model Agency. Roy flipped it over, expecting to see a large amount of small type, but the back was blank.

"Fair enough. At least they ask your permission. They'd have to do that." He smiled his big smile and raised the Champagne glass. "Here's to five pounds an hour. Addie, you're a wonder!"

***

The following day, there were several phone calls to Hartigan's shop. Maria was the third caller.

"Really, Addie, you do need a phone. I'll see what I can arrange."

"A phone?" It was something Addie had never considered. "Do you think so?"

"Of course! It's not very easy to communicate with all that noise going on behind, and I was waiting a good ten minutes for that Mrs. Hartigan woman to get you. She's quite rude. She said she'd send someone for you. I was waiting ages."

Addie looked over her shoulder at the shoppers and the none-too-happy Mrs. Hartigan. "I understand. Of course, I see your point." She turned towards the shop, her voice slightly raised for all to hear. "Yes, I do need a phone. Please arrange it for me."

Chapter 22

WANTING TO LOOK HER VERY best, Addie called to Grafton Street's Switzer's. Maria accompanied her. They purchased dresses, shoes to match and a beautiful coat with accessories, all at a special discount price for selected Berkley Model Agency people. The shop assistant fussed and flattered. Addie signed with a flourish. Afterwards, they had lunch at Jammet's Restaurant in Nassau Street. Heads turned, and some introductions were made. Addie took to her newfound status with elegance as Maria hovered in approval.

The following Monday evening arrived, and the first training session: Liz, unfortunately could not attend, so the meeting with Addie was postponed until the following Monday when the course of five classes would be completed.

Addie wore the red dress and Maria gave her special attention, introducing her to the other trainees as a Berkley model with photographic experience. Gladys, bathing in the reflected glory, never left her side. The pictures from Addie's photographic session were used to demonstrate aspects of posture and reaction to direction. There were forty-eight contact prints, and a very large picture on an easel was revealed with a flourish. Not for the first time that week, Addie was the subject of admiring and some envious glances. The picture in full colour showed Addie in the red dress looking into the camera lens, head tilted. She was stroking a big black Persian cat while holding up a long slim cigarette packet. Someone clapped amidst the *oohs!* and *ahhs!*

"Now look what you've done to me mascara!" Gladys dabbed her eyes. "You look like a film star. Doesn't she? I discovered her, you know!"

The five-day course in modelling focused mainly on preparing the girls for ramp work and an upcoming show at Butlin's Holiday Camp.

"It's your shape, girls, all the curves in the right places, the fuller figure. That's why you've been chosen. Six of you will be chosen for the upcoming show—four fuller figure ladies and two plus sizes. Good luck and welcome to Berkley's." And so, ended the first session.

***

"Practise, practise, practise, ladies. Casual wear, jacket off the shoulders, change hands, turn, stride, look and learn." Experienced models showed them how. Maria demonstrated posture and movement always to music. A recorded voice played a commentary.

"Listen to the words, keep the rhythm of the music. Practise and practise again."

"You love what you are wearing. Show it. Show it to me." Liz appeared from time to time, observing without a word and then departing.

The clipboard was very much in evidence. "Dignity, aloof, smiling, show it, ladies, show it to me."

It was the third night, and there had been a particularly demanding ten minutes of activity with a barrage of instructions and two quick changes. Gladys had flopped into a chair, her face flushed with effort, legs apart.

"Gladys Moroney! Upright! Upright! Once a model always a model. Show it to me!"

And so it went on till Friday night and the last session, the crash course completed.

Liz herself put them through their paces and presented each of them with a certificate and a folder with their name and the Berkley logo on the cover, inside the pictures from their first introductory session plus their terms and conditions. Newly recruited models would receive five pounds an hour for photographic work and two pounds an hour for ramp work. She made a short congratulatory speech, singling out Addie for special attention.

There was great excitement when they were advised by Maria that each girl would need to attend an audition for advertising work the following week. Four of the fuller-figure girls were chosen for the Butlin's fashion show. All were advised that the payment for their classes would be deducted from their first professional assignments.

There was Champagne, wine and finger food; music played, and everyone congratulated each other. Press cameras flashed— public relations—and they captured a group shot with Maria, Liz and the new Berkley girls.

"A word." Amidst the hubbub of excited chattering and congratulations, Liz, with a broad, friendly smile, took Addie to one side. "The sponsors are delighted with the photoshoot. Marcus Deering tells me that everything is on schedule and they'll be going to press next week."

"How is Mr. Deering? I hope he didn't mind too much about the cat." Addie laughed.

Liz looked to the floor and then lifted her head to give Addie the benefit of steely grey eyes, now showing a complete absence of mirth, cold and hard.

"The cat-throwing incident has not been commented upon. But don't ever attempt to do anything like that again under the Berkley name. I may still have to pay the consequences." Her expression softened slightly. "I think we've all been tempted to do something similar to Marcus, and it was rather spectacular. But people like Marcus Deering are the life blood of the modelling industry, and if you want to get anywhere, you're going to have to curb that temper of yours."

***

Sunday, Harkness's shop, the local men were in for the newspaper. The noise level and laughter, louder than usual that morning, was replaced with an immediate silence as Roy entered the shop.

He looked around, aware he was the centre of attention. "Morning, all," he greeted with a questioning smile.

"That's the last one, I kept it for you." Billy Harkness slapped a Sunday paper down on the counter. "Sold out every copy, and it's only eleven o'clock."

"Thank you" Roy looked puzzled.

For once, the chubby index finger ceased its search in the change tray as Mrs. Harkness raised her head to present Ray with a grim, jowly glare. "Has she no shame, that wife of yours?"

"What?" Roy looked around at the mostly amused faces.

"Page three," someone said, opening a newspaper and placing it on the counter.

The full-page, full-colour picture of Addie, her hair tumbling around her face, haughty, arrogant eyes fierce and challenging, stared back at him. Roy's initial reaction was one of admiration and pride until he noticed how the front of the dress gaped open revealing, and blatantly suggestive, Addie's shoulders bare, her image filling the space. It appeared as if she were naked with the heading in large letters: FOR THE WOMAN WHO KNOWS WHAT SHE WANTS. A wisp of smoke curled upwards from the tip of a long slim cigarette held between fingers with tapered, ruby-red painted nails. At the bottom of the page was a picture of the long slim cigarette pack and the title GOLD CREST.

"I know what she wants, all right."

No one knew who said it, but the comment served to break the uncomfortable silence. There were some murmurs of approval and a low wolf whistle followed by Mrs. Harkness climbing, awkwardly from her perch, crossing herself and leaving the shop.

Roy placed his sixpence on the counter.

"That's my beautiful Addie." He smiled as best he could lest he should betray his discomfort. "And a slab of Cleeve's Toffee, please."

Taking the two purchases, he left the shop without a further word.

***

"Where's the cat?! And the bar?! And I was holding the pack in my hand! And the dress! You can hardly see the dress! That's not the picture they showed me!"

Addie's expression matched the one in the press ad as she turned furiously to Roy, the newspaper spread open on the kitchen table.

"You look fabulous," Roy comforted.

"But it's like a sex picture! It's too revealing! I'd never have agreed to that!"

"Oh, I don't know." Grandad Hugh rubbed his spectacles and replaced them on his nose. "It's very like one of those pictures of Jane Russell you see at the cinema. You look very beautiful."

"Well!" Addie looked at the picture again, arms folded, considering. "I suppose it does. You can see the top of the dress, and I am a professional model."

James went very red in the face. Debbie agreed with her Grandad, and Ian thought it was great that his ma was in the paper.

"Can I bring it into school? You're famous!"

Chapter 23

MARCUS DEERING AND THE ADVERTISING people had done their work well. Street posters, magazines and newspapers—wherever Addie went her image greeted her. Even the bus shelter at the crossroads carried a large poster of the glamorous Gold Crest Girl glaring out challengingly at the neighbours.

The Jeffries ran the gauntlet of comments. James's new girlfriend proudly began to smoke Gold Crest cigarettes. Ian defended his ma's honour at school.

"Your ma has big tits."

Debbie met every challenge with, "My mother is beautiful, you're jealous," and Roy just smiled good-naturedly, accepting all comments good, bad and ugly, while Addie, in her newfound role as a professional model, accepted it all as part of the job, the role of the celebrity, revelling in the head-turning and attention.

The phone was installed at the expense of Berkley's. Addie's first call was Laura Anne Robinson. "Congratulations, Addie! How wonderful you look! I'm taking you to the Shelbourne for lunch. We have to celebrate."

There was another visit to the Grafton Street fashion shops, and at the Butlin's fashion show, Addie was the star, gracing the catwalk like a seasoned professional to special applause. The red dress featured on request from the cigarette manufacturers, who agreed to sponsor the event featuring the Gold Crest Girl and Fashion for The Fuller Figure.

Addie, en vogue, was invited to various functions and attended, Roy by her side, handsome, charming and smiling.

Liz made brief appearance at every event, always elegant, always aloof, always in charge, never available for anything more than a cursory exchange of pleasantries, always arriving late and making an entrance, always hesitating at the doorway waiting to be seen before entering a room.

"There you are, Addie. Maria tells me how well it's all going. The ad agency and the cigarette people are ecstatic. Is this your husband? So nice to meet you, Roy, you must be so proud of your beautiful wife!"

Another fashion show loomed within the week, a small affair in a Wexford Hotel.

The signature red dress would be on display again, and Maria enquired if would Roy be prepared to take part as an escort for Addie on the catwalk.

"It's Liz's idea. A suit would be provided as payment for his appearance. What do you think, Addie? It's by way of being an experiment, and we think Roy would be really excellent. He's very good-looking."

Addie didn't hesitate. "Pay him the proper hourly rate and the suit, I'll make sure he does it."

At first, Roy resisted the idea, but Addie persisted, and in the end a payment of five pounds and a new suit won the day.

The concept of ladies' fashion accompanied by a male escort on the ramp captured the imagination of the media, and Roy proved to be the perfect partner. Unassuming and obviously smitten by the beautiful Addie and what she was wearing, he casually strode the ramp, smiling and attentive. With growing interest, Liz, out front, studied the effect on the audience, heads turning to comment, nodding approval. The attendant buyers were impressed. It was all smiles, except for one person: Marcus Deering sat, arms folded, looking out of place amongst the well-dressed patrons. He was not smiling. In fact, as Liz watched, Marcus turned to speak to Jim Nolan, and it was obvious he was not pleased.

Riding on the crest of a wave, Addie could hardly wait for the twenty-eighth of the month to arrive when she would receive her first pay cheque.

Two long, cream-coloured envelopes with the Berkley Model Agency crest stood out like beacons of hope in contrast to the usual drab, brown-windowed bills on the tiled floor of the porch. Addie was hardly aware of Michal the postman's hasty retreat, pursued by Mac the black Labrador, normally kept behind the garden gate, as she gathered the envelopes from the floor, and with a cursory glance at the usual titles—gas, electricity—deposited them in the drawer of the hall table. Retaining the cream, sleek, gold-crested ones with their promise of riches, she headed for the kitchen table to sit and open them at her leisure.

Inside was a cheque and two sheets of A4 headed paper.

Pay Adelaide Jeffries Four Pounds Eight Shillings
signed Elizabeth Berkley.

Addie recoiled in disbelief. *There must be some mistake!* She scrutinised the sheet with the Berkley heading. It was a statement:

Attending photoshoot for Gold Crest Cigarettes
3 hrs @ amateur rate £2.00 per hr...£6 0s 0p
Fashion Show Butlin's...£9 10s 0p
Fashion Show Wexford...£9 10s 0p

£25 0s 0p

Deductions
Travel expenses and refreshments...£2 0s 0p
Portfolio, photographs and prints...£3 12s 0p
Modelling course 5 sessions...£15 0s 0p

£20 12s 0p

Total £4 8s 0p

Designer dress generously gifted by Gold Crest Cigarettes accessories, shoes and gold Calibri lighter valued in total £74

Addie stood up and scrutinised the statement for the second time. But it was the other sheet of paper that forced her to sit down again.

It was a statement of costs from the designer shops with the bills attached, all with Addie's signature, amounting to £78.

All the advertising posters on buses, her face appearing on every magazine and newspaper, and all she received was £4.

The new phone sat on the hall table; the Berkley-paid-for phone. The number was first in her little book; Liz wasn't available, but Maria's friendly voice was soon on the line.

"Hi, Addie, how are you?"

"Four pounds eight shillings—there must be some mistake!"

Maria listened, only speaking when Addie finished, her quiet voice controlled and reassuring, explaining that Addie had been paid the going rates: £2 amateur rate and £5 professional rate. She assured her that her daily rate would increase with her experience, pointing out that she was now the Gold Crest Girl and there would be plenty more work. There would be a great demand for her as a ramp model, and no more deductions for modelling courses; the account at the fashion houses could be paid by instalments, not to mention the designer dress and accessories.

Addie's anxiety diminished as she listened, aware that £25 was three weeks' work for Roy and she had earned it in seven hours: a day's work. Next time, she'd get the whole £25.

"Addie, you have done better than any of the models I have worked with in a very short time. The publicity you have received is worth a fortune."

Addie wiped a tear away with a relieved laugh. They finished the phone call with an assurance from Maria that the agency would be in touch with the next assignment and Addie should drop in and they'd have lunch at Jammet's.

"Be seeing around town, Addie. Drop in to the agency and have a coffee. You're in demand, and there are three model shows scheduled for next month."

Addie put down the phone, her good humour restored. Perhaps she wouldn't tell Roy about the big fashion dress bills. Better not to worry him.

The other envelope with the Berkley crest was addressed to Roy. It contained a cheque for £4 0s 0p for attending the Wexford fashion Show. And he got to keep the new suit.

The phone rang. It was Laura Anne. "Lunch, it's my treat—celebration time."

Addie sat down on the hall chair, the phone to her ear and a smile on her face as they chatted.

"The Shelbourne Hotel, tomorrow lunch. I'll collect you."

"Why don't we go to Jammet's? It's really very good. I like their lunch menu," Addie suggested.

***

The phone never rang. Well, that wasn't not quite true. It did ring, but not with the phone call Addie longed for. It had been over a month since lunch in Jammet's. For a while, things had been quite frantic and exciting. Calling to Berkley's, Addie, the centre of attention, prepared for a brilliant modelling career, the role of a celebrity, all the trappings of success, but further work was not forthcoming. On one occasion, Berkley's had called, but it had been for Roy to take part in a show in Wexford. Addie had been advised that they were keeping her for more important work. Roy, out of loyalty, did not want to take part, but Addie had insisted, and after expenses was Roy £2 5s 6d the richer. The money had gone towards the bill for Hartigan's grocery account.

Addie was becoming obsessed with her image appearing everywhere she went. The Gold Crest Girl was now appearing perched on the high stool beside the black marble bar counter, stroking the black cat, cigarette pack held for the camera with the caption in big letters: *She's got what she wants...Gold Crest.*

"I don't get paid any more money?! But it's a different picture! And it's on posters and magazines. I see it everywhere." Addie, incensed, rang Berkley's and was put on to Maria.

The quiet tones informed her that she had been paid for the photoshoot, common procedure. The pictures were available for advertising purposes. Of course, when the advertising agency needed more pictures, she would be paid at a higher rate for another session, now that she had done her modelling course. Maria was reassuring.

"When will that be?" Addie enquired anxiously, aware of all the money she owed. "When will they need more pictures?"

"That's up to Marcus Deering. At the moment they have sufficient for their needs. But I'm sure they'll be calling in the near future."

"What about all the work from other advertisers? You said that I would be in demand because I'm the Gold Crest Girl. There have been fashion shows and I wasn't asked!" Addie was alarmed and angry. "What if Marcus Deering has enough pictures and doesn't call? It's not fair!" Addie's voice rose.

There was no response for some moments. Addie waited, clutching the receiver, her feeling of dread fuelled by the break in the conversation. She could hear muffled voices. Then the recognisable cultured tones of Liz Berkley came on the line.

The explanation was clear. Berkley's had made many contacts on Addie's behalf, but unfortunately other advertisers were not interested in using her because she had been typecast as the Gold Crest Girl. Also, the sponsors of the fashion shows felt that their customers were looking at Addie, paying more attention to her than the garments. Berkley's had argued her case, but though the idea of using fuller-figured girls was a success, they did not want Addie. She personally was too much of a distraction, and the concept of the femme fatale who gets what she wants was considered distasteful and not appropriate for most products. Perhaps things would change in the future, but for the time being there would not be any work. Berkley's would continue to promote Addie at every opportunity in the hope that things would improve. Maria did not come back on the line. The call ended.

Addie replaced the new phone on its cradle and stood in the doorway of the silent house. Her worst fears had been realised. How could she tell Roy and the kids? She felt alone. The letterbox rattled and some envelopes fell to the tiled floor in the porch, one with the familiar logo of one of the fashion shops; the other one she did not recognise until she picked it up from the floor. It was a bill from the phone company. Opening the drawer in the hall table, she placed the envelopes unopened with all the other unpaid bills.

***

Roy arrived home at his usual time. Unusually, the house was in darkness. No nice smell of cooking to greet his cheery "I'm home!"

Addie emerged from the bedroom with 'a migraine' explanation and headed to the kitchen to prepare something for dinner. Roy poked the fire in the dining room and joined her in the kitchen.

"Where's everyone?" he asked, sitting at the kitchen table and opening the evening paper. "Wait, don't tell me. Ian is with the Robinsons, am I right?"

"You're right." Addie put a pan on the stove. "We've got an egg and a sausage, and I'll do some fried bread."

"He's always with the Robinsons, ever since they gave him that watch."

"I think he has a nice time there. They're so well off and they feed him," she added matter-of-factly.

"I suppose James is out with his latest. What's her name?"

"Gillian." Addie cracked an egg into the sizzling pan. "And Debbie's at Guides."

Chapter 24

GRANDAD HUGH PASSED AWAY AT the age of seventy-six. The funeral was a small enough affair, the Reverend Stephen McWilliams presiding in the local Protestant church, the parishioners well represented as Grandad Hugh had been a regular churchgoer.

Under the high trees in the picturesque churchyard, friends and associates paid their respects to the Jeffries, Addie, spectacular in thrift-shop black, with Roy in attendance flanked by their saddened children. Ian, now in his thirteenth year, held back the tears while Debbie cried with total abandon. There could be no doubting Addie's grief as she dabbed her eyes, head held high.

Ian spotted Christopher and his parents amongst the gathering as they followed the coffin to the rows of headstones, behind the church. Christopher made a funny face, and Ian was not sure whether he should wave or not. Instead, he fixed his gaze on the back of his brother's head. James paced slowly in front, his shoulder supporting a corner of the oak coffin, his arm stretched to the shoulder of his uncle Frank, newly arrived from Liverpool—his mother's brother, over to claim his inheritance. He had not been long in making his feelings known.

"I won't be staying long, back on the boat tomorrow. Did he leave a will? I always felt he had a few shillings. I know I should have kept in touch, the drink's a terrible thing." The will existed, all right: all Hugh's worldly possessions had been left to Addie.

"Fair enough. I was never his favourite. I could do with a couple of quid to pay the boat fare and maybe a keepsake or two, seeing as you're goin' to be rich." The chancer's smile accompanied the hopeful raising of an eyebrow. "I always loved that old writing desk, ever since I was a kid."

Grandad Hugh had never seen eye to eye with the wayward Frank, who had departed Ireland's shores twenty years previously. Nobody knew the full story as all enquiries were met with a grim face and a stony silence.

The small procession made its way around the side of the ancient church to the small graveyard beyond. The neighbours huddled in a group, not venturing inside a Protestant church but nonetheless showing their support, standing to one side waiting for the opportunity to step forward to offer their condolences.

***

"The key to the kingdom." Grandad Hugh would lean forward in his rocking chair, fixing Ian with a gleaming eye and a twirl of his waxed moustache as he regaled the young boy with stories of his childhood. The flickering firelight cast shadows around and up to the high ceiling; blue-veined fingers reached to grasp the little gold key attached to the watch chain stretching from the pocket of his worn tweed waistcoat. He'd hold it between finger and thumb.

"The key to the kingdom. Mark my words. You'll all be rich the day I die." He'd smile in a knowing way.

"Train sets, bicycles, all you can eat, cakes and chocolate. What do you think of that?"

"A car like the O'Neills'?" Ian would play the game, and Grandad Hugh would nod his head.

"The desk holds the secret." And he would go to the black, roll-top writing desk with its many little drawers and cubby holes.

"There's a secret drawer with a lock that fits the key. If you find the drawer, you find the fortune."

Many times they played the game, but Ian could never find the drawer, and Grandad Hugh never showed him where it was.

Now, Grandad Hugh had passed away and was in the coffin. Ian walked in the procession and remembered the game. *Or was it just a game? Uncle Frank seems very interested in the desk. Where is the key? Ma must have it.* Addie had collected Grandad Hugh's things from the hospital. There had been a suitcase. Ian had seen it being carried to Grandad's his room.

Ian watched the coffin being lowered into the grave. The men stumbled on the fresh soil, keeping their balance against the weight on the long straps supporting Grandad Hugh on his final journey.

"From dust to dust..."

Ian hardly listened to the words, his eyes full of tears, his breath choking in a sob. His ma and Debbie had their arms around each other, his da was looking at the coffin with a sad face.

"Dear boy..." Lavender water and a gentle arm. Ian did not resist the comforting embrace as Doris Blackwell clucked her sympathy.

***

Back at Ivy Lodge, the mourners gathered on the lawn in front of the ivy-clad house. The dining room table had been brought out for the occasion, laden with beetroot in a bowl and plenty of sandwiches, tea and bottles of stout, even a full bottle of whisky. The neighbours supplied the chairs.

"A fine man, a gentleman, I knew him well, a sad loss, God rest him." The Gimlet spoke and eyed Gordon Robinson.

"Indeed, so I believe. I didn't know him very well," the chairman of Robinsons replied.

"That's not an Irish accent, now, is it?"

"No."

"Jaysus! You're an Englishman!" The Gimlet stood back and looked the dapper Gordon up and down. "I never saw one before."

The sun shone, and the small gathering celebrated a life well spent.

In Grandad's room, Ian and Christopher examined the big, black, roll-topped desk, the sounds from the garden filtering through the partly closed shutters.

The pocket watch with its chain, and the little gold key lay on the desktop along with Grandad Hugh's penknife, wallet and his favourite pipe.

Ian, without understanding why, could not bring himself to touch Grandad Hugh's things. The key was right there but he could not pick it up.

Christopher was not so hesitant.

"We have an old box at home with a secret drawer. It's behind a panel at the corner of the box that slides to one side."

A small floral motif, carved from wood, decorated each corner of the desk. With a bit of pressure, one of these moved to one side to reveal a small keyhole.

"The key to the kingdom!" Christopher grabbed the key and brandished it in the air. The watch swung back and forth on the end of the chain.

"No!" Ian grabbed it from him using both hands to gently return the watch and chain to its place amongst the other items on the desk. "It's private! It's not for us to open, it's Grandad's," he finished quietly.

"But he's dead!" Christopher exclaimed. "He'll never know! Give me the key! I'll open it!"

"I'm goin' to get me ma." Ian went to the door and turned to Christopher, who was scratching his head and making one of his funny faces. "You're coming too!" Ian ordered.

With a regretful look at the desk, Christopher reluctantly followed.

***

In the garden, Addie was talking with Laura Anne when the two smiling boys emerged from the house. Christopher, unable to contain his excitement, blurted out the news.

"We found the secret drawer!"

Several heads turned at the sound of the loud exclamation amidst the muted tones of the respectful mourners, none more attentive than Uncle Frank, in spite of having more to drink than most.

"The secret drawer in Grandad Hugh's desk and the gold key to the kingdom. We found it! Can we open it, Mrs. Jeffries? Please?"

Addie, having been regaled with tales of a great fortune and the key to the kingdom over the years, had always humoured her father. She assumed that the story had been invented to salvage his self-respect, having for years prevailed on her and Roy for a roof over his head.

"Is this true, Ian?"

Ian nodded his head.

With a sigh and a wistful smile, Addie ushered the boys back into the house.

"I'm coming too!" Uncle Frank quickly followed, rubbing his hands together.

It was rumoured that Grandad Hugh's family had owned a farm and property; Hugh, with the demeanour of the country gentleman, had always given the impression of wealth, but there had been no real evidence of money available. Though not really poor, they had led a financially meagre life.

By the time Addie reached the door, she was considering the possibility that the kingdom might very well exist.

The key fitted the small key hole. Addie turned it, feeling the mechanism click smoothly. The drawer slid open, long and shallow, revealing what appeared to be bank statements, a slim bank savings book, and the unmistakable shape of a handwritten cheque.

"I knew it! I knew the old boy had money!" Frank exclaimed.

Whatever expectations Addie might have had, they were soon dispelled. The bank deposit book told its story of a fortune dwindling over the years, of withdrawals and transfers to a current account. The bank statements revealed payments made to hotels, clothes stores and public houses, several payments to Weir's famous jewellery store—purchases that the family had never seen or gained benefit from, a self-indulgent life spent while his family struggled. There were several cash payments made, in the earlier days, to a Jennifer Anderson, and in latter years to another woman named Alice Dignam. The times spent away from the family were now explained: the pretend trips to do with the Church and farm business and the many visits to distant relatives in the country, never accompanied by his wife or family.

Frank and the two boys, in the absence of a hidden fortune, lost interest and returned to the garden.

The more Addie delved, the more was revealed. Grandad Hugh had been to Scotland and England on several occasions. The latest transaction had been as recent as two months previous, the cheque dishonoured for lack of funds. How often had Addie heard the saying, *There are no pockets in your shroud*? The total sum of Grandad Hugh's legacy appeared to be an empty wallet, a pipe and a penknife. Addie examined the pocket watch. It had stopped. The winder spun around uselessly, the main spring broken.

She sighed and closed the secret drawer with a quiet click. Save for the key hole, one would never guess that the drawer existed.

And so, Grandad Hugh had passed on.

"Fair play to you, Hugh. You had a pretty good time of it right to the end."

Addie smiled a wistful smile and brushed away a tear.

***

Frank got the desk. Addie handed it over with some satisfaction, pretty sure that her brother had known about the secret drawer and had hoped to gain from a hidden fortune. It was collected the following day to be sold at a local auction house, along with the rest of the contents from Grandad Hugh's room. The proceeds, with the exception of the selling price of the desk, would help cover the cost of a headstone to mark the passing of the keeper to the keys of a mythical kingdom.

Chapter 25

TUESDAY WASHDAY, AS USUAL THE van arrived early. Addie handed over the two shillings and Jimmy Whelan wheeled the washing machine on its trolley around the side of Ivy Lodge through the orchard, into the backyard and through the kitchen door.

This was Addie's one indulgence. Unable to afford to buy a washing machine, every Tuesday the washing machine man arrived. It cost two shillings for the day, and there was even an electric wringer attached. Shirts, socks, vests, sheets…everything got cleaned on Tuesday. The long clothes line stretched almost the width of the big orchard, supported in the middle by a pole, the clothes raised high to benefit from the breeze. Addie prayed for a dry day on Tuesday.

Jimmy Whelan was always prompt and punctual, arriving to collect the machine at four o'clock. Addie worked hard and the little machine whined and shuddered in protest trying to keep up. Shirt collars needed individual scrubbing at the big square sink. Sheets too big for the protesting machine were soused and scrubbed on the washboard. The first load was on; *Music While You Work* played on the radio. Addie was up to her elbows in sudsy water, back arched, her arms moving in a practised rhythm. It was going to be a long day with no rest, to have everything done by four o'clock.

The doorbell rang.

"Damn it!" Straightening her back, hands on hips, Addie tossed her head to displace the hair from her face, reddened with effort.

Ring, ring!

"Coming! Hold your horses!" Impatiently drying her hands on her apron and ready to dismiss the intruder to her precious routine, Addie headed up the hallway to the front door. The windows of the porch at the end of the long hallway faced the front path leading to the open gate in the arch of the laurel hedge. The sunlight already drying the first line of clothes reflected brightly on the shiny surface of the little sports car. *Laura Anne!*

The unmistakable figure was discernible on the other side of the muffed glass-panelled door. Dressed in yellow with a black wide-brimmed hat, Audrey Hepburn...Laura Anne had come to visit. *Two shillings down the drain, wasted.* Addie exploded a breath of frustration as she adjusted her hair in the hall mirror.

"Laura Anne! What a wonderful surprise!" She opened the door.

Glamorous, perfectly coiffed, elegant as ever, she posed on the wide doorstep. But only for a moment.

Addie held her damp hands out wide lest they come in contact with any part of the perfection as Laura Anne delivered air kisses and stepped past into the porch, twirling and confronting, smiling and in control.

"Lunch, we're going to lunch. I'm taking you to lunch. Get your glad rags on, we're going into town."

The overloaded washing machine howled a protest in the kitchen.

"No! I can't...thank you!" Addie protested. "It's a lovely idea, but I really can't." She indicated the howling machine and headed quickly to put it out of its misery, looking back to see Laura Anne quickly following.

"Of course you can!" Laura Anne waved her hands dismissively. "Washday? Just forget it. It's a birthday present. I'm taking you to lunch for your birthday."

Addie turned helplessly in the kitchen, aware of the pile of dirty washing and the general disarray. Turning off the machine, she began to tug at a large bed sheet almost totally submerged in the tepid water.

Laura Anne, taking charge, pulled out the plug from the wall socket. The machine gave one last shudder and the noise slowly subsided. In the ensuing silence, Addie wrestled with the sodden sheet.

"Leave it!" an imperious hand commanded.

Laura Anne lifted a bundle of soiled clothes from a chair and placed them on the kitchen table. Taking Addie gently by the shoulders, in a consoling tone she said, "Sit down." The gentle yet firm touch guided the slightly tearful Addie to the chair. The two women sat facing each other.

"I'd really love to go for lunch." Head bent, Addie looked at the floor. "But I paid the two shillings for the machine, and Mr. Whelan will be back to collect it at four o'clock.

"Addie, you don't have to worry about the washing. Mr. Whelan will not be coming back at four o'clock because you now own the washing machine. It's a birthday present. I rang Gordon this morning and he arranged everything. So, you can do the washing whenever you like. I'll be waiting in the garden—you've got ten minutes to get ready." Laura Anne jumped to her feet. "Really, Addie, you look fabulous as you are."

That was her parting shot as she disappeared through the back door, leaving a stunned Addie sitting on the kitchen chair surrounded by soiled, half-washed and nearly dry piles of laundry. She could hardly believe what she had heard: her own washing machine with its electric wringer.

But could she accept such a gift? She studied the machine with new eyes. An Electrolux, almost brand-new. *Well, maybe I'll do one wash and then tell her I can't keep such an expensive gift. And the kids...I'll have to be at home when they get back from school.*

"Don't worry about the children." Laura Anne was back at the door. "I've arranged for my housekeeper to collect Christopher and Ian, and you can leave a note for the older ones. Now, come on. It's nearly half past ten."

"OK." The opportunity for Addie to wear her good designer clothes had not arisen since her modelling career had come to an abrupt end, and the red dress summoned from her wardrobe. Highly tempted to strut town as the Gold Crest Girl, she resisted in favour of a very smart bottle-green suit with a bolero jacket; black bag and gloves completed the picture. No time for the hair, her crowning glory, she teased it into a mass of shining waves and loose curls. Her make-up, always a simple matter, took only minutes. Surveying herself in the mirror, she decided the only thing missing was a purse full of money. *The reserve!*

Kept in the top drawer of the dressing table, only for emergencies, the small tin box gave up its contents. Twelve shillings and sixpence: *five weeks of hiring a washing machine. Laura Anne's present will pay back the reserve in five weeks*, she consoled herself. She set aside her pride and accepted the fabulous gift, putting the money into her purse. Bolting the back door, she wrote a quick note for James and Debbie and left it on the kitchen table. With hardly a glance at the chaos in the kitchen, Jane Russell strode up the hall and out the front door. The bed sheet hung half in and half out of the large sink, cold water dripping into a puddle on the floor.

"Wow! You look stunning!" Laura Anne clapped her hands gently as Addie locked the front door and placed the key under the brick on the windowsill for all intending burglars to find. "We're going to have such a nice time." She linked Addie's arm down the path to the front gate where, gleaming and expensive, the sports car waited. "Would you like to drive?" Laura Anne offered, opening the driver's door.

"Unfortunately, I can't." Addie lowered herself into the passenger seat.

"You really must learn. Lots of women are driving these days."

"It looks very complicated," Addie commented in admiration as Laura Anne reversed the car away from the gate to turn in the space beside Hartigan's shop, where a group of neighbours stood, out to view the spectacle. The back wheels spun. Some gravel flew, rattling against the *Players Please* sign.

Stella Boyle reacted, staggering to one side, clutching one of her cronies by the arm.

"Did you see that Addie Jeffries one and her posh friend?" She sat down abruptly on the windowsill to examine the imaginary damage. "Look at me nylons." The three-day-old ladder was there for all to see. "Vandals! Road hogs!" Indignant glares followed the departure of the glamorous duo in their lovely sports car.

***

Somehow Laura Anne's hair, sleek and tightly clipped in the Audrey Hepburn style, remained unruffled by the wind as they sped along the country road to the crossroads. In contrast, Addie's tumbled loose and magnificent, streaming out behind, her head held high as she closed her eyes and felt the wind on her face. They stopped at the lights under scrutiny from the usual group of lads outside the pub.

Aware of the attention, Addie ran her hands through her hair. "I must look a sight!" She laughed.

"Hiya, Mrs. Jeffries. Give's a lift!"

One of the younger men flicked up the collar of his leather jacket and gave them the benefit of his best James Dean impression.

The lights changed, Laura Anne gunned the engine, the car surged away, and Addie looked back. The sound of wolf whistles competed with the noise of the engine. The youth still posed, and Addie waved.

"Gold Crest Girl!" He waved a farewell like Clark Gable in *Gone with the Wind*.

"You really are something else!" Laura Anne shouted, eyes on the road. "I wish I had your confidence."

Addie, not quite sure what Laura Anne had said, assumed by the expression on her face it was a compliment. "Thanks!"

Laura Anne drove with style, gloved hands flicking the instruments, changing gear, feet moving on the pedals, passing the slower moving vehicles, steering one-handed.

"It looks so complicated. I'd never learn to drive." Addie was full of admiration. "Not much reason to anyway. I'll never own a car."

In no time at all, they had reached the outskirts of the city, over the bridge of the main artery and through the Georgian-fronted squares and streets. Faces peered down from crowded buses. At the top of Grafton Street, the policeman at point duty smiled and waved them on dramatically with a white-gauntleted hand. They passed the waiting park attendants in St. Stephen's Green to turn at the corner around the Shelbourne Hotel and entered the private car park reserved for residents and members. An attendant hurried over to take the car keys. Addie retrieved her bag from the back seat and followed her companion into the plush surroundings of Dublin's most famous hotel; along a corridor they strode to the ladies' cloakroom.

There was a time when Addie would not have dared to enter such a place. But now, donning the mantle of the Gold Crest Girl, she exuded confidence. After the open-car ride, some repairs would need attending to.

"Laura Anne! Where have you been hiding?" Air kisses.

"Meet my friend Adelaide Jeffries!"

"Pleased to meet you!" Red lipstick and more air kisses, the chatter of Dublin's well-heeled. Addie smiled and twisted and turned as she was introduced.

A long mirror stretched the length of the room, and Addie confronted her image over the marble hand basin and gold taps, the full cloakroom reflected behind her. All the women in the room were dressed like Laura Anne, the image of the day.

"Don't do a thing!" The immaculate Laura Anne admired the reflection in the mirror.

"My hair's a mess." Frustrated, Addie reached for her handbag.

"Don't do a thing. Your hair is amazing. Every woman here would pay a fortune for that look. You're the Gold Crest Girl, a trendsetter!"

"Really?" Addie shook her head, and her crowning glory bounced and shone in the bright lights, dancing and settling around her face and folding in bundles of waves to touch her shoulders, auburn with natural reddish highlights.

"Come on. We've got shopping to do—our table is not booked until twelve forty-five."

"Wait a minute." Addie put a strong grip on Laura Anne's arm and guided her to a quiet corner. She opened her bag. "I've got twelve shillings," she said, reaching for her purse.

"Close that bag! This is your birthday treat. I have no money either, but I do have this." Laura Anne brandished a tortoiseshell pen. "And a Robinson Decorating Products account at the Shelbourne. I just sign and that's it. The business takes care of the rest."

"Well, if you're sure, only, recently I had an account like that, and you know what happened."

"I'm sure." Laura Anne smiled. "The same won't happen here."

"Addie! Hello! I thought it was you! I wasn't sure for a second. Your hair is different." Doris Blackwell detached herself from a group and came towards them. "How are those darling children of yours and that handsome husband? I was just talking about you the other day to my sister, you know, from the church." Doris was in full flow. "And, of course, my favourite Ian. One shouldn't have favourites, should one? Such a mannerly boy, a credit to you." Turning to Laura Anne, she put out a hand. "Doris Blackwell."

"Laura Anne Robinson, my friend," Addie introduced.

"Do you know Ian?" Doris enquired. "Such a lovely boy!"

"He's my son's best friend. We're very fond of him," Laura Anne said with a smile.

"He seems to be more in their house these days than he's in his own," Addie interjected.

Doris was off again, extolling the virtues of the Jeffries family. Anyone listening would have thought she and Addie had been friends for years.

"I must rush! I have to meet my husband—a business thing. Someone is bringing his wife, and Roger wants me to attend. I'm not looking forward to it. The woman's a terrible bore, she just prattles on and on. One can't get a word in edgeways. So sad about your Grandad Hugh, we must do lunch soon."

More air kisses and face powder accompanied with the scent of lavender water—"Nice to meet you, Laura Anne!"—and she was off across the room, no doubt to assail another group with her heart of gold before the business meeting.

Laura Anne and Addie shared a quiet chuckle.

"She's really very nice and a good person," Addie confided. "Very clever under all that chatter, I believe. Though a bit overpowering at times."

"Well, she's very well connected. That's a group of high flyers she's just joined. Very impressive! You're a bit of a dark horse, Addie Jeffries."

After the disappointment of her experience with the advertising agency and Marcus Deering, Addie was enjoying being back in the scene, striding with her sophisticated friend out through the impressive entrance and down the steps between the two statues of ladies holding beacons aloft, along St. Stephen's Green past Adams Galleries to Grafton Street and the heart of Dublin's most prestigious shopping area. Pausing to glance in shop windows, arm in arm they strode, receiving the attention of many glances, passing the famous Bewley's Café still serving breakfast, the full Irish, waitresses in black with white frilly aprons. Purposefully, they made their way to Brown Thomas and marched briskly through the cosmetics department to ascend the grand staircase to the ladies' designer labels.

"I won't be a minute." Laura Anne indicated a door marked private. "I need to see someone."

She hurried off leaving Addie alone in the most exclusive department. Addie saw her knock and enter through the door. Puzzled at the sudden departure, she looked around, inadvertently drawing the attention of a shop assistant.

***

Brown Thomas shop assistant Harold Smith misunderstood the look for one of uncertainty. He'd seen them all—the browsers, the posers, those who were likely to buy, those who were not— but this one was out of place, uncertain, unsure, so his attitude was somewhat dismissive.

"Can I assist Madam or is Madam simply browsing?"

Offended by the tone, Addie looked the man up and down without speaking. Harold stood his ground, superior attitude in place, confident of his judgement though beginning to feel slightly uneasy. There was something familiar about this woman, and she was extremely well dressed. *Perhaps I was mistaken.*

"I am interested in only your best. What do you recommend? The Dior or the Chanel?" Suddenly the Gold Crest Girl was staring him down.

"The Mary Quant, Madam." He clicked his fingers in a subtle summons, his demeanour transformed. Two girl assistants appeared as if by magic and Addie was escorted to a private viewing room with its comfortable seating and the offer of a glass of Champagne.

"So that's where you are. You haven't wasted any time!"

"Mrs. Robinson, so very nice to see you!" Harold greeted. "Please, take a seat. We are about to show Madam the latest of the Mary Quant selection."

"Madam Jeffries," Laura Anne corrected.

"Madam Jeffries." Harold repeated with a flourish, holding out his hand as he backed away and the waiting mannequins appeared, one by one, to walk and turn and stride in a private showing.

The two friends sat side by side; Addie exclaimed quietly at each creation.

"I don't think my twelve shillings and sixpence will go very far," she whispered, unable to ignore the humorous side of the situation. "One of those outfits costs about the same as Roy's six-month salary."

Laura Anne looked at her watch. "We really must go."

Thanking the fawning Harold with a promise to consider and possibly return, the two Madams left the store and headed for the Shelbourne, but not before Laura Anne with a quick apology made another visit to the private door. On the way to lunch, she explained that some of the Robinson company staff wore uniforms supplied by Brown Thomas, and the management offices were beyond the private door—"A bit tiresome, but Gordon likes to involve me in some things."

***

The Saddle Room at the Shelbourne was beginning to fill, mainly with men in business suits. Brandies and cigars seemed the order of the day in this very much male domain. It was impossible for Addie and Laura Anne to go unnoticed. Some blatantly stared, some acknowledged Laura Anne with a greeting; all smiled.

"I must get some cigarettes."

"Have one of mine." An elegant cigarette case flashed, and Addie took the Stuyvesant.

The waiter was summoned, and they ordered a packet of Gold Crest and gin and tonics. Addie reached for her bag but was intercepted with a glance and a "Behave yourself, Birthday Girl."

For a while, they sat in silence, each occupied with their own thoughts. Addie's mind was a whirl. The twelve shillings in her purse, so vital and crucial to her daily existence yet so trivial in this other world—this glimpse of how the other half lived. Even the expensive washing machine seemed of little financial consequence to Laura Anne. How Addie longed to have such things, and Ian—how could she blame him for wanting to spend so much time with the Robinsons? Tomorrow, she would return to washday and the continuous struggle to make ends meet. How she envied Laura Anne, sitting there so relaxed, acknowledging greetings with her Hepburn smile, sophisticated, the possessor of all that Addie cherished.

Laura Anne's thoughts concealed behind her smiling face were of a different kind. How many of these men knew more than her about Gordon's extracurricular activities? How did they perceive the attractive wife of a competitor with their inside knowledge? She contemplated her solitary existence here in Ireland, missing the circle of friends in London. Christopher, temperamental, spoilt, out of place, a misfit, relied on Ian's friendship. Such a contrast between the two boys. *Ian, my lovely boy. Forthright, athletic, independent and sensitive, the promise of the man to be.* How she envied Addie—how the men looked at her, the natural beauty, her strength and joy for life, her handsome husband and children who obviously adored her.

"Ian is such a lovely boy," she spoke out loud.

"Yes! He's a good lad, likes staying at your house. He and Christopher get along." Addie tapped her Gold Crest on the ashtray. "Will he do his homework at your place?"

"Yes. Mrs. Smithers will see to that. He can stay the night if that's OK?" Laura Anne added casually.

"No problem."

"I see you still show loyalty to Gold Crest." Laura Anne indicated the pack on the table beside Addie's Calibri lighter.

"Well, maybe someday they'll need new pictures of the Gold Crest Girl, and I'll be ready for them. Next time I won't be quite so naïve." Addie exhaled with a wistful expression.

They made their selection from the lunch menu.

"The duck is amazing."

Addie smiled when she saw a prawn cocktail and, with much laughter, related her first encounter with the dish and the caterpillar incident.

"We must have prawn cocktails in memory of that story." Laura Anne sipped the second gin and tonic and smiled as the waiter took their order.

"Your table at the window is ready whenever you wish," he announced.

"Thank you. We'll go in now." She turned to Addie. "It's more comfortable away from all these men."

Addie felt comfortable already in Laura Anne's company. She was enjoying herself.

They were ushered to a window alcove table, the manager greeting Laura Anne by name. Addie was introduced.

"You know Adelaide Jeffries."

"Of course," the manager agreed, unaware of Addie's name but aware she looked familiar and therefore must be someone of importance.

The gold-foiled neck of a Champagne bottle protruded above the ice in a standing ice bucket alongside the table.

"Champagne? We haven't ordered yet!" Laura Anne exclaimed.

"It's at your disposal should you wish. Mr. Forsythe sent it over."

Laura Anne looked towards the other side of the dining room indicated by the manager, where a group of people sat at a large table. One of them raised a glass in acknowledgement.

"I don't know anyone called Forsythe." Laura Anne made a slight face.

"Cigarettes," Addie said. "It's the cigarette people. That's Michael Forsythe, the advertising executive." She turned to the manager, who was waiting for her response. "Please return the Champagne to Mr. Forsythe and tell him we don't want it, thank you," she said imperiously.

"Wait! Addie, are you sure? Your problem wasn't with the cigarette people. It was with the model agency, and you said yourself they may need you again." Laura Anne advised.

"I don't care." Addie glared, and Laura Anne put out a consoling hand.

"Business is business, Addie. Don't burn your boats. Smile and we'll drink the Champagne. Wait till they need you and then get your pound of flesh. Believe me, I know how to play this game."

Somewhat pacified and respectful of Laura Anne's obvious expertise, Addie did as she was bid.

The patient manager opened the Champagne and the first course arrived.

"Now time to eat our caterpillars." Addie laughed and wielded the little fork.

And so, they sat and chatted, finding much in common, in spite of their diverse backgrounds.

It was between the duck and the tiramisu and after a large percentage of the Champagne that Laura Anne dropped the bombshell.

"We're friends." She smiled and raised her glass.

"To us! Modern women of the world."

The glasses clinked together, and they smiled across the table at each other.

"What a wonderful time I'm having. I could put up with a lot of this." Addie looked around the room with a sigh. "Back to reality tomorrow."

"You could have all this if you want." Wide Audrey Hepburn eyes blinked across the table.

"In my dreams!" Addie reached for her Champagne glass and held it up to watch the bubbles catch the sunlight from the window. "In my dreams," she repeated, "or maybe if I won the Sweepstake. Thank you for my lovely birthday present. It is so unexpected. I should be at home up to my armpits in sudsy water, scrubbing shirt collars. Instead, I'm here dining at the Shelbourne. You are so lucky, Laura Anne. You have everything."

"Well..." Laura Anne leaned forward, holding her Champagne glass, elbows on the table, her expression serious. "Things are not always as they seem. My life is not all a bed of roses—far from it. I do have doubts and uncertainties in my life."

She made a substantial visit to the wine glass. Addie waited. "I'd like to discuss something with you."

"Yes?" Addie prompted.

"We're friends?" The enquiring look asked for confirmation.

"Of course! What is it Laura Anne?"

"Well, it's about Christopher. He's a difficult child, and Gordon is hopeless. Not like Roy. Gordon is preoccupied with business, and I know that he has a part of his life he doesn't share with me. You know what I mean."

Addie was *not* sure, but Laura Anne looked so sad and upset that she made a similar face, nodding sympathetically.

"Yes, I know what you mean, and I'm sorry."

"Well, you see, Christopher..." Laura Anne hesitated. "Christopher can be difficult. He is often angry, flying into rages, difficult to cope with, refusing to eat and sometimes refusing to speak to Gordon and myself. Gordon just shrugs his shoulders and says, 'Domestic affairs, your problem.' Then Ian came into our lives. Christopher is wonderful, a transformed person when Ian is around. Ian is the brother Christopher never had. When we return to England, we won't see Ian anymore. Could Ian come to stay with us? We're very fond of him, and it would be wonderful for Christopher."

Addie sat back in her chair. "Of course! Any time! Ian really enjoys going to your home to stay."

"I don't really mean for one night. We would like him to come as Ian's companion."

Addie sat up straight in her chair. "What are you saying? Do you want Ian to stay for a weekend, a week...what?"

Laura Anne raised her eyes to heaven. "It's a crazy idea, but I might as well say it. Gordon and I were having our usual argument about Christopher, and I was saying I would find it hard to cope without Ian when we go back to England and Gordon said, 'So, bring the lad with you. Whatever it costs, bring the lad with you.' I said, 'Don't be silly! Addie isn't going to let that happen at any cost.' Well, he really got mad at that." Laura Anne laughed. "I thought that was the end of the matter until yesterday. When Gordon produced this—would you believe it?—it's a contract." Laura Anne fished a single-page document out of her bag and placed it on the table.

Wide-eyed and shaking her head, Addie looked incredulously at the document. "Businessmen, men in high positions. It always comes down to money, doesn't it? How much does he think my son is worth?" she asked scornfully, taking the offending document from the table.

"Ten thousand pounds." Laura Anne was leaning forward holding a cheque in her hand. "Ten thousand pounds. Would you believe it? He made out a cheque for ten thousand pounds and said, 'Tell Addie that Ian comes to us for the summer.' Of course, I told him it was ridiculous, and he just laughed and said, 'Show Addie the cheque and tell her. If Ian wants to go home at the end of the summer, he returns to the Jeffries and they still keep the cheque for ten thousand.'"

Addie was astonished at the amount of money being offered. It would easily pay the mortgage for Ivy Lodge, they could buy several cars. She looked at the figure on the contract for confirmation. It would take Roy ten years to earn that much. She looked at the cheque in Laura Anne's hand, a life-changing amount of money.

She knew Ian would never want to live with the Robinsons. They had often joked with him about his posh friends, and he always said they were a bit stuffy and serious and not much fun, but they had nice things and lots of money.

But now, the Jeffries would have lots of money, so there would be no reason for him not to come home.

"It wouldn't be fair, Laura Anne. If Ian goes to you for the summer, of course he would want to come back home in September to start school."

"Of course, Addie. I know Ian wouldn't stay with us. He belongs to a loving family. He would never leave you.

Take the money. It will serve Gordon right. All I have to do is sign the cheque."

Addie reached and took the crumpled piece of paper. Laying it on the table, she spread it out, flat. *Pay Addie Jeffries ten thousand pounds.* "I think your husband is crazy. What do you think?"

Laura Anne didn't hesitate. The mischievous light of revenge shone in her eyes. "Gordon Robinson may know about business, but he doesn't know much about families. I think my arrogant husband is about to lose a substantial sum of money." She took Addie's hand. "I'd love Ian to come to us for the summer, and of course he will want to come home in September. We go to the South of France to our place there, and come back to Ireland for the beginning of school. If you agree to that, Gordon says you can have the money now."

Addie sat back with the fortune of money clutched in her hand. "It looks as if Ian is going to spend the summer with you in France." Addie laughed. "Is this for real? Is Gordon serious? Would the ten thousand pounds be ours after the summer when Ian comes home?"

"There it is in black and white." Laura Anne nudged the contract on the table and Addie read the simple wording and turned the page over to make sure there was no other small print on the back. "I see Roy has to sign it too. I'll make sure he does."

The rest of the lunch was a blur to Addie, her mind on the enormous amount of the cheque in her handbag, just waiting for Laura Anne's signature.

After lunch, walking in St. Stephen's Green, Addie's mind was doing cartwheels.

Laura Anne produced a business card and handed it to Addie. "That's the phone number of our sales manager in Ireland. If Roy is interested, there's a job for him at Robinson's Decorating Products, as a sales representative with a salary and commission and, of course, a car supplied. The factory will be opening soon, and we need people in the Dublin area. Gordon is very impressed with Roy and is sure he would be a big asset to the company. That is, if he is interested."

This, to Addie's ears, was the icing on the cake.

"I don't know what to say." Tearfully, she took the card. "You're so good, you're like an angel. I can't wait to tell Roy."

"Make sure he signs that paper!" Laura Anne laughed.

"Don't worry I will."

Addie suddenly stopped.

"Just one thing."

"What?" Laura Anne looked puzzled.

"This is Nassau Street, and that's the Office of Westbury, the Model Agency's solicitors. I got on very well with Jim Jordan, and he invited me to call in anytime I needed advice. This is the time."

"Wise girl! I'll come with you."

The two women mounted the steps of Jordan solicitors, to emerge twenty minutes later with the reputable solicitor's approval, the simple, straightforward document safely stowed away along with the cheque in Addie's handbag.

It began to rain as they made their way back to the hotel. Addie didn't mind. Let the rain wash away all her debts.

"I wonder if the rain is coming through the ceiling in the hallway." She laughed out loud, and Laura Anne laughed with her. Clutching a small, collapsible umbrella between them, arm in arm they hurried back to the hotel to wait in the reception until the little sports car was brought to the front door. The black canvas top was in place. Addie and Laura Anne were escorted down the steps by a smiling porter with a large umbrella. The attendant doorman opened the doors for the ladies to board.

Two large, impressive-looking bags practically filled the tiny back seat, the Brown Thomas logo on each.

"I see you made some purchases," Addie observed, settling into the passenger seat.

"One for you and one for me. I had the shop send them over. Happy birthday!"

"Really, Laura Anne, it's too much." Addie, palms pressed to either side of her face, looked again at the two bags.

"Not at all! I'm so looking forward to Ian coming with us this summer it's the least I could do, and anyway—" she laughed out loud "—Gordon can well afford it."

They moved out into the evening traffic, two friends happy in each other's company and both fulfilling individual ambitions.

—

Chapter 26

THE LITTLE ORANGE VAN WITH the big gas company logo rattled down the country road to Ivy Lodge. Roy sighed but was thankful to be in a dry place as the tiny windscreen wipers whipped rapidly from side to side were barely coping with the rain on the windshield. *Well, at least I'm dry.* His nose twitched at the constant odour left by Moroney and his big bag of work tools. Today, he'd had a 'fitter' with him to disconnect some customers from their gas supply. The smell of gas clung to everything, becoming particularly exaggerated in the damp weather.

The new job, as experimental accounts shortage inspector, was taking its toll. He was becoming depressed, especially today. Roy was a generous, compassionate man by nature, non-confrontational, and the shortage collector's job brought with it abuse, tears and sadness at so many individuals struggling to make ends meet. Every case affected him personally, the benefits of the meagre increase in wages and the use of the little van not a great compensation.

He turned into the lane beside the house, thankful to see the lights on and anticipating the warmth, and a nice dinner.

***

Around the same time, closer to the city, Laura Anne swung into the driveway displacing some gravel as she parked alongside Gordon's car. Glad to see he was home, she hurried into the house.

In the hallway, she handed Mrs. Smithers the large bag to bring upstairs.

"Will you be having dinner at seven?" the home help enquired.

"Something light, maybe a salad, thank you."

"I fed the boys. They're in Christopher's room, and Mr. Robinson is not eating tonight. He's in the front room with a gin and tonic."

"Thank you, Mrs. Smithers."

Laura Anne joined her husband in the living room and made herself comfortable on the large sofa. "Make me one of those." She indicated the drink in Gordon's hand.

"I see you're smiling," he observed from the drinks cabinet as he poured a measure into the glass. "Should I be smiling too? Can I assume your little venture is progressing?"

She took the glass from him. Standing close, she stroked his face with a caressing hand and looked into his eyes before she answered. "I would say exceptionally well."

"And how much is it going to cost me? I see Brown Thomas had a visit, lunch at the Shelbourne—an expensive day, it seems. Contract signed?

"By Addie. Roy to sign tonight."

"Did you give her the card?"

"Yes."

"And you showed her the cheque?"

"Yes. By the way, she thinks you're mad," Laura Anne added. "She is absolutely certain that Ian will return home after the summer, and I'm inclined to agree with her."

"You could be right." Gordon looked unconcerned as he sipped his drink. "In which case, it will cost me ten thousand pounds and whatever you spent today."

"Plus," Laura Anne couldn't help smiling, "the cost of some sirloin steak and a bottle of wine. We stopped off at the butchers so Addie could have a treat for Roy when he comes home from rattling around in that van all day."

***

Turning up his collar against the rain, Roy quickly headed through the side gate into the front garden. Addie was waiting in the porch.

Putting her arms around his neck, she kissed him. "My lovely, handsome husband." He returned the kiss.

Stepping back, she took his hand and led him down the hall to the kitchen. It gladdened his heart to see her looking so happy.

"What has you in such a good mood?" He followed, beginning to feel curious.

"Wait and see." The kitchen was warm and welcoming. Roy looked quizzically around at the piles of unwashed clothes, and when he went to wash his hands, there was tepid water in the sink and a bed sheet still soaking.

"I know the place is a mess, but I only got in just ahead of you." She was at the cooker. The deep-fat fryer spluttered with freshly cut potato chips.

"What's that doing here? I hope the washing machine man isn't charging for extra time." Roy pointed at the washing machine.

"Your dinner's nearly ready. Sirloin steak! Mushrooms as well." She indicated the pan. "Done in real butter," she added with a mischievous smile.

"Addie!" he exclaimed turning from the sink to face her. "We can't afford sirloin steak!"

"Now, dry your hands. Go and sit at the fire and I'll bring in your dinner." She guided him from the kitchen. At the door, he turned questioningly. "Go!" she commanded and then added with a smile, "And pour yourself a glass of wine."

"What?!"

About to add a protest, he changed his mind and, with a resigned shake of his head, went into the warm living room.

Debbie and James were listening to the radio, the table was set for dinner, white tablecloth and a bottle of red wine, two glasses and a small bowl of peanuts. He viewed the wine with some apprehension: a 1959 Beaujolais.

"What's your mother up to?" he enquired. The bottle was already open so he poured himself a generous measure and sat down at the table.

"Haven't a clue." James shrugged. "She was out all day with Mrs. Robinson. We had chips and sausages, and she arrived home smiling and laughing with loads of shoppin'. She said she's got great news and she's tellin' you first. That's all we know."

Before Roy could comment, Addie arrived with a laden tray and placed it on the table. Turning to Debbie and James, she said, "Off you go." She smiled. "I want to have a word with your father. We'll tell you all about it later."

"Is Ian with the Robinsons?" Debbie asked at the door on the way out.

"Yes."

"Thought so. He's always staying with the Robinsons these days. I bet *he's* not havin' sausages and chips for his dinner— probably off to a hotel with the poshies. I'll close the door and let you two have your nice chat." She pulled the door closed behind her with exaggerated carefulness.

Addie placed the plate in front of Roy. "Sirloin steak, medium rare, mushrooms, chips and onions."

He leaned back in his chair, arms folded. "I'm not eating a thing until you tell me what's going on. It's something to do with the Robinsons, isn't it?"

Addie poured herself a glass of wine and topped up Roy's glass. "Yes."

Roy reached for his knife and fork.

"They want Ian to go to them for the summer."

He put down the knife and reached for his glass of wine, and Addie told him about her day. She told him about the washing machine, lunch at the Shelbourne, Brown Thomas, the cheque for ten thousand pounds and the proposition.

Roy listened in incredulous silence, reacting with numerous visits to the wine glass and topping it up twice.

"And you can give in your notice to the gas company. There's a job for you as a sales representative with Robinson's Decorating Products, with commission and a car supplied," she finished with a flourish and placed the cheque and the business card on the table.

His mind struggling to take in all he had heard, Roy put down his glass and pulled the cheque towards him, lifting it up and looking at Addie across the table.

"That's an awful lot of money. Of course Ian won't want to stay with them. Is that Gordon fella mad? Are you saying we keep the ten thousand pounds even if Ian comes home? Of course, he'll come home! No, Addie, there has to be a catch. What's the catch?"

"That's the thing!" Addie produce the document. "It's legal. I checked it out with the solicitors. There's no catch. There it is, in black and white." She placed the paper on the table and pointed at the wording.

Roy lifted it up and read carefully. "It seems straightforward to me." His brow furrowed in concentration and he read it again. "I don't know, Addie, it seems too good to be true. I see you signed it." He poured the rest of the wine into his glass.

"Of course I signed it. Roy, can you imagine what we could do with that money? And you a sales representative with your own car—a better one than the O'Neills'? You'd be wearing nice suits and you'd be finished with hard-up customers, dogs attacking you and abuse from ignorant people." She came around the table and placed her arms around his shoulders, her cheek resting against his. She spoke softly as his natural resistance began to waver.

"We could have Ivy Lodge looking the way we've always wanted, with a brand-new roof, and decorated with new carpets and wallpaper.

"But they're rich, Addie. They might influence him to stay with them, buy him things," he said, voicing his one remaining reservation in a hushed voice.

She held his face in both hands and turned his head to look at her. "But that's the thing, Roy." She smiled triumphantly. "So, will we be. We'll have ten thousand pounds and you'll have a well-paid job with commission. We'll be rich too."

They heard a car at the gate and the sound of running footsteps up the gravel path to the front door.

"I'm home!" Ian, face flushed from the rain, passed through the hall and pushed open the door. "I had my dinner, Mrs. Smithers gave us sausages and chips. Hiya, Ma! Hiya, Da! I did my homework!" He dumped his schoolbag on the table.

"I thought you were staying with the Robinsons tonight?"

"No, I said I wanted to come home."

"Come here, son." Addie put her arms around Ian and hugged him close.

"Don't kiss me, Ma!"

"The solicitors said it's OK?" Roy looked at Addie. She nodded vigorously, and he signed the document.

"A bottle of Beaujolais, Da! Very posh!" Ian left the room, and they heard him laughing with the others in the kitchen.

"I think we're safe enough with that lad. What about a little whiskey?" Standing up from the table, Roy transferred his long frame to his favourite armchair in front of the fire.

"Dessert!" Addie raced from the room, returning a moment later. With a flourish, she placed a serving of ice cream and strawberries on the arm of the chair.

"I think I'm in heaven." Roy eyed the luxurious dish and reached for a spoon.

Addie left the room again to share out the remainder of the ice cream and strawberries in the kitchen.

Roy's mind was full of happy thoughts, the figure of ten thousand pounds provoking possibilities unheard of in his world. The question of Ian and a possible controversial decision was wiped from his mind. *Roy the representative. Strawberries and ice cream. This is the life.* After weeks of uncertainty and controversy, he was ready, willing and able to accept some good news. He let himself sink deeper into the comfortable chair. Thanks to Addie, things seemed, at last, to be working out.

Addie returned from the kitchen, whiskey in hand, to find him in a deep sleep, his handsome face relaxed, his brown hands, fingers entwined, resting in his lap.

She placed the whiskey on the table and picked up the contract with its signatures. The cheque, looking a bit the worse for wear, still told the same tale. An enormous amount of money.

At last, the Jeffries were rich.

Chapter 27

SINCE THE RETURN OF THE phone and the financial fiasco of her modelling career, Addie had not used the phone at Hartigan's shop. On the odd occasion when a phone call was necessary, she used the O'Neills' phone.

Addie opened the small iron gate and approached the yellow-painted door with some reluctance. The careful, meticulous Brenda O'Neill took pride in every aspect of their small white bungalow with its two windows fronting the perfect dining room and equally perfect 'best room'. The best room was kept locked and only opened on special occasions, Christmas and Easter reputedly. The fireside rug, still in its polythene bag, lay upside down lest it should fade with the sun.

Should a neighbour need to use the phone, the key would be produced. In this haven of perfection, where all things gleamed without a trace of a speck of dust, the telephone resided on its custom-made small table and cushioned seat combined. There was a spring-up silver phone number pad and the phone directory. Shoes had to be removed at the polished door and placed on a special mat, which would be whisked away for cleaning after the visitor had left the building.

"Please may I use the phone?" Addie stood on the doorstep, two pennies at the ready.

"Of course, Addie!" The permission, though granted in a friendly enough manner, was also laced with slight disapproval.

Having unlocked the best room, Mrs. O'Neill ushered Addie in and retreated to the hall, leaving the door slightly ajar.

Addie sensed her lurking within hearing distance as she dialled the number.

"The Robinson residence." Addie recognised Mrs. Smithers' voice.

"Hello. Could I speak to Mrs. Robinson, please?"

"Whom shall I say is requesting her?"

"Adelaide Jeffries."

"Please hold on."

"Hello, Addie, how are you? I'm just back from taking Christopher to school."

"That matter we were discussing yesterday…" Not wishing Mrs. O'Neill to overhear, Addie spoke in a low voice.

"Yes," Laura Anne interrupted. "I hope you weren't offended. Gordon is such a control freak."

"No, of course not! I talked to Roy, it's agreed." Almost whispering, Addie spoke quickly. "What do we do next?"

There was silence at the other end of the phone, and Addie was afraid Laura Anne had changed her mind. She was about to speak when Laura Anne said, "OK! I'll pick you up at eleven, if that's all right? And wear your best outfit. We're going to the bank."

"Everything all right?" Brenda O'Neill was at the door, dust cloth at the ready.

"Great! see you then, bye!" Addie returned the phone to its cradle. "Yes, Mrs. O'Neill. Things couldn't be better!"

"It's just that when people ask to use my phone it's often an emergency of some kind." The duster was giving the phone a thorough work-over.

The overjoyed Addie smiled broadly. "No emergency! I was just on about our new car. We're deciding what make to buy, and I probably won't need to bother you again. We're getting a new phone installed."

"That's nice." Mrs. O'Neill folded her arms as Addie headed for the door to collect her shoes.

"Thanks for the use of the phone. Bye!"

Addie left Brenda O'Neill with something to discuss with the neighbours. Running the seventy-five yards along the road to Ivy Lodge, her was mind flying with excitement and relief, around to the back of the house and into the kitchen. The washing machine stood in the same place from the previous day, surrounded by unwashed clothes. The sodden bed sheet still hung from the sink in water now quite cold. Her watch said ten past ten; no time to attend to the kitchen, she'd have to get ready. Laura Anne would be here at eleven. *I'll buy new clothes*, she laughed to herself, *and sheets*.

The cheque and the contract were still on the table where she had left them the night before. *Ten thousand pounds.* She smoothed out the paper with her fingertips. *What if Laura Anne doesn't turn up? Is it all a dream?* The two signatures stared back from the page of the contract. Her name was on the cheque. Laura Anne was on the way.

Shortly, back in the kitchen, dressed in her nicest clothes and feeling a million dollars, she heard the unmistakable sound of the little sports car. Closing and locking the back door, she hurried around the house to the front gate.

The neighbours were out in force, cars a rarity on the country road, especially sports cars driven by an Audrey Hepburn lookalike.

"Pride comes before a fall, mark my words."

"That outfit she's wearing was in *Woman's Way* magazine last week."

"Poor Roy, she's spending every penny that man earns."

"I believe your woman with the car is feedin' young Ian. Sure, he's never at home these days."

Addie couldn't hear the words over the sound of the engine, but by the expressions, she knew herself to be the butt of their remarks.

This time, Laura Anne was careful not to spray gravel on the sign as she reversed at the shop.

"We're so excited that Ian is coming away with us for the summer. I'm sure he'll love our place in the south of France." They chatted as they headed through the suburbs.

"What did he say when you told him?"

"Oh! He's really excited too."

Addie, dismayed that she had, in her excitement, neglected to mention anything to Ian, gave the most obvious response. "Good. I was afraid he might not want to come. Christopher would have been so disappointed." *France!* Addie hadn't thought of Ian going so far away. "Will you be there for long?"

"Most of the summer. I'll go out with the boys next week and Gordon will come out later. You and Roy must stay at the villa sometime. When we aren't using it. Gordon can give Roy some time off from his new job at the company." Laura Anne laughed and nudged Addie, who smiled weakly. Everything was moving rather fast.

"That would be nice."

"He'll need a passport for France and some light clothes, but you can leave that to me. We'll need a passport for Roy when he joins the company—sometimes our reps need to go abroad—it can all be done at the same time." Laura Anne waved a dismissive hand. "Exciting, isn't it? It's all arranged for Roy to meet up with Peter Hackett, our sales manager. Roy will have a choice of car. The senior reps drive Rovers."

With mixed emotions, Addie clung to her bag with the contract and the cheque. *A Rover car, how wonderful! And everything else, the money, the reps job. I'm sure Ian will love France, it's such a wonderful opportunity for him to see the world—sunshine, the Riviera, and we might be going too.* She stared silently ahead, in her own world, her mind tumbling through all the details. She was hardly aware of the trip into town.

"Here we are." Laura Anne expertly parked almost opposite to the bank in Harcourt Street. Addie helped to click the soft top into place and they sat for a minute, close together, in the confines of the small car.

"All set, Addie? Your new life begins here. Any doubts?" Laura Anne looked enquiringly.

Addie took a deep breath.

"None," she said.

"Right. Give me the contract and the cheque, I'll need these for the bank."

Addie handed them over, first the cheque—"Sorry it's a bit crumpled." She laughed nervously. "Worn out from us looking at it."—and the contract. Laura Anne checked quickly for the signatures.

"Well, everything seems in order. Let's go."

Waiting for two cars and a bus to pass by, they crossed the street and strode through the elegant doors into the bank.

They were very quickly attended to, the manager appearing through a panelled doorway: a tall man, grey at the temples, immaculate suit, more Randolph Scott than Clark Gable.

"Laura Anne." He held her hands, kissing her on both cheeks. Addie stood to one side, surprised by the familiar greeting.

"And this is my friend Adelaide Jeffries," Laura Anne introduced.

He turned his smiling attentions to Addie, who, not sure whether she was going to get the same treatment or not, stood her ground.

"Andrew Dixon," he introduced himself. "Adelaide, so nice to meet you. May I say, the advertising posters don't do you justice."

"Be careful of this one, Addie. He has an eye for the ladies," Laura Anne informed. "He's also married to Gordon's sister."

"This way, ladies." They were ushered through a doorway into a wood-panelled office with comfortable chairs. High curtains framed a tall Georgian window. There was a filing cabinet and a low mahogany sideboard. Andrew indicated the chairs and waited until they were seated before taking his place behind a large, dark-wood, highly polished desk.

"Straight to business, ladies." He rubbed his hands together and smiled his smile. "Coffee or tea?" He glanced at his watch. "A bit too early for something stronger."

"Tea would be fine," Laura Anne confirmed for them both.

"Now, I have taken the liberty to proceed with all things. Addie, can I assume you are prepared to open a bank account with this bank?"

Addie nodded.

"We could open a current account and a deposit account. How much is the sum?" He looked at Laura Anne.

"Ten thousand pounds." She signed the crumpled cheque and handed it across the desk with the contract. He perused both carefully and handed the cheque to Addie.

"May I suggest you put, say, five hundred into your current account for daily use and the rest on deposit until you get advice on investments?"

Addie studied the cheque, hardly aware of what the bank manager was saying. Such a staggering amount of money.

"Yes."

"Please sign the back of the cheque and these two forms." He handed Addie a beautiful platinum pen. She signed her name at the appropriate places, carefully screwed the top back on the pen and went to hand it back.

"Please, Addie, keep it with the compliments of the bank. Consider it a symbol of the beginning of our relationship. We will always be here to look after all your needs. My door is always open to our special clients. Welcome!" He stood up and reached across the desk to shake hands.

After some pleasantries, Andrew Dixon led them to the door and they said their goodbyes. Addie fished the temporary cheque book from her bag, unable to keep the smile from her face.

"I'm dying to write a cheque. Let's go and buy something. I'll get you a present—you've been so good to us."

"Just write a cheque to yourself and cash it here at the bank.

"What?!" Addie looked at the cheque book. "How much can I write it for?"

"Well, you've got five hundred pounds in your current account, so you can write it for that much if you want."

Addie put her hand out for support on the bank counter. "So much money! I can write a cheque for six months of Roy's wages and they'll give it to me it in cash?"

"Absolutely!" Laura Anne laughed. "But perhaps twenty pounds would be enough until you get your head around all this."

Chapter 28

No! I'm not going!" Ian looked at his parents. "I don't have to."

Addie, taken aback, sat down at the kitchen table. She looked across at Roy. Things had happened so fast she had not considered how Ian might feel.

Twenty pounds in her purse and ten thousand in the bank. *He has to go. Of course he wants to go!*

Roy just looked back helplessly. A moment passed. He turned to Ian, earnestly, and spoke in a quiet voice.

"You don't have to do anything you don't want to, son."

Addie put her face in her hands.

"I know about the deal." Ian put his hands on his hips. "You want the money more than you want me."

"No, son!" Roy was on his feet. "We don't."

Ian sat down at the table, his eyes full of tears. "Christopher told me all about it. His dad gave you ten thousand pounds for me to go with them!"

"We were going to tell you all about it, but things happened so fast. We're sorry, you don't have to go anywhere." Roy reached out, but Ian pulled away.

Taking her hands away from her face, trying to stay calm, Addie looked at Ian. "Why? Why do you not want to go to France? You'd have a wonderful time."

"You'd like that, wouldn't you. They keep me, and you keep the money!" Ian jumped to his feet and ran out of the room, slamming the door behind him.

"I don't blame him." Roy stood crestfallen, near to tears. "We've made a terrible mistake. The poor lad."

Addie took the copy of the contract from her handbag.

"We never meant him to stay with the Robinsons. He's got to understand that." She went to the door and called. "Ian! You've got it wrong! Mr. Robinson has made a big mistake. Of course we're not giving you to the Robinsons. How could you think such a thing? It's just not true. Christopher has the whole thing all wrong. Come back here immediately." She called in a kind voice but there was no mistaking the command, the tone familiar to Ian.

She returned to the table.

"Addie, what are you up to? We have to give that money back!" Roy whispered fiercely, his eyes on the door. "Go after him."

"Ian!" Addie called, not moving from the table and putting out a hand to stop Roy when he moved to stand up.

"Wait!" she hissed.

They waited, sitting silently.

The door slowly opened, and Ian came in and stood looking at them, no longer crying, arms folded, his expression defiant.

"Sit down." Addie pushed out a chair.

He didn't move.

"Please, sit down and I'll explain." Addie, her voice gentle and inviting, stood and put her arm around his shoulders.

Reluctantly, he sat down.

"We're sorry." Roy anxiously tried to catch his eye, but Ian wasn't prepared to look at him.

"We're not sorry. We have nothing to apologise for." Addie pushed the contract across the table, her finger pointing at a section. "Read that, just there. See for yourself. 'If Ian doesn't want to stay, he returns home after the summer,'" she read out aloud. "We know you're not going to stay with them, and of course we wouldn't want you to. We would be horrified at the thought of it."

Ian read it a second time.

"And we keep the money when I come home?" He looked up, relief beginning to show on his face.

"That's the arrangement. I'm afraid Gordon Robinson is not a very good judge of loving families." Addie hugged him again.

"Don't kiss me!" He laughed in relief.

"So! I can go to France in an aeroplane? They have a villa, a swimming pool and a speed boat, and the sun shines all the time. It doesn't rain, and it's lovely and warm. When am I going? I can't wait!"

"The day after tomorrow," said Addie. "You can stay as long as you want to. Now, off to bed and dreams of France."

Roy was leaning back in the chair, beaming in wonderment and relief.

"Good night, son."

After Ian had departed to his bed, Addie produced glasses and the wine bottle.

"Maybe a whiskey for me," said Roy. "I think we deserve it. That was a close one with Ian, but he seems happy enough though. The day after tomorrow...that's a bit soon, isn't it?"

"Why not?" Addie shrugged. "They'll call and collect him on Thursday. Sure, the lad's looking forward to it."

"What happens next? I suppose I get in touch with this Peter Hackett." Roy sighed and rubbed his eyes. "Sales rep, salary and commission, nice job. I hope I'm up to it. Maybe it's a bit risky leaving the gas company."

"Roy! Are you joking?" Addie looked incredulous. "You are going to be the best rep Robinson's Decorating have ever had. I know you—you're brilliant with people—and Gordon Robinson himself is offering you the job. Driving around in a big Rover car, clothes allowance, wearing lovely suits. It's the job you've dreamed of."

Chapter 29

THE NEXT TWO DAYS PASSED quickly with so much to do. James and Debbie took the news in their stride. All that concerned Debbie was the fact she would now have a room to herself without curtains surrounding the bed.

"Only until September!" Addie stressed. "He's coming home in September."

A suitcase, new underwear, two short-sleeved shirts, new sandals...Laura Anne had insisted they should not buy too much in Dublin—"The shops on the French Riviera are far more suitable for summer wear."

Addie reluctantly agreed.

Ian was very proud of his suitcase and passport. Dressed in his new clothes, he sat in the porch looking down the path to the open garden gate in the gap of the high laurel hedge, waiting for the appearance of the big Mercedes. The Robinsons would be arriving to collect him at seven thirty.

"It's only half past six," Addie called. "Come and have your tea, your dad is home."

"It's thirty-five minutes past six," Ian corrected, looking at his watch. "I'm not hungry."

"Come and sit at the table. You won't be having tea with us for two months. It's two rashers, sausages, an egg, white pudding and chips!"

Ian, with a last glance down the path, hurried along the hall to the dining room. Even the imminent arrival of the Robinsons and a trip to France could not outshine the proposition of such a feast.

"And chocolate éclairs for afters," Debbie said, pulling out a chair for him to sit down. "This is how we eat in the Jeffries house, like real poshies."

Teenager Debbie, in compensation for her little brother's French trip, had paid a visit to the local music shop, and her new pride and joy, a Philips record player had been playing Bill Haley and Mario Lanza at a high volume almost continuously for the day. A trip to Dublin's clothes stores was promised for the following Friday.

She beamed across the table and wagged her finger. "You'll probably fall in love with a French girl, Ian. They are very chic and *like ze sexy Irish boys*," she teased.

"Debbie! behave yourself!" Roy admonished with a laugh.

Ian smiled. "Maybe I will." He produced a comb from his back pocket and ran it through his hair, Marlon Brando, *On the Waterfront*.

Later, Addie and Debbie were in the kitchen washing the dishes when the bell rang.

"It's them!" Ian ran up the hall to open the front door. Roy, reading the newspaper in front of the fire, just had time to put on his shoes before Ian led the visitors down the hall and into the living room.

"Mr. Robinson, Mrs. Robinson, come in, come in, sit yourselves down." Roy put away his newspaper. Debbie, couldn't take her eyes from Laura Anne, who greeted them, surprisingly, with a kiss on both cheeks. Addie, having hurriedly dried her hands on a tea towel, came in from the kitchen.

"Let me take your coats."

"No, no, thank you, we won't be staying." Gordon stood in the middle of the room, the centre of attention, taking in his surroundings. "I really wanted to meet Ian's brother and sister. Hello, James...Debbie."

Dutifully, they stepped forward to shake hands.

Beaming, Gordon turned to Roy. "What a fine-looking family. You must be very proud." He cleared his throat and looked at Laura Anne and then at Addie. "I hope you don't mind, I have small presents for James and Debbie."

Addie raised her hand in silent protest as Gordon produced two neatly wrapped boxes and passed them to the smiling teenagers.

"Really, you shouldn't...there's no need, thank you." Roy smiled. "Are you sure you won't stay for a drink?"

"No, thanks, we really must rush. You're very kind. Perhaps a quick word about your employment at Robinson's?" Looking at Roy, the smaller man drew himself up to his best height.

"Children, we'll leave the men to have a chat. Take Christopher out to the kitchen." Addie ushered them out the door into the hall but came back into the room when she realised that Laura Anne wasn't following.

"That's fine, Addie, no need to disappear. Laura Anne is my business partner. What I know she knows—best way to have it, don't you think? I'm sure things are the same between you two. Now..." Gordon continued briskly. "I'm sure you need to give your current employer at least two weeks' notice. As far as I am concerned, the job is yours. I have personally instructed Peter Hackett, our Ireland sales manager, and he will be expecting a call from you." He took an envelope from his pocket. "Here are the terms of employment. Please read them. I am sure you will find them favourable. You come highly recommended. I have made my enquiries, and I am sure you will be a valuable asset to Robinson's Decorating Products. All you have to do is say 'yes.'"

"Yes! Thank you, Mr. Robinson"

"Gordon!"

They shook hands.

"Now, we really must be off."

All smiles and small chat, they made their way to the front door and down the garden path, Christopher and Ian leading the way, laughing, heads together, sharing the excitement.

"Ian, come back here and say goodbye properly!"

About to climb into the back seat of the big car, the two boys stopped. Ian dutifully returned, presenting his face for the lipstick kiss.

"Don't worry, Ma. I'll be back home in time for school in September," he whispered.

"I know. Don't forget to send a post card from France." Addie grabbed Christopher. "And one for you too!"

Christopher, to his surprise, received the same treatment.

Roy hugged his son. "Be good and behave yourself, see you in September."

They stood on the step and watched the big car drive away. The two boys in the back seat.

"Well, that's that." Addie linked her husband's arm. Roy wiped his eyes and blew his nose into a big white handkerchief.

Ian stuck his head out the window as the car gathered speed, waved and shouted something.

"What did he say?" Roy looked at Addie. "I couldn't hear, I was blowing my nose."

"See you in September," Addie said. "He said see you in September."

"That's what I thought he said." Roy smiled weakly.

They turned and made their way to the house.

"I'm not that keen on that Gordon fella. He's a bit too complimentary about everything, and he didn't need to give them presents." Roy closed the front door.

"You don't have to like him. Sure, you'll probably never see him again." Addie shrugged.

"A gold watch!" James, in the hall, held up his wrist. "Eighteen jewels!"

"And mine's a locket watch on a gold chain, with my name engraved on the back and the date," said Debbie.

"Very nice." Roy left them standing in the hall, oohing and ahhing, and headed for his chair in front of the fire. He sat down, leaning back, and closed his eyes.

"Well, I hope all this doesn't end in tears," he said to no one in particular.

Chapter 30

THE GAS COMPANY VAN PULLED into the car park of Robinson's Decorating Products. It was a week since Ian's departure, a week full of activity. Roy had contacted Peter Hackett and after a friendly exchange had agreed to come to their offices the following Monday.

Roy had handed in his notice to Roger Blackwell, who seemed not to be surprised, assuring Roy he wished him well and then confiding that Gordon Robinson had spoken to him personally requesting a reference and informing him of the job offer.

"We'll be sorry to see you go, Roy, but between you and me, I advise you to take the job. I have no doubt that it will suit you and your abilities." The chairman's words heartened Roy, boosting his confidence.

Taking the wide steps two at a time, Roy glanced curiously left and right, taking in the spectacular aspect of his new employer's premises, and pushed open the high glass door. Polished granite floor filled the area, reflecting the lights set high up in the ceiling.

"Hello, Roy, you're expected." The smart-looking girl with a bright friendly smile extended a hand.

"I'm Jackie," she greeted from behind the long, low-slung, dark-wood desk.

"I think I've got the right place," Roy joked, taking in the company logo in big silver three-dimensional lettering on the wall behind her head.

She laughed as she indicated some seating alongside a large, glass-fronted product display cabinet. "Take a seat."

She glanced at the switchboard on the desk. "Peter, Roy Jeffries is in reception." She spoke softly into the receiver, then looked across the reception to where Roy was examining the product display. "Bill Sweeney has been assigned to show you the ropes. He'll be down in a minute."

"I didn't know Robinson's made so much stuff. What's that?" he asked, peering through the glass.

"It's a paint roller, Roy. You're looking at the future."

Roy turned. The aspect of the man striding across the reception area did not match up with the deep melodious voice. Bill Sweeney, senior rep, a portly five feet four inches, perfect suit in pinstriped charcoal grey, white shirt cuffs, older than Roy by a couple of years. Danny DeVito. With a big smile and hand outstretched, he was the epitome of a salesman from his shiny loafers to the top of his equally shiny bald head.

They shook hands.

"Friends in high places." Bill leaned close, prolonging the handshake. "Orders directly from head office, apparently. They don't come higher than Gordon Robinson. I am to show you the ropes. Peter Hackett, our sales manager, wants to see you and then I'll give you the grand tour."

They left the reception area and headed along a carpeted corridor. Pale wood-panelling interspersed with inset glass fronted showcases reached to the ceiling on each side. Roy could hear the buzz of conversation punctuated with the sounds of typewriters, male and female voices. The air of busy activity appealed to him as he strode beside Bill Sweeney.

"A bit different from the gas company, very modern..."

They stopped at a door bearing a plate: 'Peter Hackett Sales Manager' in neat letters.

Bill knocked and pushed the door open. "I'll see you when you're finished. I'll be in the reps' office." He left Roy to his meeting with Peter Hackett, who greeted him with a smile and a welcoming handshake.

"Glad to have you aboard. Welcome to Robinson's, take a seat," he said, indicating a low coffee table with four cushioned chairs. "Would you like a coffee or tea?"

Roy, used to the Beaky style of management, was slightly taken aback. "Tea would be fine, thank you, Mr. Hackett." He sat in one of the comfortable chairs.

"Peter, please, Roy. We're a team here, no need for surnames."

A woman appeared through a door to one side and Roy was introduced as the new representative.

"Tea, please, June, and maybe some chocolate biscuits?"

Having clambered to his feet, Roy sat down again as the girl, with a polite smile, nodded in his direction, said, "Yes, Mr. Hackett," and departed through the door to the secretary's office.

Peter Hackett sat down opposite to Roy. "Cigarette or a cigar?" He nudged the open cedarwood box and onyx lighter across the coffee table.

There followed an induction to the Robinson Philosophy. Roy listened with increasing amazement to a world he hardly knew existed. "The Robinson Irish dimension does not manufacture. It sells and distributes products throughout the country, divided into the three provinces—Munster, Leinster and Connaught—which are subdivided into districts. You'll initially be assigned to the Dublin district with Tom Delaney."

The tea was delivered, and the secretary withdrew discreetly. Explanations relating to remuneration followed; the basic salary was half again as much as Roy was earning with the gas company, plus commission.

"The more you sell the more you earn. There are targets which, if exceeded, would result in bonuses, trips to the sun, electrical equipment, many opportunities to make even more money, a pension scheme, three weeks holiday and a car supplied with petrol and travelling expenses plus a clothes allowance."

Peter Hackett leaned back and blew a smoke ring at the ceiling.

"So, Roy. You see, our representatives are our strongest resource. This is purely a sales and distribution driven organisation. You will be one of the most important people in the company. Should you prove to have the potential chairman Gordon Robinson sees in you, you will make a great deal of money. Have you any questions?"

Roy, quite staggered at the information and still trying to equate his new position with that of riding a bike around the streets collecting pennies and shillings in a bag in all weathers, managed to conceal his elation.

"Just one question, Peter. When do I start?"

"Friday. Hook up with Bill Sweeney at ten o'clock, production meeting at two thirty, and you can meet the team. Monday morning, you start on the road. You'll have the weekend to swot up on the products you'll be selling."

They exchanged pleasantries for a while, discovering some common interests—teenaged kids, school sports.

Ten minutes later, Roy had joined Bill Sweeney for a tour of the building and an introduction to Robinson's product range and the list of potential new business opportunities in the Dublin area, with an appointment list.

He was rather surprised when requested to leave the keys to the gas company van in reception.

"An arrangement has been made for it to be collected. These are the keys to your company car. It's in bay six in the car park." Bill Sweeney laughed at Roy's look of surprise. "You're an employee of Robinsons now." He handed Roy a card. "Present this at that store in Grafton Street between now and Friday and pick up a suit—I'm afraid it will have to be ready-made until you have time to be fitted. Now, let's start with the product room."

Eventually, after a thorough exposure to all the various decorating products from tile grout to the latest innovation, the paint roller, and everything in between, plus a tour of street maps and hardware shops in the Dublin area, they left the building and headed for the car park.

The streetlights were coming on, and the evening rush would be beginning shortly.

"It's a Rover, not new," Bill explained, "but a great car. Last year's model, 20,000 miles on the clock. See you Friday." About to leave, he turned with a smile. "I'm glad we're working together." He pointed at the bulging briefcase—product catalogue, brochures, all the information needed for the job—in Roy's hand.

"Get swotting up on that lot in the meanwhile. It's your bread and butter." With that, Bill walked away towards his own car, leaving Roy to drive home and tell Addie everything.

Chapter 31

I T HAD BEEN A WHIRLWIND of events for the young Irish boy, first to London and the Robinson home in Kensington.

The trip on the Princess Maud from Dunlaoghaire to Holyhead had been exciting, every wave lifting the steamboat and pitching into the next trough. The Irish Sea grey and forbidding, the two boys had stood above deck, gripping the rail and playing a game of survival in a storm, red-faced with the wind.

Laura Anne had watched from the safety of the cabin doorway, pleased at Christopher's unusually boisterous behaviour. On the previous trip, he had remained below decks claiming seasickness. *Gordon would be pleased and approving of Ian's influence*, she couldn't help thinking. *Well, he will be seeing enough of them for the next two months.* Business keeping him in Dublin, he had vowed to join them as soon as possible.

Laura Anne had been slightly taken aback when they had to wait for the cattle below decks to disembark first. Three different boats operated the Holyhead crossing, and she was unaware that one of them also carried livestock. The three travellers had stood at the rail and looked down at the milling cattle, Laura Anne with a handkerchief to her face.

"What a pong!" Christopher had held his nose. The smell had still lingered in the air as they'd left the boat and made their way to the taxi rank and the station for the train to London.

For Ian, everything was a new experience—"It's the express!"—countryside flying by, sudden blackness as they entered a tunnel to explode into bright daylight at the other end, then houses and streets and a darker sky on arrival into Paddington Station.

242

Always, there was someone waiting in attendance to load their luggage onto a trolley and guide them through the throng of people. Everyone seemed in a hurry.

It was evening time when they had arrived: the evening rush in London.

"The buses are red! The policemen have high helmets! The voices sound strange."

Ian followed as they hurried to yet another taxi, two attendants helping with the luggage, their backs bent against the heavy cases and bags, one a man, the other a youth not much older than Ian.

Ian reached out a hand to help as the younger man handled the heavy trolley up some steps.

"It's all right, sir." The young lad, puffing from his exertions, stopped Ian's helping hand.

Puzzled, Ian took his hand away. "Why can't I help?" he asked.

"You're rich, sir," said the lad. "It's my job, but you can give me a good tip if you like."

Ian stepped away, unsure of his feelings and not knowing what 'a tip' meant.

Christopher handed the lad a sixpence. "There's your tip. Do a good job."

"Thank you, sir." The lad took the sixpence.

The taxi was black with seats facing each other.

"That's where the queen lives, it's a palace." They asked the taxi man to stop so Ian could see the soldiers in red marching up and down and standing in sentry boxes.

"They're like my toy soldiers! Look at their big, high hats!"

"Busbies," said Christopher. "They're called busbies."

The lights of Piccadilly Circus left Ian amazed. They drove along Shaftsbury Avenue where big posters advertised the shows outside the glittering theatre entrances.

"*Hopalong Cassidy*!" Ian twisted in his seat and craned his neck. "Hopalong Cassidy with his horse Trigger. Wow!"

"Maybe we'll book for the show." Laura Anne smiled. " Would you like to see *Hopalong Cassidy*?"

"Yes, please!"

At about eight o'clock, they arrived in a street lined with big houses with steps and railings. A man came down the steps to help with the cases. He wore white gloves and a dark suit. A girl greeted them from the top of the steps.

"This is Ian, my friend," Christopher introduced.

"Master Ian." The man shook hands, and the girl, smiling, bobbed up and down.

"They look after us and the house," Laura Anne explained.

Again, Ian attempted to help with the cases but was not allowed, this time by the taxi man. He quickly followed Laura Anne and Christopher into the big house.

For two weeks, they stayed at the Kensington residence. Ian often thought of the Gimlet and his friends in Ireland wondering why he could not be friends with the people who worked in the house.

"You may treat the staff in a friendly manner if you wish," Laura Anne told him, "but do not become familiar. They understand their place and are not your equal."

"But I like them, and they're grown-ups. My ma always says I am to respect my elders." Ian stood his ground.

Laura Anne frowned. "This is London, and things are different here."

"But the girl is Irish and nobody told me her name," Ian argued defiantly, and Laura Anne, experiencing a side to the young man she had not seen before and unaccustomed to such logic from one so young, was not sure how to reply.

"That's just the way it is in this house," she said more sharply than she had intended.

They did get to see *Hopalong Cassidy* in Shaftsbury Avenue and had hamburgers and chips at Wimpy and visited Carnaby Street, but the highlight was Hamley's toy store in Regent Street. Gordon arrived but only stayed briefly, his intention being to join them in France after two weeks.

Finally, it was time to head for the Mediterranean, and now Ian was more used to his position in the Robinson household, he took everything in his stride.

Their destination: the Carlton Hotel, perhaps the most exclusive hotel of all on the fabulous Riviera coastline.

Chapter 32

B LUE, BLUE, SKY, NOT A cloud to be seen. Blue, blue sea changing to a translucent green and gold rippling over almost white sand: Europe's most famous beach front, Cannes, the French Riviera; the Croisette boulevard lined with the most exclusive shops—Cartier, Vogue, Yves Saint Laurent— and hotels, each with its own beach front and boardwalk pier where the occupants of the many tenders and Mediterranean cruise ships would alight, and white-clad attendants escorted the Rich and the Famous across the Croisette to their hotel receptions...

***

A blue speedboat appeared from beyond the headland travelling fast, curving, a white wake streaming behind. At the controls, Gordon Robinson expertly manoeuvred between the slow-moving tenders, heading for the Carlton and the beginning of his annual two weeks' break.

The three figures waved from the pier as he approached, cutting back on the power of the twin engines. He had travelled the distance from the small harbour at Cannes la Bocca in a matter of minutes.

The project in Ireland now completed, the two weeks' break would be a welcome relief, giving him time to check out Laura Anne's plan and have a look at this Ian fellow. In general, Gordon approved. Christopher seemed to be responding well in the relationship; it seemed that the experiment had its benefits.

Prising the young lad away had been the plan: isolate him from the family and work on his natural instincts. The father was an added bonus; all reports indicated he was doing extremely well, his figures exceptional in the first month of sales. The mother was ambitious, strong-minded; her weakness was her aspiration for better things. Gordon smiled to himself at the prospect of manipulating these people, especially the woman, perhaps conquerable in time, the man a different matter, principled and confident in himself. Gordon saw no weakness there.

As he neared to the three waving figures, it came to him in a flash. *Of course! The wife! She is Roy's Achilles' heel.* He cut the engines and coasted in.

"Hello, Ian. Welcome to the joys of the Riviera."

"Hello, Mr. Robinson."

In a matter of minutes, the luggage was on board and they were on their way, speeding across the blue Med, heading for Cannes La Bocca and the short drive to their summer home.

"Would you like to take the wheel?" Gordon and Ian stood side by side at the controls, Laura Anne and Christopher lying back on the comfortable seats at the stern.

"Yes, please!"

"Gordon..." Laura Anne warned.

"The lad's fine. Not a sail in sight. Here, Ian, just keep her full ahead. Aim for that point." He indicated a sun-soaked headland in the distance. "That's the throttle. Put your hand there to control your speed." He turned to a locker, lifting the lid. "Cold drinks?" He looked back to Ian and then at the disapproving Laura Anne. "He's doing fine."

Ian experimented with the throttle, and the fast boat bounced into a wave, sending a spray of salt water in the air.

Christopher jumped up to join him. Laura Anne put up a hand in protest but held back at a glance from Gordon.

Ian moved to one side. "Do you want a go?" Christopher looked uncertain. "Here, I'll slow it down a bit." Ian eased off on the throttle and Christopher took the wheel.

"Look at me! I'm driving Dad's speedboat!"

"Be careful," Laura Anne called, but she was not alarmed. It was what she'd wanted, and she was happy to see Christopher at the wheel.

They were nearing the small harbour with more craft about, so Gordon took back the controls.

"Well done, lads! We'll take her out tomorrow and do some fishing."

The marina at Cannes la Bocca boasted some fine yachts and many berths for the owners of the surrounding residences. The Robinsons' approach had been sighted by the attendants, and the baggage was soon stowed in the boot of the car. Gordon took his position behind the wheel.

The open car surged up the cliff road bordered by bougainvillea and the gateways to fine villas on its short drive to the gates of Falcon Dip: the Robinsons' summer home.

"Here we are." Christopher pointed. "Are the Poulsons here?"

"They arrived last week," Laura Anne said. "They're staying with us for a while."

Falcon Dip, an expansive estate, boasted a long, straight driveway flanked by plane trees. Ahead through the windscreen, Ian spotted the arched doorway of one of the oldest residences in the district. They drove between the high sandstone gate pillars, passing a gatehouse as large as Ivy Lodge.

"Look at the bullet holes in the wall! The Germans did that during the war." Christopher pointed, and Ian craned his neck to see.

"Wow!"

Ahead, Ian caught his first glimpse of the two-storeyed villa with high green-shuttered windows and an ornate balcony running its full width. Two people waved from the steps in front of the vast studded double doors.

The area around Cannes boasted several of these country villas, a reminder of pre-war France and all its attractions—the proximity of Monte Carlo casinos and Cannes movie industry, the playground of stars of the Silver Screen during the thirties and forties.

After the Second World War and the German occupation, Falcon Dip had been left vacant, its American owners disenchanted with France, preferring to spend their leisure time in the warmth and security of Florida. During the war, a German detachment under a notorious commander had occupied the villa, using it as a base, and the beautiful property had fallen into disrepair.

Gordon Robinson, always a man to make the best of a financial opportunity, had bought the property at a very competitive price. A great deal of restoration work was done and the beautiful house had become a showpiece for Robinsons Decorating Products, to attract and indulge international customers and favoured clients. Many now vied for a privileged stay at the Robinsons' villa.

Gordon reserved two months of the year for himself and the family. Irene and Georges lived permanently at the gatehouse, cooking and serving meals for those staying at the villa.

"Bonjour, Madam et Monsieur. Bonjour, Christopher." They smiled a greeting. Laura Anne and Christopher received air kisses; Gordon stood to one side smiling and nodding.

Irene reminded Ian of Iris Blackwell, big and smiling but browner and less wobbly. He was introduced as Christopher's friend and received his two kisses.

"Come and see the pool!" Christopher rushed up the stairs and pushed open the big heavy double doors. Ian followed into a tiled porch and across a large area through a doorway to one side of a wide stairway, along a short corridor to an expansive kitchen and living area, out onto some more steps to emerge from the back of the house. He stopped, dazzled by the bright sun.

Christopher ran across a wide patio to some more steps leading to another level with little paths and rose beds. More steps led to a pool, sparkling in the sunlight. Beyond and far below were the terracotta roofs and white buildings of Cannes with the Mediterranean shimmering shades of blue to the distant horizon.

Switching his gaze and shielding his eyes, Ian watched Christopher join some people at the pool. He quickly followed down the steps. There was a woman reclining on a sunbed; two figures splashed in the pool.

"This is Ian, my friend," Christopher said.

"Hello, Ian." The woman's voice sounded strange, foreign like Ingrid Bergman, and her eyes very blue, though her hair was blonde. She smiled and raised a casual hand, surprised when Ian stepped forward to shake hands.

"Pleased to meet you," he said politely.

"Oh!" She sat up and took Ian's hand. "I'm Ingrid Poulson, and I am also pleased to meet you."

Getting to her feet, she beckoned the two girls in the pool. "Come and meet Ian."

The two girls laughed and shouted, "Hello! Hello!" They both had blonde hair like Ingrid, one about Ian's age, the other a bit older. The water glistened on the girls' tanned bodies, their teeth white and smiling in faces shining with fun and friendliness. Ian had never seen girls more beautiful. *Hayley Mills in the movie Pollyanna.*

"Come in for a swim!" they called.

With a shock, Ian realised that the girls were naked. He could not believe his eyes. To his horror, Christopher had stripped to his underpants and dropped them to the ground. Ian looked down at his feet, aghast at the thought that they would expect him to take all his clothes off.

Christopher kicked his underpants to one side. "C'mon, Ian." He ran and jumped into the pool, surfacing a moment later, laughing and smiling.

Ian, frozen to the spot, looked back to the woman.

"It's all right, Ian. The men usually keep their swimming trunks on," she encouraged.

With a mumbled apology, Ian turned and headed back towards the house, moving quickly, his mind a whirl of confusion. *Why had they no clothes on? People always wear clothes!*

At the door, he met Laura Anne, who took in the situation in an instant.

"Christopher! Come in now!" she shouted. "And put on your bathing trunks."

"I want to go home!" Ian brushed past her. She put out a hand to stop him. He half turned, repeating angrily, "I want to go home."

"It's all right, Ian. We just caught them by surprise." She spoke comfortingly and slowly, explaining, "They're our house guests, Freija and Sarah. That's their mother. They're here for the next two weeks." She put a consoling hand on his arm. "When we are together, they always keep their clothes on. They're naturists. Nils Poulson, their father, is important to Gordon's business. He has a large wholesale company in Denmark."

She crouched and bent to look up into his eyes. "All right?"

He nodded.

"You, poor boy, you must have got a big surprise."

Ian, glad that he didn't have to take all his clothes off, smiled ruefully.

Laura Anne smiled and said, "They're very beautiful, aren't they?"

"I suppose so...yes," he said in a steady voice. "Very beautiful."

"I take it you don't want to go home."

"No."

"Come and I'll show you your room." She put an arm around his shoulders and guided him through the door.

Christopher followed them in his underpants, his hair and body dripping wet.

"Behave yourself and stop showing off. And stop dripping all over the floor. Go and dry yourself!"

All the bedrooms on the second floor had double glass-panelled doors from floor to ceiling, opening out onto a wide, wrought-iron-railed balcony running the length of the house. Each room had an adjoining bathroom, some with connecting doors.

"This is your room." Laura Anne opened the tall doors to the balcony, allowing the warm breeze to disturb the net curtains. They swayed gently; floor-to-ceiling presses lined the wall facing the window.

"Plenty of room for your clothes, and there's an adjoining door to Christopher's room. This is your bathroom. Come and see the view from the balcony."

They went through the flimsy curtains and looked out over the terraced garden with the pool and the roofs of Cannes to the sea.

She put her arm around his shoulders, and they stood watching Freija and Sarah make their way from the pool towards the house.

"I hope you'll be happy here. If you feel unsure or uncomfortable about anything, talk to me."

Christopher came out onto the balcony and joined them. "It's great, isn't it?"

Laura Anne put her other arm around his shoulders. "It's my most favourite place...outside London," she corrected. "Now, have fun." She stepped back into the room. "Oh, and Christopher, you must knock on Ian's door and respect his privacy. We'll eat at seven thirty—a barbecue at the pool. Some friends are coming over to mark the beginning of our holiday." She left the two boys on their own.

"Watch this, follow me!" Christopher ran along the balcony; Ian followed. "That's my parents' room. That's the Poulsons', that's the girls' room." All the rooms had the same tall doors.

Christopher stopped at a small shelf on the rail. "Watch this!" He flicked a switch, and water shot high into the air from an ornate fountain in the centre of the pool. He flicked the switch again, and the water stopped in a cascade leaving ripples on the surface.

"Wow! Can I have a go?" Ian flicked the switch.

"It's great fun in the pool when the fountain's on, we'll do it tomorrow." Christopher turned the fountain off again.

On the way back along the balcony, they passed the girls' room. The doors were closed, but they could hear voices. Christopher stopped and knocked on the glass.

"I'm going to unpack my clothes." Ian kept moving. At his door, he looked back. Christopher was talking to one of the girls. She smiled and waved.

Christopher beckoned. Ian smiled and shook his head before stepping through the doorway into his room. He sat on the bed, wishing he had gone back and unable to understand why he hadn't.

"Come on!" Christopher was at the door. "They want to talk to you."

Ian looked at his watch and began to unpack his clothes. "Tell them I'll see them at the barbecue." He opened one of the presses.

Christopher sighed and sat on the bed. "I don't get it. They're just girls." He looked up at Ian, puzzled, genuinely surprised that the usually confident Ian seemed so unsure.

"They were naked, you could see everything," Ian said, a bit red in the face. "It's not right."

Christopher smiled knowingly. "There's nothing wrong with it. It's natural," he said knowingly. "They're naturists."

"I see...naturists," Ian repeated.

"You don't know what they are, do you?"

"No," Ian admitted.

"It's like a religion." Christopher nodded sagely. "They don't believe in God, but they believe in Adam and Eve, before they ate the apple. So they don't wear any clothes." He nodded again, looking very serious. "They have nudist camps where everyone is naked, and nudist beaches. But they wear clothes when they're with people who don't belong to the religion."

"Oh!" said Ian. He looked at Christopher and made a funny face. "I think I'll change my religion," he said, and they both laughed. "Naturists!"

Christopher pulled off his underpants and ran around the room "I'm a naturist."

Ian laughed.

Christopher waved his underpants over his head. "Join the naturist religion!"

Ian stripped to his underpants and jumped onto the bed. "I'm a naturist!" he shouted, laughing.

"No, you're not!" Christopher jumped on the bed pointing. "You're wearing underpants. Naturists don't wear underpants. You're *afraid* to be a naturist."

"No, I'm not!" Ian pulled off his pants and jumped up and down.

A defiant look on his face, Christopher stopped jumping. "You've got loads of hair." He pointed.

Ian sat down on the bed, casually drawing a towel across his lap. "You have as well, only it's blonde and not so noticeable."

From where he was sitting facing the window, Ian detected a movement on the balcony. One of the girls was outside watching. Christopher, unaware, stood up to demonstrate.

"Look, I'm circumcised. Why aren't you?"

For some reason, Ian's shyness had diminished. Not knowing what the word circumcised meant, he just smiled knowingly. Impulsively, he stood up, facing the window, allowing the towel to fall away. "I'd better get on with my unpacking."

He checked the window as he turned to the suitcase, but the girl was gone. *I wonder which one it was,* he speculated, disappointed to see no further movement from outside.

Selecting a pair of shorts and a shirt, he began to dress.

"You have an erection!" Christopher pointed triumphantly.

"No, I haven't!" Ian denied, quickly sitting down again.

"I saw it!" Christopher said. Unaware that the reason for Ian's arousal had been standing the other side of the curtain behind him, he asked, "Are you a queer?"

"There's nothing queer about me!" Ian retorted indignantly.

"It's all right if you are." Christopher smiled. "I like girls and I like boys too."

"So do I," said Ian. "What's queer about that?" He looked puzzled.

"Nothing, I suppose." Christopher stood up and headed for the door of their adjoining room. "We always wear long trousers for dinner," he said. "I'm going to get dressed. I'll see you later."

"Thanks," said Ian with a smile. "Close the door after you. See you later."

When Christopher had gone, Ian lay on the bed. He had an hour to spare before the barbecue. He wondered which girl had been watching, Freija or Sarah, their image and how they were in the pool strong in his mind. He had never seen naked girls before and the memory was far from displeasing. And his friend Christopher...*what was that word?* He couldn't remember. The breeze blew the curtains. Warm air invaded the room, and Ian felt content and in control, far from home and the cold rain.

***

"Ian!"

He jumped from the bed, looking at his watch. *Eight o'clock! I must have fallen asleep.*

Laura Anne was below the balcony, calling.

"People are arriving. Aren't you going to join us?"

"Sorry, I fell asleep. I'll be there in a minute."

The case was open. He found a pair of long trousers, black and flared at the bottom, very nice. Four shirts hung in the tall press, ironed and waiting. They felt new and perfect to his touch. He selected a white short-sleeved one with a paisley collar and a paisley strip on the pocket. There were two pairs of shoes, casual suede slip-ons and a shiny black pair, and ankle boots with high Cuban heels. The shirt fitted perfectly. *What a contrast to darned socks and James's hand-me-downs.*

Sitting on the side of the bed, he tried on the black Cuban-heeled ankle boots with zip and buckle on the side. They were a bit difficult to fit, but once his feet were inside they felt perfect. He stood up in front of the tall mirror, legs apart, studying his reflection. Black hair slightly curled, he brushed it into shape at the sides, a duck arse at the back, Tony Curtis style. He was tall for his age, and the boots added even more height. He turned up the collar and checked himself out, standing sideways. Then he spotted the jackets, three of them on hangers concealed by a second door on the big wide press. He pulled back the door, revealing more clothes and what looked like a dark suit—even ties.

He selected the jacket that reminded him most of James Dean—light blue with narrow labels—and slipped it on. *Perfect.* The mirror told him he was ready to face the world. Feeling a million dollars, he headed out the door and down the stairs, moving quickly, shoulders swaying, the shiny boots clicking on the wood stairs, Fred Astaire nimble and stylish.

At the back door, he paused, but only for a moment. Through the glass, he could see lights and people at the pool on the lower level. It was nearly dark now. The fountain danced high and sparkled in the lights.

He descended the first set of steps, turned sideways, elbows slightly bent, dancing down to the next level.

Laura Anne came to meet him. "My, you are such a handsome boy!" She took his arm. "Come and meet these people."

"Thanks for the clothes. I love them. I never had clothes like these before."

"I'm glad they fitted you. You're dressed perfectly for a young man in the South of France."

Impulsively, he kissed her on the cheek, bending down to do so. "You're fantastic," he said.

Debbie Reynolds tightened her grip on his arm, and they made their way down the last few steps to join the party.

"Just a group of our friends," Laura Anne had said.

Even Christopher looked smart wearing a blazer with a badge on the pocket and grey trousers.

Ian cast an eye around for the two girls from the pool. He could not spot them, though there were quite a few blonde heads in the company. Then he saw Mrs. Poulson. She was in a small group at the barbecue, a blonde, tanned man beside her with two other women, blonde as well, all with drinks in their hands, chatting and laughing. Gordon Robinson beckoned Ian to join him.

Laura Anne, still attached to Ian's arm, made the introductions.

"Meet Ian Jeffries. His father is attached to our new Irish outlet in Dublin. Ian and Christopher are best friends."

Ian shook hands and received several lipstick kisses. Some of the people had French accents. One lady introduced her son, Lucas, a lad about three years older than Ian with a smiling face and a confident manner, who shook hands and leaned forward, close to Ian's ear and whispered in a French accent, "I believe you have the black pubic hair."

Ian recoiled in surprise, feeling his face beginning to redden, but Lucas's smile was friendly.

"You have an admirer. It is the girl from Denmark." He indicated with his glass, and Ian followed his eyes to the group at the barbecue. The two blonde ladies had turned and were looking at him. The girls from the pool, Sarah and Freija, had transformed, wearing long dresses and high heels, tanned brown, Sarah's hair almost as white as her dress. They looked like they had stepped from the movie *High Society*.

Lucas was amused by Ian's reaction. "Come and say hello. Freija is my girlfriend. She is the one who told me about your pubic hair." He laughed. "By the way, what age are you? You look much older than Christopher."

"I am," said Ian, who was only two months older, but he was not going to share the information with his new French friend.

Laura Anne stepped to one side. She had not overheard the whispered comment but was not necessarily dissatisfied with Lucas's obvious interest in Ian. In fact, she had been counting on it. Despite Ian's tender age, she felt he could cope, and she had not been wrong in her judgement. The Poulson girl would unwittingly play her part.

Christopher joined the two apparently older boys, his demeanour less childish than a few short months previous.

Laura Anne, pleased at the progress, took her husband's arm. "It's all going very well."

Gordon shrugged an *I told you so*.

Christopher lifted the lid of the large ice box with a swift glance in his mother's direction. She nodded imperceptibly. He retrieved three beers.

Lucas took one.

"I'd prefer wine." Ian had spotted Georges moving amongst the guests with a bottle of white. Christopher wasn't keen on the taste of beer, and he held the can in an unaccustomed, nonchalant hand.

The older of the two girls, smiling, stylish, confident, glass in hand, detached herself from the group beside the pool and strode across the grass. Lucas went to meet her. Ian hesitated, aware that the younger girl, Sarah, had stayed where she was. He watched Lucas and Freija share a brief kiss. His eyes moved to Sarah. She was still standing half turned away but not sharing in the conversation. As he watched, she looked straight at him and smiled. It was a shy smile, a smile that excited him in a way he had never experienced before, only at movies, especially those starring Tammy and Debbie Reynolds.

Ian studied her face with disbelief at his feelings. She turned away but then looked at him again over her shoulder, this time her expression uncertain. He realised that he was staring. Freija and Lucas laughed gently.

"I think it's love," they whispered loud enough to reach Ian's ears.

"Sarah!" they called. "Come over here."

The younger girl, now smiling broadly, joined them.

"We met this afternoon." Ian stepped forward to shake hands. She stepped close and kissed him on both cheeks. Her light scented perfume, the softness of her cheek and the closeness of her face surprised the love-struck Ian, who managed to retain his composure, concealing his confusion even when she remained close alongside him, her arm around his waist. Mustering all his resources, and remembering every movie he'd ever watched where the boy gets the girl, he casually put his arm around her shoulders and said with a laugh, "The luck of the Irish."

The comment was greeted with laughter from those in earshot, including Laura Anne, who had moved closer to observe how her protégé was doing. Once again, Ian was the centre of attention; the laughter was genuine and friendly and obviously appreciative. He looked around, smiling at everyone. Sarah squeezed his waist harder and laughed up into his face, and Ian felt happy to be with these people who treated him in such a grown-up fashion.

A bell sounded, and people's attention moved to three round, white-cloth-covered tables arranged on the lawn. Ian had been so preoccupied with the whole occasion that he hadn't noticed the tables or the small raised platform, where a group of musicians were playing music.

People moved to take their seats, Georges and Irene were at the barbecue making up large serving dishes and platters of seafood to be placed in the centre of each table. Champagne corks popped, and the mood was becoming more celebratory.

"Come and sit with us." Sarah transferred her arm from around Ian's waist and took his hand. Lucas and Freija were already at the table with the Poulsons. Ian saw that Christopher was heading to a table where the Robinsons were taking their seats along with several other couples. He reluctantly released her hand.

"I'm sitting with Chris," he said apologetically.

"Come and join us!" Laura Anne called to Sarah, who looked at her mother and, receiving a smile and a little backhand wave, took Ian's hand again.

They sat side by side at the table, Christopher on the other side of Ian. Sitting next to Sarah was a French woman whom Ian had met earlier. She smiled and, to Ian's amazement, offered him a cigarette. He assumed she was joking, but she nodded encouragingly. He looked around the table. Almost everyone was smoking.

"No, thank you," he declined. "I don't smoke."

"I do." Christopher reached out. The French woman looked across the table at Laura Anne, who hesitated, made a slight face, but then nodded.

Gordon was smoking a large cigar and chatting to the man next to him. He looked at Christopher but remained silent. To Ian's further surprise, Christopher produced a Zippo lighter from his pocket and reached across to light the French woman's cigarette for her, then lit his own cigarette with a flourish and inhaled deeply to exhale in the most professional manner. He sat down and blew a smoke ring in the air.

Ian watched on in admiration. He had once had a drag on an unattended cigarette when his mother had left the room, resulting in a fit of coughing and tears streaming from his eyes. It wasn't the first time, he had seen Christopher give his cigarette performance, but it was the first time in front of his parents—a fact evidenced by the expression of astonishment from across the table.

Another large platter was placed on the table alongside the first with red, angry-looking lobsters, black eyes shining in the light. Sarah reached out, along with most of the others, and took one and placed it on her plate. She expertly cracked the claws with the back of her knife and poked the white meat out with a fork-like instrument. The body meat was already exposed and ready to eat.

Smiling, Ian did the same. The meat tasted delicious. "White wine with fish," he said, seeing the familiar Chablis label on the wine across the table. The image of his ma and da, the kitchen table, James and Debbie, a special occasion, a bottle of wine, sprang into his mind and he was at home in Ivy Lodge.

"Ian." He tore his eyes from the label. Sarah was holding out a fork with succulent white lobster meat for him to take. A warm breeze moved her blonde hair, she smiled, red lips and blue eyes for him. The image of home fled from his mind.

"Monsieur." Georges poured Chablis into a glass.

"Merci," Ian said, and washed down the succulent morsel.

Chapter 33

EVERY DAY BROUGHT A NEW experience to the teenaged Irish boy who had never before experienced the heat of the Mediterranean sun, the refreshing temperature of a swimming pool and all the other delights experienced by the well-heeled in a warm climate.

Unaware of his natural friendliness and charm, he impressed all he met. He responded to the attention of girls with a naturalness that was very disarming—the handsome Irish boy with the big smile and the easy manner—especially with Sarah.

It was in the afternoon on a particularly hot day. Christopher, Sarah and Ian were lounging by the pool, making frequent visits to the water to cool down. Lucas and Freija sat in the shade.

Standing up, Sarah held out her hand to Ian. "I'm going for a siesta would you like to come?"

"Yes! What's a siesta?" Ian jumped to his feet. "Come on, Chris."

Christopher was about to get up but, at a meaningful look from Sarah, sat down again.

"What's a siesta?" Ian repeated as they made their way to the house.

"It's when the sun's very warm and you want to cool down. It's cool in the bedroom and you go to bed for a rest."

"Oh!" said Ian, not particularly interested in going to bed in the afternoon.

"Do you know the song 'Secret Love'? Doris Day sings it." She looked at him intently. "'Once I had a secret love'…" she began to sing quietly.

"Yes." He smiled at the invitation in her eyes. She turned and ran swiftly up the steps and into the house.

He hurried after her, through the doors and into the large lounge. He could hear her footsteps as she headed upstairs.

With a feeling of anticipation, he quickly followed, slowing down when he reached the long landing. Sunlight flooded through the open doorway of her room. "...'that live within the heart of me'..."

Pulse racing, Ian felt the beads of perspiration form on his forehead.

She must be in the room, it's like a Hollywood Movie. James Dean and Natalie Wood, Rebel without a Cause. We're alone in the house, everyone's outside. He was suddenly aware that he was only wearing his swimming trunks.

"'All too soon my secret love'..." her voice continued.

His mind raced. *What would James Dean say?*

The room was the same as his. Sarah was sitting up in the bed, her figure silhouetted against the bright sunlight from the high window.

"...'became impatient to be free'...Hello."

He could not make out the expression on her face, but her bikini lay on the polished floor.

"Hello," he repeated and stepped forward, closing the door behind him.

***

At the pool, Lucas and Freija looked after the departing figures. Sarah's tune drifting back to them, they exchanged a glance.

"I think our Irish boy is going to have a nice time." Lucas laughed.

Chapter 34

Laura Anne paraded her new charge proudly amongst the Elite of Cannes. At the Carlton Hotel, at the Marina, on the Croisette, Ian smiled and chatted his way through every situation with old and young alike.

Christopher, to Laura Anne's delight, spent his time with Ian, obviously; the best of friends, always together, tantrums and tears a thing of the past.

The Robinsons' cabin cruiser, Gordon's pride and joy with its new name 'DÉCOR 8' emblazoned on the hull, took many trips along the coast to San Tropez, Niece, Antibes and Monte Carlo, seeking out quiet beeches. The Poulsons, naturists and nature-seekers, discarded swimsuits when swimming in the warm sea, their casual indifference to nakedness influencing everybody else.

"If you can't beat them, join them." Gordon dropped his trunks and ran into the warm sea to splash about in wild abandon, much to almost everyone's amusement.

Christopher, at a warning glance from Laura Anne, kept his trunks on.

Ian, at first, was uneasy and quite uncomfortable, but he soon became accustomed to the idea. In fact, he found Gordon quite amusing. Freija and Sarah, however, were a different matter, his assumed indifference to their nakedness often belied by how his body reacted. To his relief, nobody seemed to notice.

Tall and athletic, skin tanned to a golden brown, his hair jet-black, Ian had taken to the sun. Mrs. Poulson would often hug him, delivering one of her lipstick kisses, and say,

"Where's the Irish Boy gone?" Her daughters would look on sympathetically and Ian would grin and bear it.

***

"Do your family miss you?" the Danish woman asked one day, at the pool. The question took Ian by surprise. With all the newfound experiences and the distance from home, he had not thought of the family for some time. Mrs. Poulson frowned quizzically. "They must miss a lovely boy like you." Her accent was no longer strange to his ear.

"I don't know," he said. "I suppose so."

"Here, send them a postcard. I have plenty of them." She took a card from the pile in front of her and fixed him with an earnest expression. "I like to sit here and write my cards and letters. It is important to keep in touch with family and friends back in Denmark."

Ian took the postcard. It had a picture of Cannes on it.

"You write on the back of it, here." A red varnished nail indicated. "You put the address here, and where you're staying, here, so your family can reply. I'm sure they'd love to hear from you. Do you have brothers or sisters?"

Ian told her about James and Debbie and then all about his beautiful mother being a famous model with her picture in all the Irish newspapers and on the sides of buses and posters, and how his dad was tall and, people said, good-looking, like the actor Van Heflin. In no time, he was chatting away, describing his family and the big old house with holes in the roof where the rain came in. He laughed as he related the incident of the chamber pot and told her about the neighbours and his friends at the pub who called him Curly.

Rhoda Poulson's interest increased as Ian, who had not thought of his family for some time, animatedly described his life.

"Holes in the roof and the rain coming in, porridge for breakfast, eating sugar sandwiches, labouring in the garden. Your poor father riding a bicycle all day in the rain and your poor, beautiful mother with no money. You must never have to worry about money again. It is the waste of a good life. The world is at the feet of a boy like you."

Ian had spoken about his family with amusement and pride, and was taken aback at her reaction. He scratched his head, puzzled and unsure of his feelings.

Laura Anne, arriving in time to hear the last part of the conversation, made herself comfortable on a recliner.

"The girls and Christopher are walking into the village, Sarah asked me to tell you," she said.

Ian propped himself up on his elbows and looked towards the house. Sarah in white shorts and a bikini top was beckoning from the steps. Her blonde hair danced in the sunlight. She was smiling as she called his name.

"Ian, come with me, we are going to the village." Her voice floated on the warm breeze, and all images of his family fled from his mind.

"Coming!" he called, jumping to his feet. "Excuse me, thanks for the postcard." He ran across the grass and took the steps two at a time. They disappeared into the house holding hands.

Rhoda Poulson sighed. "Oh, to be that age again. I think those two are in love." She shook her head and reached for her pen to continue with her postcard-writing.

Laura Anne lay back and closed her eyes. "Gordon was saying that he and Nils are going to San Tropez tomorrow on a business trip."

"Yes," Rhoda confirmed. "Forever the businessmen."

Laura Anne, as if the thought had just occurred to her, sat up. "Why don't we go with them? Do some shopping have some lunch, make a day of it."

Rhoda nodded. "Yes. I'll ask the girls would they like to come with us. I'm sure the boys wouldn't be interested."

"Oh, I think the boys should come as well. We can go to the sports shop, and Christopher was saying he'd like to go to the war museum. We can do the sights. Ian hasn't been to San Tropez." Laura Anne lay back and waited for Rhoda's reaction. It did not take long.

Rhoda, eyes closed, murmured, "Or...we could do what you said first. Just the two of us, do some shopping and have a nice lunch."

"Sounds nice."

"What about Ian?"

"We can do the sights another time."

"What about breakfast and lunch?"

"Georges and Irene can look after them."

***

The following morning, the sun as usual made its ascent into a blue cloudless sky as the Mercedes, with Norman at the wheel, surged out between the gate pillars of Falcon Dip. San Tropez was about one hour's drive away; they would arrive in time for the business meeting at eleven o'clock. The women on the wide back seat of the open car, good friends for many years, chatted with familiarity. The conversation eventually turned to the young Irish boy.

"He is so charming and polite, very well-behaved." Rhoda lit a cigarette as she spoke. "Not like so many of the young people today. It is unusual for a teenage boy to pay so much attention to older people. We had a conversation about his family. Are they very poor?"

Laura Anne considered how to answer.

"No, they have come into some money lately and want Ian to widen his experience of life. So, we offered to take him for the summer. He and Christopher are such good friends. Perhaps he will stay with us in London for a while."

"That's very unusual. I certainly wouldn't have one of my girls go to live with another family," Rhoda remarked.

"Oh, the Irish are quite casual about such matters. As long as Ian goes back to them for Christmas, everything is fine. I think your girls like him," Laura Anne deflected. "Especially Sarah."

"Well," Rhoda laughed, "I hope his old-fashioned good manners rub off on them."

Chapter 35

Splash! Ian reached high to catch the beach ball. The water up to his waist in the pool, the fountain cascaded around him.

"Give me that ball, Irish boy!"

Off-balance, Ian fell back, Freija on top of him in a frenzied, gleeful attack, bodies disappearing beneath the surface in a tangle of arms and legs. The ball bobbed free. Christopher and Sarah struggled for possession, laughing and shouting as the other two emerged still holding on to each other in a frantic game of piggy-in-the-middle that had very little to do with the beach ball.

It was midday, the sun at its highest.

After breakfast, the foursome had made their way to the pool. In the absence of grown-ups, their manner was more casual, their glances and attention to each other more meaningful. They had made themselves comfortable on the recliners.

"Beer! Who wants a beer?" Christopher opened the ice box.

"Is there wine?" Freija rose from the sunbed. She had, without comment, discarded her bikini.

Though Ian had become more accustomed to the concept of nudity, in the absence of the grown-ups this was different. He looked at Sarah, who smiled at him and reached behind her back to undo her bikini top.

"Maybe we shouldn't," he said.

"Shouldn't, what?" Freija laughed in his direction. "Go nude?"

"No. Take the beer, I mean."

"Oh! Being nude is OK but drinking beer is not?"

"Yes."

"So, you agree that going nude is OK," she challenged, smiling.

Seeing the trap, too late, he mumbled, "I suppose so."

"You don't have to if you don't want to," Freija taunted.

Christopher opened a beer. "I'm a nudist and proud of it." He wriggled out of his swimming trunks and held the beer aloft.

"Cheers!" He reached into the box. "There's wine!"

Freija took the bottle from him.

"And glasses!" Sarah was on her feet; they poured the wine into three glasses.

Ian took a beer. Nobody commented on the fact that he had removed his swimming trunks.

In the heat of the mid-morning sun, they drank quickly and thirstily. A second bottle of wine was produced. Christopher, who was developing a taste for beer, drank greedily. Everything that was said became more amusing, and Christopher, ever the clown, made them laugh. Ian and Sarah sat close together on the sunbed. Freija began to catch Ian's eye.

"Piggy-in-the-middle! Girls against the boys!" Christopher kicked a beach ball into the pool. Laughing and jostling, they jumped in after it to play the most exciting game Ian had ever participated in. Freija and Sarah, competitive and athletic, competing with the boys at every opportunity, the boys responding in like manner, the game becoming a personal tussle, the beach ball an excuse for physical contact. The frantic activity increasing, Ian became more and more the target for the two girls, Freija totally uninhibited, Sarah less so.

"Lunchtime!" Christopher climbed from the pool as Irene and Georges appeared from the house with a large basket and white towel robes.

Reluctantly, out of breath from the exertion, Ian disentangled himself from the girls' clutches, and the beach ball bobbed free. Freija climbed from the pool and donned one of the robes.

Irene busied herself at the table under the large sun shade, laying out plates of food.

Ian and Sarah remained in the pool together, gaining their breath, aware of their closeness, reluctant to join the others.

"We're going back to London soon." Sarah looked up into his face with a sad smile. The sunlight danced around her, reflecting in the water. She pressed against him. Her small hand on his waist. Golden hair framed her beautiful face.

Ian looked to his friends at the table and up to the blue sky, feeling the warmth of the sun, the cascade from the fountain. His gaze travelled to the house with the balcony, the long curtains stirring in the warm breeze.

"Will you be coming back to London with the Robinsons at the end of summer?" Sarah asked.

He looked back to her upturned face.

She smiled and continued, "If you go to Christopher's school, we'll be in the same class. We'll see each other every day."

"Have you got a boyfriend in London?" he asked.

"Yes," she said. "You."

***

Time passed quickly, and the day for the Poulsons' departure approached. Ian and Sarah were inseparable, spending every minute of each day together.

It was the evening, two days before the imminent departure; the parents had gone to Cannes for the evening, and Christopher, Freija, Lucas and some of his friends were at the pool, playing music, a small party to say goodbye.

Ian and Sarah were on the balcony. She took his hand.

"I want to say goodbye properly," She led him to the girls' bedroom.

Chapter 36

QUIET, SMOOTH, LUXURIOUS, RESPONSIVE, LEATHER upholstery, gleaming dashboard with its array of dials and tell tales...Roy eased on the Rover 2000's accelerator and felt the instant surge of power. Traffic lights up ahead, he shifted smoothly through the gears, slowing down on the outside lane as he brought the big car to a stop in the evening traffic. The engine hummed quietly. The windscreen wipers smoothly arched across the windscreen, coping easily with the rain. The 46A bus on the inside lane came to a shuddering noisy halt. Fogged-up windows concealed the passengers from view. The lights changed, and Roy accelerated away, checking in the rear-view mirror, leaving that part of his life behind. He exhaled, smiling in contentment, immersing himself in the satisfaction of knowing that he would never need to use the bus again.

The traffic in front had come to an abrupt halt; red lights flashed. He hit the brake, too late. The heavy car seemed to gain speed on the wet surface. *First day, crash*. Roy wrenched the wheel and pumped the brakes, jackknife, side on. The back of the Ford Fiesta flew towards him. *Impact?* He stared out the side window as the car slewed to a stop. Horns blared. No impact. The driver of the car in front, unaware, moved on. Engine still running, Roy engaged the clutch. The bus driver, drawing alongside and the passengers all looked out and down, shaking their heads with eyes to heaven. *Rich guys in their big cars—more money than sense.*

Relieved at his escape from disaster and aware of blaring horns and irate stares, Roy headed for home, now fully concentrating on his driving.

It had been an eventful day. Being a man who did not do anything in a rush, Roy always weighing up the pros and cons, usually leaving Addie to make the decisions, and his head was spinning from the pace of it all. He would be happy to reach home and put his feet up.

***

Since Ian's departure, Addie, now a rich woman, was filling every day, reconstructing her life.

The telegram arrived on a Monday morning. Roy had left for work and Addie was in the kitchen discussing new flooring with the contractor when the doorbell rang. She excused herself and opened the door to a uniformed chap from the post office.

"Telegram for Mrs. Jeffries." He handed her a small brown envelope.

A telegram...always bad news. Addie took the small envelope and opened it with some trepidation.

> Sorry not in touch. Still in France. Will have Ian
> home in time for school.
> – Laura Anne

I wonder what he'll think of the new kitchen, Addie speculated with a smile.

That afternoon, the model agency called on behalf of Marcus Deering. Addie was needed for a new advertising campaign, this time featuring the Gold Crest Girl on television.

"Really, Adelaide, this is a big opportunity for you. The Berkley Model Agency will provide all the training you will need. More money, of course. We have always promoted you, working hard, putting your name forward at every opportunity,

271

our Gold Crest Girl." Liz Berkley had phoned herself with the good news.

The familiar, cultured tones jarred on Addie's senses. About to hang up the phone with a curt refusal but at the last second remembering Laura Anne's advice about burning boats, she encouraged Liz to tell her more. When would she be needed? What would the budget be, and how long would the campaign run for? She also implied she might not be available on certain dates.

"Details, details. Come in to the agency tomorrow and Maria will tell you all." Liz, not used to being questioned, was at her most imperious.

"No, thanks. Too busy." Addie smiled in satisfaction, aware of the sound of disappointment in Liz Berkley's voice.

"Well, of course, Adelaide. Let me think about things and we may be back to you."

As soon as Addie put down the phone, she regretted her impetuous refusal. She liked being the Gold Crest Girl—the recognition and the compliments. About to dial the agency number, her pride took over and she put down the receiver, not making the call, instead imagining Liz's smug voice answering. *It's for the best*, she comforted herself. *We don't need the money.*

Television, imagine being on television.

"Damn! I shouldn't have turned her down," she said out loud and then reasoned to herself, *I couldn't do it anyway, with the roof being fixed and re-equipping the kitchen and, of course, the driving lessons. We'll get a television as well.*

She sat on the new phone table and seat combined, a more expensive one than the O'Neills', and smiled in contentment, thinking of all that money could buy.

Twenty minutes later, when she was in the kitchen about to start getting the dinner ready, the phone rang in the hall.

"Hello, Addie."

"Hello, Marcus." She recognised the clipped tones.

"Why are you not taking the job?" It was a question and an accusation rolled into one.

For the second time that day, Addie was tempted to put down the phone. "I don't like you."

"Well, I like you. But that's beside the point." There was a smile in his voice. He continued before Addie could comment, "Liz is upset and confused. This is a great opportunity, and the money would be very good. She cannot understand why you turned her down."

"I don't like her either." Addie's tone was offhand, uncaring.

"Again, that's incidental." She could still detect the smile in his voice.

Addie, unwittingly, had used the greatest bargaining tool: disinterest in what the other person was selling.

Marcus hesitated. "I have someone here who would like to talk to you." Marcus's voice was now serious. "It's Michael Forsythe. You met at the photoshoot—he's from the cigarette company. I want you to listen to what he has to say. I'm handing the telephone over to him."

"Hello, Mrs. Jeffries, Michael Forsythe here."

Addie remembered lunch at the Shelbourne Hotel. It seemed like such a long time ago.

"Hello, Michael. We enjoyed the Champagne."

"My pleasure."

After a few pleasantries, he came to the point.

"I have a proposition for you. It is very simple. There is only one Gold Crest Girl, and that is you. We are not interested in using anyone else. This puts you in a very strong bargaining position regarding a fee, so we are prepared to pay you the top rate.

"I'm listening." Addie could hardly contain her interest.

"We would be dealing with you directly. Your contract will be with the cigarette company and not with the model agency. This is television, Addie. There will be total control of what goes on air, and you will be consulted throughout the entire process. All support advertising, press, posters et cetera will be passed by you."

The conversation concluded with Addie agreeing to attend a meeting the following week to discuss the details. Two weeks later, the contract was signed, and Addie was the Gold Crest Girl again.

Meanwhile, Roy progressed from strength to strength in his new job, popular with both staff and customers. There was some talk about James joining the company as a junior rep, and Debbie was proving to be a star student though her main talents featured on the sports field. Ian's name cropped up from time to time, always in the context of how much he must be enjoying himself.

So taken up with their newfound success and confident of Ian's return for school and the Christmas term, Roy and Addie hardly gave their son a thought.

***

"Not even a postcard," Addie commented as they sat around the kitchen table. It was the weekend: Sunday morning breakfast.

"Young lads wouldn't think of sending postcards." Roy reached for a piece of toast. "Anyway, he'll be home next week for school."

"Talking with a posh voice." James laughed.

"Or an English accent." Debbie joined in. "Or French."

"We should have given the Robinsons our new phone number." Roy looked at Addie.

"And how would we do that? Sure, we can't contact them. We don't know where they are. They should be back in England by now."

"What if he's not coming back?" Debbie said. "What if he decides to stay with the Robinsons?"

Addie looked furiously across the table. "Don't be ridiculous! There is no question of him not coming home. He doesn't even like them. This is his home, blood is thicker than water. He's back to school next week." Addie glared, punctuating each point with an index finger jabbing into the tablecloth. "Gordon Robinson is not like your father, and Laura Anne is not like me. Ian's mother and father." Unexpectedly, tears pricked her eyes as the niggling doubts, latent in her mind, began to surface.

"I was only joking," Debbie protested. "Sorry."

Addie brushed her eyes with the back of her hand and stood up. "It's all right, Debbie. I want no more talk about it."

Roy followed her as she left the room.

In the porch, she stood, looking out into the garden, arms folded, tearful. He put his arms around her.

"What's the matter? You know Ian is coming home." His voice was soft and comforting. "Laura Anne's telegram. What's changed?"

"Nothing." She tried to smile. "I just had a doubt for the first time. It was when Debbie said it—it took me by surprise. Of course he's coming home. He's our son."

Roy hugged her close, and they stood together, looking both occupied with their own thoughts. Had their judgement been blinded by the money?

"I'll try to find their address tomorrow at work," Roy said. "We need to know what the arrangements are for Ian coming home. I might have to go to London and collect him. Peter Hackett—he'll have an address."

Monday morning, instead of heading out to his district, Roy set off for the depot. This would cut into his day, and several calls would have to be abandoned as a result, which would not please Peter Hackett, sales manager, but Roy couldn't help that. Once Addie got an idea into her head, there was no room for arguing.

"I want to know where Ian is and I want to know now."

Roy parked the car and headed through the reception area for Peter Hackett's office.

"Is Peter in?"

275

"Not yet. Take a seat."

Roy sat down and looked at his watch. Weekdays at the depot; he knew he should be out on his district and not here. After a quarter of an hour waiting and becoming anxious, he stood up and began to pace the polished floor. He was about to leave when Peter Hackett arrived accompanied by three other people, two men and a woman, smartly dressed with English accents.

The receptionist was on her feet. With a frown and a cursory nod, Peter Hackett passed Roy.

"We'll be in the boardroom, Sheila. The usual please."

"Yes, Mr. Hackett. Roy Jeffries is here to see you."

He stood for a minute, obviously displeased. His secretary appeared from her office along the corridor and, at a nod from him, greeted the British contingent in a familiar manner and led them off to the boardroom. With a murmured apology and an assurance that he would be with them right away, he walked slowly across the floor to Roy.

"What are you doing here? That's some of the top UK brass I just picked up from the airport. They wouldn't be pleased to find one of our reps hanging around the depot at ten o'clock on a Monday morning. Surely you have appointments. What do you want? It better be important."

This was not the way Roy expected things to happen. He had anticipated finding the sales manager in his office. "I can't discuss it here. It's personal."

"Sheila, I'll be in the small conference room. Tell Anne to look after them." He glared at Roy. "I'll give you five minutes!" he said and strode away. Roy followed.

During the short walk along the corridor, Peter Hackett had time to consider why Roy, who should be out with customers, was making this unscheduled visit to head office. His initial irritation had diminished to be replaced with curiosity. The English contingent could wait a while. Anne would ply them with coffee and chocolate biscuits.

"What's this all about?" His customary smile was back in place as they took their seats. "The door is always open to my sales force."

"Gordon Robinson." Roy came straight to the point. "I need to contact him."

Peter Hackett sat back and looked quizzical. "You need to contact Gordon?" He paused. "And why would that be?" He leaned forward, looking Roy straight in the eye. "Have you got a complaint? Are you unhappy about something? Does the work not suit you? You realise that you can't go straight to the owner of the company if you have a problem?"

"No, I love the work, everything's fine. It's personal, nothing to do with business."

"If you tell me what the problem is, I might be able to help."

Roy stood up. "I'd better get back to work. I'm sorry for bothering you," he said, his disappointment obvious on his face. "It's private, you know, family stuff."

"Sit down. Look, I'm your sales manager. I'm afraid any business to do with Gordon Robinson must come through me. You understand, Roy?" He smiled kindly. "I'd like to help." He thought for a minute and came to a conclusion. "I'll tell you what I'll do. I'll contact him, let him know you're looking for him, and if he wants to contact you, I'm sure he will. He's on holiday at the moment in the south of France, and I wouldn't say he'd appreciate being disturbed." He looked questioningly. "Are you sure you want to go through with this?"

"I know he's in the south of France. Tell him I want to talk to him."

"OK, if that's what you want, I'll call his secretary."

Roy left the room satisfied that he had at least set the wheels in motion towards Ian's return home.

But they did not hear from the Robinsons.

Roy waited until after the sales meeting on the following Friday to confront Peter Hackett again, and Peter assured him he had made contact and the Robinsons were still in France. Gordon Robinson had said he would contact Roy on his return.

"When will that be?"

"He didn't say. He's not in the habit of explaining his actions to members of his staff, and that includes me." Hackett, noting Roy's worried expression and feeling kindly enough towards this man who was fast becoming one of his best salesmen, sighed, shaking his head. "Tuesday, I think. He'll be back in England next Tuesday. One of the English contingent said he had a meeting arranged, and Robinson is getting back for it."

"Will his family be with him?" Roy looked perplexed.

"What's that got to do with anything? I don't know, and I'm certainly not going to ask!" Peter Hackett retorted angrily. "Look, Roy, you had better tell me what this is all about. Obviously, you're worried about something, and I don't want it affecting your work."

Roy restated that it was a personal matter and thanked Peter for his help. Realising he was not going to be enlightened, Peter sought further assurance from Roy, restating company policy on the error of mixing business and family matters.

Roy headed for home in the evening traffic, not looking forward to updating Addie. If only there was a way to get in contact with the Robinsons, talk face-to-face. He was sure that they were not up to anything underhand. *If only we had got an address I could go to London and confront them.* How naïve they had been, blinded by the money, not thinking things out. Foolish and greedy.

Peter Hackett had been decent enough about it all. *Maybe I'll leave it a few days and talk to him again.* He considered telling Peter the whole story. After the lecture on company policy regarding mixing family matters and business, this seemed out of the question, but Peter had a direct line to Robinson and probably knew the address in London. By the time Roy reached home, his mind was clear. He'd ask for the London address and threaten to give in his notice if Hackett didn't give it to him.

"Tuesday? Back in England on Tuesday!" Addie folded her arms and glared. "Ian should be in school! Robinson's coming back for a meeting! Where's Ian? Is he still in France? What's going on, Roy? I think they're keeping him, not letting him come home! It's Laura Anne, all smiles, and scheming." Tearful and angry, she appealed to an equally bewildered Roy who had just told her about the meeting with Peter Hackett.

"Of course they're not keeping him!" Roy frowned wearily. "You got a telegram from Laura Anne," he reasoned. "It said they'd have him home in time for school."

"But school started last week."

"Obviously, they've been delayed, France is a long way away. I'm sure we'll hear soon. If not, I'll go over to head office in London and see Robinson or find out where they live."

But the decision was taken out of Roy's hands when he received a summons to Peter Hackett's office the following day.

"I don't like this situation, and I don't like personal issues interfering with business." He looked across the desk at Roy. "So, let's get past this as quickly as possible and get you back to doing what you're paid for. I'll update you on the important stuff first.

"I have been in touch with Gordon Robinson, and we had a long chat." He glanced at his computer display. "You have been on a trial period and the company is satisfied that you are up to the job. I have recommended you be made permanent." He smiled. "Of course, this means an increase in your commission. Your basic salary remains the same and your targets are increased. You'll be left in the Dublin area for the time being, however, in the future we may need to move you elsewhere."

Roy, expecting some news about Ian, paid scant attention to information that would have normally been music to his ears. He waited expectantly.

Hackett cleared his throat. "They're expecting you in London. I don't know what it means, it's not my business. I believe your son is over there and is looking forward to seeing you. Two return flights have been booked for Wednesday morning, same day flight. We'll need you back for the sales meeting and I can only afford to have you away for one day.

Chapter 37

COLLINSTOWN AIRPORT: DEPARTURES. ROY ARRIVED to find Bill Sweeney waiting.

"Hackett's something else. Wants us to visit the factory in London together, have the grand tour, kill two birds with the one stone, mercenary bastard. I've got the tickets, he wanted me to look after you, seasoned traveller and all that."

Roy was glad to see his workmate. This would be his first time flying. Never having been on a plane before, though somewhat nervous, he was excited but more so at the prospect of seeing Ian again and bringing him home. *I hope he hasn't developed any airs and graces about himself. Those Robinsons are a toffee-nosed bunch. He's going to find things a bit changed around Ivy Lodge since he left. What a difference that money made.*

Addie had remained indignant over the Robinsons' irresponsible and haphazard attitude towards Ian's return to school.

"I had to call Henno and apologise for the absence. He wasn't very pleased. I told him it wasn't our fault. But I couldn't tell him about the Robinsons. It was really very awkward."

However, Ian's imminent return overshadowed everything. He would be returning to a far different Ivy Lodge than he had left.

The flight was called and Roy joined the short queue to board the plane.

Bill handed him his boarding pass. "We're in row six, A and B. You can sit by the window."

They crossed the tarmac with the other passengers, mostly businessmen catching the early flight to London. Up the steps, they were greeted by a smiling air hostess.

"Very nice," Bill muttered. "Wouldn't kick her out of the scratcher." But Roy was not interested, preoccupied with his surroundings, the narrowness of the aisle between the rows of seats, the low ceiling. The plane was much smaller than he had anticipated.

"Put your bag up on the rack," Bill instructed. "You can take off your jacket and hang it on that little hook. Your table is in front of you when you sit down and put on your safety belt."

Roy, impressed with Bill's knowledge, obeyed. Ducking low, he deposited himself on the seat beside the window. "There isn't much room," he commented as the overweight Bill squeezed into seat B.

"You're sitting on my safety belt." Bill twisted and turned.

"Sorry." Roy raised himself up in the confined space.

"You're in my seat!"

About to sit down again, Roy was confronted by a bulky, red-moustached fellow standing in the aisle, his tone friendly enough.

"You're sitting in my seat, I'm beside the window."

Roy looked at Bill. "Am I?"

"An aisle seat," Bill said. "The window seat is A, and you're in C."

"But I always have the window seat." The tone was slightly frosty now.

"Take your seats and fasten your safety belts." The safety belt sign flashed above their heads. The air hostess advanced along the aisle. "Please take your seat, sir."

The plane began to move, the sound of its engines increasing in volume. Roy looked out his window, fascinated by the rotating propellers. They seemed so close. He could see the rivets in the metal wing, and everything was shaking.

Roy looked at Bill who appeared totally unperturbed. The man with the moustache, looking disgruntled, had taken his seat and was adjusting his seat belt.

The plane taxied out for take-off. *Sweets. The stewardess is giving out sweets.* Roy nudged his companion. "Free sweets! That's a nice touch."

"They're for your ears." Bill took a sweet and unwrapped it. "And don't ask me, 'Do you use them as earplugs?'"

Roy laughed but only realised the significance when the plane began its ascent and his ears popped.

"We're above the clouds!" He looked out the window, transfixed by the sight. "Wow, blue sky. The clouds are like a carpet." A gap appeared. "There's Howth! We're over the sea."

Bill nodded sagely and glanced sideways at his companion. This new man, so suddenly dropped into a senior sales position, alongside experienced men like himself, was a subject of some speculation. There was no doubting Roy's popularity and his obvious success with Robinson's customers. Rumour rife, it was assumed by some that Roy had contacts in very high places and therefore was a man to be watched. It was even suggested by some that the spectacular Mrs. Laura Anne Robinson had a soft spot for him or that he was a relative who knew where some of the skeletons were hidden.

"So, this will be your first time to The Big Smoke?"

"Yes, first time to London. I'm looking forward to seeing my young lad, Ian. He's been with the Robinsons for the last few months. They took him to France with them."

Bill, unable to believe his good fortune with this gold mine of information, could hardly control his obvious curiosity. "Oh, So they're friends of yours, then?"

"I suppose you could say so," Roy speculated. "Well, Addie and Laura Anne are friends and, of course, Ian and Christopher are great pals."

"Friends in high places, well for you," Bill said, smiling and nodding his head. "I suppose you'll be back and forth to see them quite a lot, then."

"I wouldn't say so. I'm just going over to collect Ian to bring him home. Fair play, Gordon even paid for the return fares, decent man."

"Ah, yes, he's a decent man, all right," Bill said with a sigh, aware of some individuals who had suffered at the hands of the ruthless head of Robinson's Decorating Products.

The irony was lost on Roy, who nodded his agreement with a smile.

Chapter 38

HEATHROW AIRPORT: THEY PASSED THROUGH arrivals and the waiting travellers collecting bags from the carousel. Two suited individuals were waiting for their arrival, sales reps from head office. Bill Sweeney introduced Roy.

"You're with me. Enjoy the flight?" the smaller of the two greeted Roy in a friendly manner. "I'm to take you into Knightsbridge for eight forty-five and then we meet up at the factory for the grand tour. We'll be back in London, to Robinson's house about two o'clock."

Roy parted company with Bill Sweeney. "See you later."

He was swiftly led out to the car park; the English rep was anxious to get ahead of the traffic. "Strict instructions. I've got to get you to the school before nine."

"What school?" Roy was puzzled.

"Oh, the one Robinson's son goes to. We're to be there at eight forty-five. Don't ask me why. I just do what I'm told. Especially when the supreme boss does the telling." He glanced at the car clock. "Should be there in time."

Roy sat back. *Why do they want me to go to Christopher's school?* He patted his inside pocket, reassured by the bulk of the two return tickets. *Obviously, Christopher is in school—maybe they want me to pick up Ian from there.*

Roy had never seen so many cars before. High buildings loomed on either side as the traffic slowed to a crawl. They were in the streets of London. Piccadilly Circus, red buses, policemen with high helmets. White gloves flashed, as police with stern faces on point duty kept the traffic moving. The Mall, Buckingham Palace, people appearing in their droves from the underground trains to flood the pavements, across the Thames and Big Ben. Fascinated by it all, Roy twisted from side to side, ducking his head to peer up at the skyline, then back to the streets.

"Just a quick tour—I was told to take you the scenic route. Here we are."

They pulled into a space on a wide street, ornate railings and steps leading to Georgian doors spanned by high windows. Residential London.

They sat; the Englishman looked at his watch. Then Roy saw them.

On the opposite side of the street, a large limousine, black with a driver wearing a cap, pulled up. There were people in the back of the car. Roy could not make out the faces too well. The driver opened the back door, and Christopher Robinson emerged in his school uniform. He was laughing and looking back into the car. A figure quickly followed, taller, black hair, tanned face. He was also laughing. At first, Roy did not recognise Ian. It was probably because of the uniform. Ian was in the same school uniform as Christopher.

Roy watched as the limo pulled away from the kerb revealing a group of boys and girls at the high gates of the school, all immaculate in similar uniforms. The two boys joined the group, and there was much activity. Roy rolled down the window. The sound of their voices drifted across to him. Ian appeared to be the centre of attention, Christopher beside him. A group had gathered around them, boys and girls. Ian was talking. Roy couldn't make out what he was saying, but he was smiling, and the others were reacting to his words. He appeared to be confident and somehow in charge.

The group split up as they moved through the gates. Then Roy saw the beautiful girl standing to one side, blonde hair, almost white, her head tilted to one side in greeting, her eyes on Ian, smiling as she spoke. He detached himself from the group and, to Roy's astonishment, he kissed her. Not a 'hello' kiss. It was the kiss of familiarity. Christopher said something that provoked a friendly push from Ian as they followed through the gates. Ian had his arm around the girl's waist, her head momentarily resting on his shoulder, blonde hair white against the dark-blue uniform blazer.

Roy reached for the door handle, but the car had started to move out into the traffic.

"Stop! That was my lad back there!"

"Sorry, mate, no can do. We have to join the others for the grand tour at the factory."

The car had picked up speed in the now-lighter traffic heading out of the capital.

"Is that your lad, Ian Jeffries? I never made the connection, of course! You must be very proud. Great young lad, very popular with everybody. Scored two tries in our last match—big lad, fast.

Roy stared out through the windscreen as the English rep extolled the virtues of this Irish boy who had made such an impression on everyone.

"It's a nice perk, the company paying the school fees," the voice continued as Roy listened. "I couldn't have afforded a posh school like that. My young lad is doing very well there. Best school in England, guaranteed place in Eton or any of the best colleges." He glanced at Roy, who was still staring straight ahead. "Great chance in life for our young lads. You must be highly thought of, Roy. Robinson knows how to keep his best reps happy.

"Yes," said Roy. "He sure does."

Chapter 39

To Roy, preoccupied with the revelations about Ian, the factory visit was a blur. *He must have been going to the school for some time. Rugby. He never played rugby at school in Ireland. And the girl...what was he doing kissing her like that? Sure! He seemed happy, though, and the English rep. with his kid at the school, all paid for by Robinson.* Roy's head was spinning. He longed to talk to Addie. *It's a pity she's not here. What would Addie do? Probably order me home and give that fancy young one a kick up the backside.* He couldn't help smiling at the thought.

He was delivered in front of the Robinsons' house in residential London promptly at two thirty and climbed the steps to the well-kept royal-blue door with its shining brass.

He rang the bell, unsure of his intentions, deciding to keep his powder dry until he had assessed the situation. Stepping back, he took in the Georgian frontage. Tall windows, three storeys and a gate with steps leading down to a basement. Fine living in the centre of London.

The door opened. "Come in please, sir. You are expected." A soft-smiling, diminutive woman in a black dress with white frilly apron summoned him into a wide hallway. "Mrs. Robinson will be with you right away." She peered at Roy and then said in a conspiratorial tone, "Excuse me saying so, but your son is the image of you." Indicating a doorway, she ushered Roy through into the drawing room before he could comment.

The room was typical, heavy curtains framing long windows looking out onto a London square. There was a marble fireplace and a gold-framed oval mirror. Roy stood, ignoring the plush settee and other comfortable chairs. Ill at ease, he turned to face the open doorway.

"Roy, how nice to see you." Laura Anne paused before entering, as always smartly dressed in the latest fashion, her appearance complementing her surroundings. She came over and shook his hand. "No Addie?"

He dismissed the niceties came straight to the point. "No. I'm just here for one reason and that is to collect Ian and bring him home. Where is he?"

Laura Anne did not respond immediately. She moved to the centre of the room and turned to face him. "He and Christopher are just finishing their lunch. They'll be here in a moment. I'm surprised Addie didn't come. I was so looking forward to seeing her. How are James and Debbie?"

"Fine, thank you," Roy answered with a perplexed expression, aware that something was definitely amiss. He took a step forward. "I want to see my son right away, please."

Laura Anne stood her ground, looking up into his face, her expression hardening. "I have just told you he will be here in a moment. Please, sit down. We need to talk this through, and it cannot be done without Ian. I really am disappointed Addie isn't here. We did include a return plane ticket for her, after all, and my dealings were with her from the start. We had a perfect understanding."

Roy reached inside his jacket and retrieved the envelope. He looked at the other tickets for the first time. Raising his eyes, he looked at Laura Anne. "There are no tickets here for Ian! What's going on?"

"Dad! What are you doing here?" Ian and Christopher were at the door.

Laura Anne quickly went to stand beside them. She took Ian's arm.

Roy looked grim and determined. "I'm here to take you home, son."

Ian looked at Laura Anne, who shrugged.

"But I'm not going home now, Dad. I'll be going home at Christmas. Isn't that right, Laura Anne?"

"Whatever you want. It's up to you," she said calmly.

Roy held up his hand. It was a gesture of puzzled incredulity. "What's this? Why are you in that uniform?"

Laura Anne, about to speak was quietened by another impatient gesture from the aggrieved Roy. "I want to speak to Ian, alone," he said firmly.

Ian looked at Laura Anne again.

"It's all right." She squeezed his arm and then said equally firmly, "Ten minutes. Ian is playing for the school rugby team this afternoon at three o'clock."

Roy and Ian were left facing each other, both mystified by the circumstances.

"Sit down, son, and tell me what's going on here. What's all this about?" Roy kept his voice low. He wished Addie was here to help handle the situation.

"No problem, Dad. I'll be going home at Christmas, that's all. It was all arranged when we were in France. Laura Anne sent a telegram."

Roy was about to contradict but decided not to. Better to let the lad speak. "And the uniform? You're going to Christopher's school?"

"Only for one term," Ian quickly replied. "And then I'm going home at Christmas. It was all in the telegram."

"Oh!" Roy sat back in the chair and then spoke, his expression enquiring, his voice soft, casual, non-accusing. "Just one term. Has this got anything to do with the girl I saw you with this morning?"

Ian went very red in the face and looked at the floor and then up at his dad with a mixture of defiance and a plea for understanding. "Yes. Her name's Sarah, she's my girlfriend. She's from Denmark."

"I see. That explains a lot. She looked very nice." *Addie would know what to say.* "I'd like to meet her sometime." He paused and then continued. "We're getting the roof fixed."

"Great!" Ian rubbed his hands together and looked at his watch. "The match starts at three o'clock. I've been picked for the school team. I scored two tries on Saturday. Why don't you come to the match?"

The door opened halfway and Laura Anne called, "The car's waiting."

"I'd better go, Da." Ian got up and Roy followed suit. They stood opposite each other.

"I'll tell James and Debbie you were asking for them. They miss you, and your ma sends her love. I'm sorry I can't go to the match. The plane is organised for four o'clock." He reached out, and they hugged spontaneously. "Keep in touch. We want to know all your news," Roy said as Ian turned and, with a mumbled "OK," hurried out the door.

Roy could hear voices out in the hallway and shortly the sound of the front door closing. Laura Anne came into the room, talking and smiling.

"I've asked Maureen to bring us some tea. She's Irish, you know, I think from Wexford. She's very fond of Ian. Such a wonderful young man, everybody likes him. You know he's doing ever so well at school and of course, the rugby. The sports coach says he's an exceptional talent..."

Roy, remained silent, deep in thought, hardly listening to what she was saying. It seemed that, though Ian wasn't coming home right away he nevertheless had no intention of staying full time with the Robinsons. He also seemed happy and in control.

The girlfriend's a bit of a surprise but that will fizzle out. Teenagers, puppy love...when he comes home at Christmas he'll fall for someone else. In a way, it's just as well Addie isn't here. She'd probably get angry and spoil it all. A bit high-handed all the same, enrolling Ian in the school for the autumn term. The Robinsons, an arrogant bunch, used to getting their own way. Well, they underestimated the strength of a loving Irish family. Blood is thicker than water.

"You should have told us about the school in England," he interrupted abruptly.

"What?" Laura Anne stopped in mid-flow, looking indignant. "You received a telegram explaining the position. It was very specific. In fact, it was a request for your approval. Ian was quite anxious to stay in London until Christmas. Gordon, had it sent to you from head office. When we did not hear from you, we assumed you were in agreement." Tilting her head and raising her chin, she gave Roy the full benefit of her most fierce look of disapproval.

"That's not what it says here." Roy calmly retrieved the telegram from his pocket and handed it over.

Laura Anne's expression darkened as she read the words. "*Gordon!*" She said his name quietly but furiously. "Look, I'm sorry, Roy, but this is *not* the message you should have received. I want you to know I put no pressure on Ian. It's his decision to stay. Christmas isn't far away. I know he misses you all." Her expression softened, and she reached out a conciliatory hand.

Roy stood up.

"I'll be off, then. Perhaps you'll contact Addie and explain things. I'd better go and catch that plane."

Chapter 40

THE ANCIENT METAL STAND BOASTED six tiered rows of seats and flanked one side of the rugby pitch. Painted green with ornate wrought iron, some of the less traditional members of the school board felt it should be replaced with a more modern version. Opposite the stand, the other side of the pitch, the playing fields stretched, green and well-kept, to the school building. Matching the green stand at one end was the pavilion. Today, an inter-schools match, the stand was almost full, occupied by enthusiastic pupils from both schools attempting to out-shout each other as the participants engaged in a pretty heated hard-fought contest. Rugby and reputations paramount at both schools, and this was a cup match. Sarah Poulson with eyes only for Ian chanted her encouraged with the others.

Amongst the teachers and parents, seated in the centre of the stand, Gordon, Laura Anne and Christopher cheered enthusiastically especially when Ian was involved. The under-sixteen cup was a hotly contested affair. Ian, at fourteen, was one of the youngest players but by no means the smallest or the weakest, and he revelled in the contest.

"So how did it go with Roy, then?" Gordon turned to Laura Anne.

"Fine." She smiled. "I'll tell you all about it later."

There was a scrum at the far side of the pitch opposite to where they were sitting. The ball came back on the Kensington side. Ian kicked for touch. The ball arched high in the air, clearing the line.

A tall spectator reached high to take the ball down with one hand. Roy, about to throw the ball back onto the pitch to the nearest player to him, changed his mind. The temptation was too much. The posts too inviting. He took a step forward and drop-kicked the ball from where he stood. All eyes watched the oval shape soar high and straight to begin its decent between the posts.

"See you at Christmas, Ian," he called and then turned and strode away across the grass towards the exit.

"Who is that fellow? Dammed cheek!" the headmaster, sitting beside Gordon, exclaimed indignantly.

Gordon Robinson was probably the only one whose eyes had not followed the course of the ball.

"Roy Jeffries—Ian Jeffries father and an important man in Robinson's Decorating Products," he answered, his eyes never leaving the back of the retreating figure on the other side of the playing field. He turned to Laura Anne. "Make sure Ian knows that Sarah will be coming to us for the Christmas Holidays. We'll take them skiing."

***

"Who was that?" enquired one of the players.

"That's my dad," Ian answered proudly. *I wonder if he can talk Ma into letting Sarah stay with us for Christmas.*

END